CAMP FORD

JOHNNY D. BOGGS

LEISURE BOOKS NEW YORK CITY

A LEISURE BOOK®

May 2007

Published by special arrangement with Golden West Literary Agency.

Dorchester Publishing Co., Inc.
200 Madison Avenue
New York, NY 10016

ISBN-10: 0-8439-5838-3
ISBN-13: 978-0-8439-5838-6

The name "Leisure Books" and the stylized "L" with design are trademarks of Dorchester Publishing Co., Inc.

Printed in the United States of America.

*For nine friends and fans of the game
who'd make my starting lineup any time:*
Butch Anderson
Kent Anderson
Mike Anderson
Paul Palazzo
Chuck Scott
Cotton Smith
Jack Smith
Perry Stokes
Frank Wooten

PROLOGUE

All these years later, and what strikes me most, what I remember the most, are the smells. Not the stink of death, of offal and decay—although I still have nightmares once or twice a year, waking up with the taste of bile, the pungency of the stockade embedded in my nostrils—but scents we take for granted: pine tar and grass, chewing tobacco and goober peas, leather and the sour odor of sweat. Strolling through the woods, I will be overcome by emotions from just a hint of rosin. I can walk past a florist, and feel the tears well, brought on by the aroma of fresh roses. I close my eyes and see them again, the good and bad, my friends and enemies, Sweet's Guards and turncoat razorbacks—Ward Keener, Mike Peabody, Pig Oliver, Sharky the Seaman, Captain Conall McGee, and Jane Anne Bartholomew—feel the knot on my head and the crack in my skull.

I am ninety-nine years old, and have seen wars and depressions, automobiles and moving pictures, the beauty of spring, terrible brown clouds of dirt that some said portended Armageddon, and, more recently, a horrible end to a grueling war that many fear might just spell the beginning of the end of our Earth. I have seen my children, grandchildren, even great-grandchildren grow up, and, in agonizing cases, die. I have outlived my wife by twenty-one years. I have been honored, saluted, chastised. And I have seen countless games of baseball played across these United States that I fought to preserve as a mere teenager. I have cheered Wee Willie Keeler, and have cursed at, and been cursed by, Ty Cobb. I have played on great, and a lot more mediocre, teams in the National Association of Base Ball Players after the War of the Rebellion, worked as an umpire in the Texas League from 1889 to 1894, managed that league's Corsicana Oilers for J. Doak Roberts for two seasons after the turn of the century, and traveled with the Providence Grays—admittedly playing little as an aging catcher—for two glorious seasons, 1878–1879.

Every spring or fall, I am invited to some function or other relating to this game we call America's pastime, be it a National League, American League, Texas League, or even some college contest. Every year, a newspaper reporter asks me what was the greatest team or game I ever saw, and I always offer some nonsensical reply that befuddles the reporter until he dismisses my answer as the rambling diatribe of an ancient old coot. This year, 1946, *The Sporting News* invited me to attend the World Series games at Sportsman's Park, and, before the opener, a reporter with the *Globe-Democrat* asked me how the Cardinals or Red Sox would fare against the best teams I had seen over the course of my ninety-nine years.

I answered that, actually, when I was born in 1847, baseball itself was just an infant, so that ninety-nine years is a bit misleading, that the first game I recall seeing was an exhibition in Rhode Island when I was eleven, and kept on spitting out flapdoodle until the reporter asked me to name the best team I had ever seen.

"Can I name two?" I said.

"OK," the reporter agreed.

"Easy," I said. "Mister Lincoln's Hirelings and the Ford City Gallinippers. Played one game at Camp Ford, Texas."

He didn't mention those teams in the next day's paper, nor in any other editions during what turned out to be one of the greatest championship series ever played, probably writing me off as senile. As I don't know that I'll live to see another World Series, or even another opening day, another baseball game, or ever be asked again to name the greatest team or teams, I am logging my thoughts on these Big Chief tablets I purchased at the Pelegrimas Five & Dime in St. Louis, hoping someone will find it after I'm gone, and decipher my babbling and prehistoric scrawl. Or, if I do reach the century milestone, and if I am invited to another baseball game, and if a reporter asks me once more to name the greatest game I ever witnessed between the two best teams, I will hand him this memoir and say again:

"Easy. Mister Lincoln's Hirelings and the Ford City Gallinippers in a one-game championship at

Camp Ford, Texas. They were playing for stakes much higher than any World Series."

Read this story, if you desire, and draw your own conclusions.

PART I

"But it is needless further to comment on the meritorious features of our American game, suffice it to say that it (is) a recreation that any one may be proud to excel in, as in order to do so, he must possess the characteristics of true manhood to a considerable degree."

Henry Chadwick
Beadle's Dime Base-Ball Player:
A Compendium of the Game

CHAPTER ONE

Before the opening game of the 1946 Series at Sportsman's Park, a dozen reporters from St. Louis, Boston, and the national papers began a verbal assault of Ted Williams, the American League Most Valuable Player "who shined the brightest on a Boston team full of stars"—at least according to a cliché-inspired columnist in one of the New York dailies. Seems that these scribes agreed on one thing: Ted Williams is the biggest S.O.B. ever to play the game.

"You gents must have never met Ty Cobb," I interjected over a mouthful of hot dog the members of the press and we VIPs had been served. "Or Pig Oliver."

"No, I knew Cobb," said a rotund chain-smoker from the Boston Record. "But the thing about Ty Cobb is that everyone knew what made him tick."

"Who the blazes is Pig Oliver?" another reporter blurted, but the Record man told him to shut up, that he had the floor.

"The problem with Williams is," he continued, "nobody can figure him out. He lives for the game, you *see, but he also lives for himself. Other than that, he's one tough nut to crack. Excepting that he hates the press, 'specially me."*

With that, he crushed out his cigarette, and, with a tobacco-stained grin, fished out a flask from his hip pocket, which kept the attention on him, and allowed me to finish my hot dog before being escorted to my seat down the first-base line, nowhere near the seats of the real VIPs like Rogers Hornsby or Happy Chandler, but I did not mind. Like every other fan who had arrived early on that sweltering afternoon, I watched Ted Williams take batting practice with some interest, but my thoughts didn't really settle on that tall drink of water wearing the No. 9 Red Sox uniform.

I thought of my father. He, too, proved to be a hard one to figure out, perhaps the hardest nut of them all— can't say I ever really knew, or, rather, understood the man—and maybe he lived for himself. He definitely lived for the game. Sort of.

Henry Wallace MacNaughton called himself an apothecary, and he ran a little drugstore in Newport on Rhode Island Sound. He seemed to be more of a dreamer, though, and I'm not sure I would have had clothes on my back or shoes on my feet if it hadn't been for my mother, or, rather, my mother's family. Mother claimed Easton bloodlines, and the Eastons ran one of the largest shipping lines in New England. Why, you could hardly ever scan the "Maritime Journal" in the *Daily News* without reading that at least one Easton ship had docked at the port of Newport. I never asked her what she saw in my father, and my grandparents on the Easton side never questioned their only daughter's judgment. She did love him, though, or else she wouldn't have put up with his tomfoolery, followed him halfway across the continent and back, or erected that marble monument over his grave at Island Cemetery.

My most vivid memory of my father came when I was eleven while walking home from school with my best friend, Mike Peabody, on a warm but windy late April afternoon. The door to the drugstore had been flung wide open, but when I stuck my head inside and called out for my father, I received no reply.

"You think something's happened?" asked Mike, ever the worrier.

Before I could think of an answer, my father's voice boomed from across the street: "Winthrop! There you are!"

Winthrop. How still I cringe when I hear that name.

I managed to shut the door to the apothecary, but not lock it, and back onto the sidewalk just as my father raced across Thames Street, dodging a glistening phaëton driven by a furious Episcopal minister. Father grabbed my arm, almost separating my shoulder from its socket. "You have to see this, Winthrop. Come on, Mike. You, too."

Miraculously I retained my footing, freed myself from my father's grasp, and followed his gangling gait down the street that led out of town toward Fort Adams. "Stimulating," my father said to no one in particular. "Invigorating. Fascinating." Most likely, he also added a few other -ing words that I have forgotten over the course of eighty-eight years. During our hike, I shot an occasional glance at panting Mike Peabody, who fired back a curious look at me only to receive a shrug in reply. We stopped an exhausting walk later at a field overlooking Brenton Cove. A crowd had gathered at the field, but my father pushed his way through the throng before halting and dropping to his knee, motioning for Mike and me to stand close beside him.

"They're playing baseball!" He said this as incredulously as if he had said: "They're walking on the moon."

They were some monkeys from the harbor, a few soldiers from Fort Adams, and the Green Mountain Club from Boston, and, boy, did those Massachusetts ballplayers stand out in their plaid knickerbockers and green shield-front shirts with white piping. I had always admired the uniforms of sailors and soldiers, but had never seen civilians in snappy uniforms, especially not while playing athletics.

This was the Massachusetts Game of Baseball, quite different from the version played today, or the style popular in New York in 1858. Instead of a diamond, a square field had been laid out with the batter—we called him a striker in those days—standing halfway between first and fourth base. The bases were four-feet-high stakes driven into the ground, sixty feet from each other, and the bat resembled a round piece of lumber that I had seen Mike Peabody's dad use over the heads of unsavory patrons at his groggery near the harbor.

"They're having a convention in Dedham in two weeks," Father said, "to adopt rules and sign clubs, and, by jingo, I think Newport should be a part of this. It's history, Winthrop. Why should Massachusetts enjoy this game and not Rhode Island?"

A heavy-set Green Mountain batter drilled the ball over the pitcher's head, but the sergeant playing what we would call center field caught it on the first bounce, which prompted a smattering of applause from onlookers. Only the Green Mountain fellow kept running, reaching all the way to third base before the slow-to-understand soldier threw the ball to the pitcher.

"He's out!" the sergeant yelled. "I caught it on the bound!"

"That's not the way we play the game," the Green Mountain Club captain answered. "The ball must be caught in the air, before it hits the ground."

The soldier made a beeline for the Bay Stater, telling him what he thought of his game, that he had made a fine catch, and that batter should be out. Mike Peabody punched my arm, and whistled. Back then, he didn't care much about baseball, whether the game followed Massachusetts or New York rules, but, like his father, he enjoyed a good brawl, and he held high expectations that one would soon break out.

Father intervened, withdrawing a pamphlet from the inside pocket of his waistcoat. "He's right, Sergeant. Rule Number Nine here states . . . 'The ball must be caught flying in all cases.'"

"And it's a rule I guarantee you that we shall adopt in Dedham on the Thirteenth," the Green Mountain captain answered.

"Well," the sergeant said with a snarl, "we don't play that way in Hoboken."

The burly man on third base then made a rather indelicate comment about Hoboken's populace, and Mike Peabody got his wish.

* * *

"So who won the contest?" Mother asked that evening, after placing a bloody slab of beef over Father's eye.

"It was fifty-nine to six," I answered, "when the constable and some officers from Fort Adams stopped the riot. At least, that's what the scorer told me. In Green Mountain's favor."

"We would have gotten more tallies," Father said in defense of the home squad, "if the game had continued."

"Of course, Henry," Mother said, but she gave me a knowing wink before instructing me to wash up for supper.

From that day forward, I never lost interest in baseball, and tried to recreate the game—albeit without fisticuffs—and instruct my classmates on the particular rules over the next few weeks. I retained the pamphlet my father had lost when the Fort Adams sergeant had punched him in the head, often consulting it for various rule interpretations or asking schoolmaster Mr. O'Quinn for his advice, Mr. O'Quinn being a firm believer in how sporting events led to manhood and gentlemanly endeavors. Mike Peabody, ever my faithful companion, stuck with me, and actually proved to be a capable first baseman, and several other friends, always willing to experiment, gave it a chance, but most preferred rounders, cricket, or sneaking to Mike Peabody's dad's tavern to watch the fights, listen to the swearing, and perhaps get a taste of the whiskey and beer being served.

Having become fascinated with the way the Green Mountain player could throw the ball with such finesse, velocity, and movement, I wanted to be a pitcher, but my knowledge of the game—not to mention the fact that Jimmy Bliss could pitch better than anyone this side of Greenwich Bay—relegated me to catcher, though I was a tad small.

By the time school let out that summer, we had assembled a decent club, and scheduled regular matches on Saturday afternoons against the sons of the Fort Adams officers at the field overlooking Brenton Cove. The Army boys, like their fathers fond of the New York version of the game, didn't care much for my rules, but I insisted we use the regulations adopted by the Massachusetts Association of Base-Ball Players at Dedham that spring.

Our games became spirited affairs, and soon drew a handful of officers, officers' wives, girls from the Narragansett Subscription School, and a few parents, including my mother. Father rarely attended these contests, and not because he found himself too occupied with forming the Newport Base Ball Club. Fact is, his obsession with baseball had withered, as Henry Wallace MacNaughton had become a leader of the New England Abolition movement.

Even among the staunchest Abolitionists—and many lived in Rhode Island and Massachusetts—only a handful had ever read a sixteen-page pamphlet titled "How to Conquer Texas before Texas Conquers Us" written and published by Edward Everett Hale. This Boston-born, Harvard-educated minister had become so obsessed after the annexation of Texas as a slave state that he preached how Northerners should settle in Texas to keep slavery from spreading. A decade later, Fred Olmsted published a controversial book called *A Journey*

Through Texas, which several Abolitionists excerpted in pamphlets that they distributed at rallies and stump speeches, one of which, along with a newly printed version of Hale's prose, found its way into my father's hand.

Thus, by August of 1858, my father had become less infatuated with baseball and obsessed with the thought of a free-soil, cotton-growing colony in Texas. Before the month was out, he had sold his drugstore as well as our home on Bellevue Street and had begun preparations to move our family to this faraway wasteland called Texas.

"I don't want to leave Newport," I told my mother. "My friends are all here. I've known Mike Peabody all my life."

"You can always write Mike, and he can write you."

"But what about our baseball club?"

"I'm sure they play baseball in Texas." She tousled my hair. "And if they don't, you can teach them, just as you taught Mike and Andy and Jimmy and Mister O'Quinn and all your friends."

"But why? Why do we have to go?"

Smiling, she pulled me close. "It's a noble cause," she said softly. "Freeing the Negro, occluding this blight. I'm proud of your father. This takes a lot of courage."

"He'll forget about it." My mood turned surly. "Just like he forgot about the Newport Base Ball Club. Just like he forgot about my birthday party that time. Just like he forgot about that medicine that would cure the gout. Just like he forgets about everything. He'll find something new in Texas, and he'll tinker with that for a week or two, and then find something else."

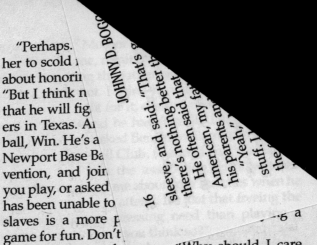

"Perhaps. ... her to scold ... about honori... "But I think n... that he will fig... ers in Texas. A... ball, Win. He's a... Newport Base Ba... vention, and join... you play, or asked... has been unable to... slaves is a more p... need than playing a game for fun. Don't...

I pulled away from ...her. "Why should I care about a bunch of ignorant darkies?"

Mother surprised me yet again. Her backhand sent me reeling.

The Fort Adams boys defeated the city club, 100–47, in my last game in Newport before leaving for Texas. I struck out three times, dropped the ball twice as much, and once sent the ball sailing well over the third baseman's head, allowing three runs to score and prompting laughter and insults from spectators and players alike. The loss left a bitter taste in my mouth, so Mike Peabody suggested we go to the back of his father's tavern, an invitation which I readily accepted. In an overflowing trash bin behind that bucket of blood, Mike found a bottle of Scotch, its neck broken but several fingers of amber liquid in the bottom, and we poured some into a rusty airtight, never considering the dangers of broken glass or lockjaw.

I coughed up my first swallow of the raw whiskey, wiped phlegm with my sweaty shirt

ood stuff. Father says

ran single-malt Scotch."

, too, for I was first-generation

ther having left Edinburgh with

d siblings in 1834.

Mike said, "well, Papa don't serve this

heard him tell a drummer that he just gets

fancy bottles from Mister Zeske and fills 'em

up with the hogo he serves regular."

"It's still good," I lied, forcing down another swallow of coal oil.

"Wish you wasn't going to Texas," Mike said later, pushing his sweat-drenched red bangs off his forehead. "I was starting to enjoy our baseball matches, but now Andy Turner says I'll have to play catcher, and he's going to make Sean take over first base."

"Didn't take Andy long to anoint himself manager," I said with a sour face and hoarse voice before pouring the rest of the liquor into the tin can.

"Still," Mike repeated, "I wish you wasn't leaving."

Passing the can to my friend, I admitted that I didn't want to leave Rhode Island.

"Hear Texas is full of wild Injuns, snakes, gumbos, and highwaymen."

"Mother says they're mostly hardshell Baptists, at least, where we're going."

"Where's that?"

"Jack County," I answered with utter contempt.

"Hope you don't get scalped."

"I hope you catch better than you played first base."

With a snigger, Mike downed the rest of the

"Perhaps." Mother surprised me. I had expected her to scold me, remind me of the commandment about honoring thy father, but she remained calm. "But I think not. I think he will preach Abolition, that he will fight for it, even against the Southerners in Texas. And he hasn't really forgotten baseball, Win. He's asked Benjamin Cornay to lead the Newport Base Ball Club, to attend next year's convention, and join the association. He's watched you play, or asked me about your matches when he has been unable to attend. It's just that freeing the slaves is a more pressing need than playing a game for fun. Don't you think so?"

I pulled away from her. "Why should I care about a bunch of ignorant darkies?"

Mother surprised me yet again. Her backhand sent me reeling.

The Fort Adams boys defeated the city club, 100–47, in my last game in Newport before leaving for Texas. I struck out three times, dropped the ball twice as much, and once sent the ball sailing well over the third baseman's head, allowing three runs to score and prompting laughter and insults from spectators and players alike. The loss left a bitter taste in my mouth, so Mike Peabody suggested we go to the back of his father's tavern, an invitation which I readily accepted. In an overflowing trash bin behind that bucket of blood, Mike found a bottle of Scotch, its neck broken but several fingers of amber liquid in the bottom, and we poured some into a rusty airtight, never considering the dangers of broken glass or lockjaw.

I coughed up my first swallow of the raw whiskey, wiped phlegm with my sweaty shirt sleeve, and said: "That's good stuff. Father says there's nothing better than single-malt Scotch."

He often said that, too, for I was first-generation American, my father having left Edinburgh with his parents and siblings in 1834.

"Yeah," Mike said, "well, Papa don't serve this stuff. I heard him tell a drummer that he just gets the fancy bottles from Mister Zeske and fills 'em up with the hogo he serves regular."

"It's still good," I lied, forcing down another swallow of coal oil.

"Wish you wasn't going to Texas," Mike said later, pushing his sweat-drenched red bangs off his forehead. "I was starting to enjoy our baseball matches, but now Andy Turner says I'll have to play catcher, and he's going to make Sean take over first base."

"Didn't take Andy long to anoint himself manager," I said with a sour face and hoarse voice before pouring the rest of the liquor into the tin can.

"Still," Mike repeated, "I wish you wasn't leaving."

Passing the can to my friend, I admitted that I didn't want to leave Rhode Island.

"Hear Texas is full of wild Injuns, snakes, gumbos, and highwaymen."

"Mother says they're mostly hardshell Baptists, at least, where we're going."

"Where's that?"

"Jack County," I answered with utter contempt.

"Hope you don't get scalped."

"I hope you catch better than you played first base."

With a snigger, Mike downed the rest of the

whiskey. "Couldn't be no worse than you, Win, the way you played today."

I punched his arm, and we began a fine wrestling match among the refuse behind the dram shop, which ended in a draw as soon as the whiskey took hold, and then we covered the trash with our own refuse, sicker than dogs, but still believing that Mike Peabody's dad served mighty good whiskey.

My first hangover, but certainly not my last, probably didn't subside until a train carried Mother, Father, and me across the Ohio River.

CHAPTER TWO

Father set up shop in the corner office of a limestone building on Jacksboro's main square, peddling the products he had had shipped from Rhode Island: Hazard & Caswell's Pure Light Straw Colored Cod Liver Oil, Alpine Hair Balm and Dr. Sanford's Liver Invigorator. Mostly, though, he tried to sell Texians on the concept of emancipation. I pushed what I considered a much nobler pursuit.

Ever so slowly, I garnered a modicum of success. I can't say the same of Father, although no one ran him out of town on a rail.

It is easy to think of Texas in the years before the Rebellion as a land full of whip-wielding slaveholders and buckskinned Secessionists who cursed Negro and Abolitionist alike and would eventually liken Abraham Lincoln to Santa Anna. Certainly a handful of slave owners called Jack County home, and more than a few despised my father's political views, but history would record northwest Texas, on the edge of the Indian frontier, as a nest of strong Unionists, not all of them Abolitionists, of course, but men and women who accepted and tolerated the espousings of Henry Wallace MacNaughton more than they bought his Yankee hair balm. You see, traveling theatrical combinations seldom stopped in Jacksboro, and since Westerners loved entertainment, Father's Saturday afternoon stump speeches drew crowds, who sometimes cheered, sometimes heckled, but mostly just listened politely before meandering off to do their shopping, drinking, or gambling.

At the beginning, that is. By 1861, the mood of the people had turned less tolerant and more violent.

Naturally—after school and chores—I championed baseball, which proved an equally hard sell in Jack County.

It just occurred to me, as I write these words in my hotel room, that I inherited at least one trait from Henry Wallace MacNaughton: obsession. I must have been as compulsive as he was, focused on spreading the gospel of baseball while he preached Abolition and the evils of enslavement.

"Baseball," said Eugene Oliver with a snort. "Sounds like a game for slinks."

"It is a manly endeavor," I replied.

" 'Manly,' he says." Eugene elicited a number of giggles from our fellow classmates. " 'Manly,' coming from a yank named Winthrop."

My ears colored a rich crimson as those giggles metamorphosed into guffaws.

"Out here," the thick-waisted, pockmarked boy went on, "manly endeavors are poker,

mumblety-peg, horseracing, and scalpin' red niggers. You ain't no man. By thunder, I bet you wear
a corset and chemise under that girl's dress."

Mother, you see, had not adopted the Texian
ways of attire, and, looking back, I concede that I
presented a rather ridiculous sight in my kilt suit
of checked cassimere, surrounded by a handful of
children in itchy homespun and wide-brimmed
slouch hats. Eugene Oliver, the dirtiest and
smelliest of them all, towered over my classmates
and me. His father raised hogs on Lost Creek and
his older brother worked—rustled, if you believed the street-yarns told over dominoes at Father's drugstore—cattle in the Keechi Valley. I
had seen Eugene provoke fights at school before,
always thrashing his victim before our schoolmaster threatened to send him home to help his
father tend hogs if he didn't stop. There was no
way I could beat that lummox in a fair fight.

So I hit him with my baseball bat.

Not in the head, mind you. I wasn't so provoked to risk murdering the ruffian, but I did
chop him hard at his knees, and down he went,
screaming and writhing in pain as I flung the bat
aside and jumped atop of him, pounding his
meaty face with my bony fists. We both
screamed, him in pain, me in enraged fury.

Never had I been provoked to draw blood. I
scarcely recognized the animal I had become, and
wanted to stop, especially once Eugene begged
me to quit, but I punched and punched, distantly
hearing another shout, that of fetching Lucy
Covey as she screamed for the schoolmaster, June
Rainey, to stop me from killing poor Eugene.

Lucy didn't care a whit for any of the Olivers; she feared I'd be hanged for murder.

How many minutes passed, I did not know. I knew nothing but brutality. Eugene's screams had become sobs as I flailed about, but when I drew back to hammer him again, a vise almost snapped my wrist, and suddenly I went hurling backward, landing with a thud that knocked the breath from my lungs.

When my vision cleared, when I understood that I wasn't going to die, I stared at a bronze, mustached face shaded by a black hat. At first, I thought Mr. Rainey had laid me out, but that couldn't be. For one thing, June Rainey kept his face clean shaven. Besides, he lacked backbone to break up any fight, and, more importantly, he probably desired me to maim, if not kill, that callous oaf.

"You all right, boy?" a firm voice drawled.

Unable to talk, I merely nodded.

"What's your name?"

I coughed first, tested my mouth, and risked speech. "Win MacNaughton."

"New hereabouts, ain't you?"

"A couple of months, I fathom."

"*Fathom?*" The man pushed back his hat and cackled. "*Fathom?* Hell, no, I reckon you ain't been here long."

He extended a massive paw, and I cautiously took it, cringing as his fingers tightened, almost crushing the bones in my hand, then yelping as he jerked me upright roughly.

Momentarily I considered him a rough friend who had kept me off the gallows, perhaps a constable sworn to keep the peace even if it meant aiding the likes of Eugene Oliver. Kneeling, he dusted off my kilt suit while whispering in a most menacing tone: "You ever use a piece of lumber like that again on Gene, Win MacNewton, and I'll use this Bowie knife on your innards. Savvy?"

My throat filled with sand; my bowels quaked. I nodded again as my eyes located a massive pig-sticker scabbarded on his right hip, next to a single-shot horse pistol shoved inside the belt.

"He ain't much," the man said, "but he is my only brother."

I knew then that I was at Pig Oliver's mercy.

Eugene had managed to stand and wipe the tears off his cheeks when Pig Oliver turned around. "You ought to. . . ."

Eugene never finished, because his big brother cuffed him viciously, and the young rowdy dropped to the ground again, his nose pouring blood.

"You got what you deserved, boy. Now get up. I'm takin' you home. Pa'll tan your hide."

When the dust had swallowed the disappearing Olivers, Mr. Rainey picked up my bat, offered it to me, and said: "So, Winthrop, show us how this sporting affair is played."

As far as Eugene Oliver is concerned, he never tormented any of the fifteen children enrolled at Mr. Rainey's subscription school after that day. He even started playing baseball during recess or on the rare Saturday mornings when I cajoled enough people to try a game. Mostly we just played toss. I am not saying Eugene and I became the best of friends, merely that we formed an uneasy truce. He couldn't hit well, or catch, but he had a strong arm and accurate throw. His brother played with us, too, when he wasn't sleeping off a drunk or riding about the countryside, chasing Indians, horses, cattle, buffalo, or simply looking for trouble.

In those games, everyone wanted Pig Oliver on his team. As a catcher, he intimidated anyone who reached third base by running a thumb over the blade of his massive knife, daring the player to try to score. If someone challenged him, he was apt to throw the ball at that person, and, if he hit you, it hurt. On the bases, he would bowl over anyone in his path, once even clubbing a second baseman with a pistol barrel. I've often wondered if Ty Cobb were somehow related to that son-of-a-bitch. Yet I admit, as much as I disliked Pig Oliver, as much as I feared him, I wanted him on my team, too. If you listen to radio broadcasts of baseball games, you've probably heard an announcer say of Joe DiMaggio or Stan Musial: "He tore the cover off the ball." Well, on several occasions in '59 and '60, Pig Oliver did just that—literally—stopping the game until we could rewrap the ball with calfskin or make a new one.

Our contests were mostly makeshift affairs. Instead of driving stakes into the hard Texas earth, we used cow patties for bases, unaware that we were adopting a New York rule, which substituted Massachusetts-mandated stakes with canvas bags much like the ones used today. No one ever stepped on the dung on purpose, excepting the rawhide Olivers, but rather followed a gentleman's agreement on where the base was. Although I possessed a couple of fine bat-sticks (as we called them then) from Newport, most players preferred the local version, often thicker than the rules allowed, made from neither ash nor maple or pine or hickory, but gnarled juniper.

Back in New England, I had never been good enough to pitch, but that's what I did in Jack County, especially considering that Pig Oliver proved to be a much better catcher than me. So did Lucy Covey's younger brother, Ryan.

Gradually I began to take a liking to my new home. Jacksboro no longer appeared to be a blight at the end of the universe populated by uncouth b'hoys and hellions. The baseball games turned into fine frolics, if the contestants not always followed the rules or showed manly athletic ability and fine sportsmanship. Off the field, I developed a taste for strong coffee, burned grain often substituted for real beans, and Mrs. Covey's rhubarb pie. Mr. Rainey, who often umpired our baseball exhibitions, instilled in me an appreciation for William Shakespeare and Honoré de Balzac, even mathematics, something my instructors in Rhode Island had failed to accomplish. I worked in my father's store on Saturday afternoons while he preached free-soil sermons. I sang in the choir at the Methodist camp meetings (the only services around, and my parents constantly reminded me that we were Presbyterians!), and wrote Mike Peabody each Sunday evening, posting the letter the next day, relating all my adventures in baseball games and chasing wild Comanches. The latter, as well as most of the former, I exaggerated, although Indian raids became commonplace, especially during the spring, and the first funeral I ever attended came in April of 1860 after Mr.

Covey and a neighbor were killed—by Kiowas, according to Pig Oliver, who found the bodies— while tending stock near Snake Creek.

In three years, Mike Peabody wrote back twice. I hadn't expected much more from my best friend. Never the most disciplined fellow, Mike took to writing as well as children take to cod liver oil. Nor did his letters say much, which is about what I expected, too.

Perhaps the best thing that happened to me came in the form of my wardrobe. At last, Mother adopted the Texian dress as I outgrew my kilt suits, cheviots, Newport ties, and silly sailor hats. I got to wear collarless flannel and muslin shirts, duck trousers, floppy hats, even boots that I didn't have to lace up. Chas Lauderdale, whose son Buck (when he attended school, an occurrence so rare Mr. Rainey would applaud when he saw him sitting at his desk) played right field, taught me how to ride, offered me a nip from his flask every now and then, and let me fire his Navy Colt when deep in his cups, then made me clean and reload it.

I'm not saying that I ever considered Jacksboro some sort of Utopia, but I came to accept it for what it was: a friendly town with mostly friendly people.

For Christmas, 1860, when I was thirteen, I opened a package underneath what passed for a tree. Mother smiled as I pulled away the brown paper and stared at the shoes, biting back my disappointment, fearing that she had ordered some new hideous pair of embroidered slippers or ill-fitting operas that I would have to wear to church, school, and the Covey Ranch. Somehow, I managed to crack a false smile in my granite face, and pulled out the shoes, mumbling a barely audible and unconvincing "thank you" before noticing that these had canvas uppers, not leather. They weren't dress shoes, but high-top athletic tie-ups.

Of course, they didn't have spikes, not then anyway. If you've ever read *Beadle's Dime Base-Ball Player* of 1860, you might recall a line about the bases being made of double-thick, heavy canvas "as there will be much jumping on them with spiked shoes." But cleats were a rarity in those years, and the Beadle's book focused on New York baseball, while at the time I preferred the Massachusetts game that used wooden stakes for bases, not sawdust-filled bags. Cleats, though allowed by the rules, weren't really needed, and didn't become common until after the Great Rebellion.

As I marveled at this treasured gift, my memories flashed back to that spring day in Rhode Island and the Bostonians from the Green Mountain Club, their knickerbockers and pretty shirts, and canvas shoes that completed those dashing uniforms. When I pulled on my shoes and laced them up, they fit . . . well . . . maybe a bit too large, but felt more comfortable than my stovepipe boots. It certainly beat running barefooted around our field filled with stones, prickly pear, and cow dung.

"Do they fit?" Mother asked.

"Yes, ma'am. Only, I hope I stop growing." I could scarcely control my excitement. My words ran together. "I hope they still fit when spring comes and we can have some contests. Can I take them over the Coveys tomorrow, show them to Ryan? Please."

"Do you mean Ryan Covey?" Father asked in a rare display of humor. "Or Lucy?"

Covering her mouth with both hands, Mother laughed.

"Well . . ." I couldn't think of a proper response. Of course, I meant Lucy.

Father shook his head, picked up the latest issue of the *Liberator*, and went back to reading, although I noticed a smile betraying his granite countenance, too.

"I thought Lucy Covey doesn't like baseball," Mother said after regaining a measure of composure.

"Well . . . I'd still like for her to see 'em." Quickly I added: "And Ryan."

"*Them*," she said sternly. "See *them*. I swan, I don't know what . . ."

She never finished for Father lowered the *Liberator*. " '*I swan*,' Regina?"

I took my baseball shoes to the Covey Ranch the following evening. Ryan shrugged with a nonchalance I found annoying. Lucy, however, found them interesting, said they undoubtedly would make me run faster, that she couldn't wait to see me wear them come spring. That came from the same Lucy Covey who never once watched us play during recess or on Saturdays.

I thought I might kiss her then, but I didn't. No, I never kissed Lucy Covey, never saw her much after that Christmas, and I often wonder what happened to the Covey family.

Instead, I hugged her, wished her and her mother and brother a happy New Year, and tried to sound enthusiastic when she showed me the scarf she got for Christmas. It was a hand-me-down from her mother, the silk bringing out the blue of Lucy's eyes, a little frayed, and it suddenly struck me how poor the Covey family must be after the death of Mr. Covey. Ryan, if he had gotten anything that Christmas, hadn't shared it with me. No rhubarb pie was served for dessert. Instead, Mother had brought over leftover stew and bread peppered with dried cranberries. When I started to ask for seconds, she stepped on my new athletic shoes, stepped hard, and those canvas uppers didn't offer much protection. I bit back my request.

Lucy hugged me again before we left, her blue eyes dazzling, and thus the year 1860 ended with me looking forward to the following spring. My dreams were being answered.

Those dreams ended with the coming of the new year and spring. And war.

CHAPTER THREE

They held the vote in three precincts on February 23, 1861.

Only one question appeared on the ballot, asking for the rejection or ratification of the Secession Ordinance passed during the Austin convention, February 1st.

Father voted against Secession, signing his name, he announced to us that evening, with a flourish and adding his personal thoughts: "Glory to the Union. Freedom for all men!" In fact, when the votes were tallied, Jack County remained true to our country. Seventy-six voted against Secession to fourteen ballots for ratification. My new home didn't go this alone, either. A handful of counties near the Red River and other points decried the idea of leaving the Union, but in the end Texians voted overwhelmingly to join South Carolina and the other Secessionists—Seceshs, Union loyalists would soon call them. The following month, after a convention in Montgomery, Alabama, Texas ratified the Confederate Constitution.

My father had seen this coming.

Back in November, Lincoln had won the Presidency, and talk at Father's drugstore became more and more heated. Most townsmen wanted to remain in the Union. The few slave owners voiced war. Ruffians spoiled for a fight, eager at the chance to whip those damnyankee tyrants. The Olivers, as far as I could tell, did not care one way or the other. In December, South Carolina became the first state to withdraw from the Union, and others followed. Father's stump speeches no longer drew quiet crowds. Instead, angry mobs tried to shout him down: "You damned Black Republican!" "You fool Bourbon Democrats!" he would blast back. "You are about to enter a fight you cannot possibly win. Our just Lord God will not allow you to win."

Much of this, my thirteen-year-old brain could not process. At first, I could not imagine how things would change. Whether I lived in the Confederate States of America or the United States of America meant little. I just longed for warmer weather so I could play baseball again, and show off for Lucy Covey. It didn't take long, though, before I learned how this move to dissolve the Union affected me.

When spring came, my classmates shunned my suggestions of baseball, opting instead to play chuck-a-luck, tag, or some other game . . . without me. Neither Lucy nor Ryan Covey showed up for school that spring, and Mr. Rainey declined to address my concerns about them, although I once heard him whisper to Mother that Mrs. Covey couldn't afford to pay the subscription, fifty cents per month per child, and, when he had told her that wasn't necessary, she had straightened her back and cursed his charity. Pig Oliver had joined a ranging company to protect the border from Indians and a possible Federal invasion—paranoia running high among the Secessionists—and brother Eugene had too many chores to attend school. Buck Lauderdale, at sixteen, became the first of my classmates to enlist in a Confederate unit, and the citizens of Jacksboro threw a gala ball to honor him before he departed for Houston with his father.

Both died before they "saw the elephant", I heard—Chas of dysentery and Buck of snakebite in Louisiana.

I had lost my catchers (Pig Oliver and Ryan Covey), my right fielder (Buck Lauderdale), my first fan (Lucy Covey), and most of my friends. My Rhode Island heritage transformed me into a Yankee, reviled by true Texians, and Mr. Rainey stopped calling on me in class, probably for my own good. I blamed Father. After all, had Henry MacNaughton simply been a Unionist, he would have had more supporters than detractors, but he was an Abolitionist, a warmonger who suggested that Texians and Arkansans could not defeat New Yorkers and Bay Staters. I wanted to hate Father for causing all my troubles, yet he was the only one who would play toss with me. Both of us had plenty of time, for he had closed his drugstore the first week of April, I suspect for his own safety, although the pittance he earned, especially after the Secession vote, hardly made it practical to keep the store open.

Yet I remained stubborn, so, when Saturday

rolled around, I pulled on my athletic tie-ups, grabbed a ball and an ash bat, and headed for the field in town, bound and determined to round up enough players for a game. I didn't tell my parents, just sneaked out the house.

To my surprise, a crowd had gathered at the field, the largest I had seen in Jacksboro, and I almost shouted with joy, thinking those fools had seen the error of their ways, had started up a contest without me. I moved toward the throng, stopping when a woman shook her head in disgust and tossed a yellow paper on the ground, hurrying past me without as much noticing my presence. Sticking the bat under my arm, I fetched and unwrapped the paper. My stomach roiled.

AUCTION!!! AUCTION!!! AUCTION!!!
I, Leonard Weaver, having sold my farm and intending to move back to Alabama, will sell at the field betwixt the borough of Jacksboro and Lost Creek,
ONE BUCK NIGGER!
ONE NIGGER WENCH!
The buck, called Joe, is about 27 years old, weighs 230 pounds, is a good field worker and wheelwright. Caused no trouble since I gelded him in 1857.
The wench, called Martha, is about 20, also a good worker, can bear children, don't eat much or say much. I will also offer for sale the following: 1 wagon, 1 side saddle, 1 very good whip, a quarter-ton of 2-year-old tobacco, 3 yokes of oxen, 2 10-inch stump plows, and 50 one-gallon whiskey jugs.
The public is invited.

Curious, I flanked the crowd and stood near what had once been second base, as the auctioneer brought out the Negro male to auction off to any willing buyer.

Men and women of color whom I had seen in Rhode Island had been freedmen, cobblers and preachers, seamstresses and sailors, educated and friendly. For the life of me, I could not recall ever seeing a slave during my short stay in Texas. I must have seen one before, because, as I said, slaves did live in Jack County. Mayhap I just never noticed them, paid them scant attention as I would a bovine or field mouse.

I noticed Joe, however. I couldn't take my eyes off him.

He had a barrel chest and shaved head, flattened nose and yellow teeth, arms thicker than three or four ash bats, but he appeared stoop-shouldered, and walked with a limp. He rarely looked up, never making direct eye contact with anyone, and he simply stood there while owner and auctioneer prodded him this way and that, inspecting his teeth the way a fellow would a horse for sale. His clothes were ragged, worn, his muscles corded, and, when his owner made him take off his shirt, I grimaced at the sight of his scarred back, permanent welts from the lashes he had received during his life in bondage.

Little wonder the lady had found this display so revolting. Another curious woman turned to flee after seeing the slave's whip marks, but I stood there, mesmerized.

"Let's open the bidding at two hundred and fifty dollars," the auctioneer began.

"Confederate or Union?" someone shouted out, and a chorus of cackles echoed his question.

Most had gathered not to bid, but to be entertained. I doubt if many Jack County residents could afford a slave, or, for that matter, a stump plow or even an empty whiskey jug. Yet apparently word of the auction had spread to the richer hamlets—Gainesville, Dallas, and Weatherford—for the auctioneer began talking at a furious pace as men in black silk hats and broadcloth suits kept the price of Joe rising.

It held at $850 for a moment. My mouth had turned dry.

"Eight and a half going once," the auctioneer said, and wet his lips. "Twice . . ."

"Eight seventy-five!" This new voice shouting caused me to shiver.

My father stepped out of the mass to my left, approached the auction block, and turned to face everyone. Timid, maybe ashamed or afraid, I tried to retreat, to get out of his sight, but rough hands stopped me. Someone cursed Henry MacNaughton.

"Eight eighty!" a graybeard stranger said.

"Eight eighty-five," my father responded without hesitation.

"Nine hundred." The graybeard sounded angry.

"Let's make it one thousand," Father said.

Muffled whispers chorused through the gathering. A bucktoothed man to my right cried out how that was an obscene amount to pay for a "castrated darky." I tried to swallow, but my throat proved too dry to work up a decent spit. Where would Father get his hands on that kind of money? $1,000 seemed so unreachable to me.

Then it hit me: Mother, or, rather, mother's parents. I could not comprehend this at first, imagining how furious my mother and grandparents would be at Father's actions. Buying a slave? What would he want with a slave? For God's sake, he wanted to free the slaves.

Seconds later, I belittled my own stupidity. He wasn't interested in owning anyone, but was trying to buy this poor man to set him free.

The Texas hard rocks understood this, too, quicker than I had.

"You can't sell to that nigger-lovin' bastard!" someone yelled out. "He'll set the buck free, Leonard. We'll have an uprisin', get our throats slit."

"Our women won't be safe!" another rowdy added.

Leonard Weaver, bound for Alabama, did not appear to give a tinker's damn about the well-being of his soon-to-be former neighbors. The auctioneer shot him a glance, but Weaver nodded and said: "Yankee money spends as good as Texas money, boys."

People began cursing Leonard Weaver with as much venom as they cursed my father.

"I have a thousand dollars," the auctioneer said, not sounding so eager any more. "Can I get a thousand and a quarter?" His eyes trained on the graybeard, but the man's head shook slowly.

"One thousand and ten?"

Nothing.

"A thousand and five?"

A few curses, followed by an eerie silence.

"Anybody interested? . . . Anyone . . . ? Sold to Mister MacNaughton for one thousand dollars."

As the clerk recorded the bid, my father told the crowd: "I aim to have the woman, too. You can drive up the bid all you want, but I will win in the end."

Now Leonard Weaver grimaced. He had surely hoped to fetch a fine price for his female slave, but Father was intimidating the buyers.

A buckskinned figure stepped forward, drew a Navy revolver, cocked it, and took aim at Father's chest.

"You make one bid, mister, and you'll pay your debt to Lucifer in hell."

"One hundred dollars." Father pulled open his shirt front. "Make your shot count, sir," he told the assassin.

"No!" I shot out from my poor hiding place, lifting my bat, running to stop this ruffian from murdering my father. Heavy arms jerked me to a stop, lifting me off the ground, and my bat fell to the dirt. I fought against my captor, but to no avail. Screwing my eyes shut, I waited for the pistol's report, but no shot was fired, and, when I opened my eyes, the man had lowered his weapon and my father was buttoning his shirt, having called the rowdy's bluff.

The rowdy, I recognized, was Pig Oliver, better armed now that he was a ranger. Quietly he disappeared into the crowd, neither looking at me, nor at Father.

"One ten!" another stranger countered, and the bidding resumed. My captor lowered me, and I grabbed my bat and ran to Father's side.

In the end, Father bought the Negress for $325. As he paid Leonard Weaver, he listened to the warnings, but said nothing, not even to me. We took Joe and Martha home, where Father freed them, signing their papers while telling Mother what he had done. She listened without comment, staring at me, likely wondering about my presence at this malicious event. What Father didn't tell my mother were the threats. Our house would be burned, the roughest of the lot said, and we would be hanged alongside our darkies. Father didn't have to reveal this; Mother knew it already.

"We cannot stay," she said as Father placed the freedom papers into Joe's callused hands.

"You understand you must leave?" Father told the big man, ignoring Mother for the moment.

The Negro nodded.

"There is a mule in the barn," Father continued. "I have written out a bill of sale along with your papers, but neither is likely to save you if you are caught on the road in Texas. You must leave now, not tonight, now. Head north, through Indian Territory, and on to Kansas. I have drawn you a map. Follow the trail till you reach the town of Lawrence, then go henceforth to the house of Ezekiel Schiff. He is an Abolitionist, a leader in the Underground Railroad. Stay off the main roads, and remember what I said about these papers. They will not protect you from fire-breathers."

How Father knew all this, I had no clue. He had all of this arranged, from the mule to the map to the name of some man I had never heard of in Lawrence, Kansas. My father never planned anything, simply did things on a whim, never thought anything through, never stuck with any idea.

That was, I think, Father at his best, strong and determined. This is how I always want to remember him: a fighter, a man with an intense sense of

justice, not the befuddled, unimaginative apothecary who could barely hold a train of thought for
more than an hour. Until that day, I had never
considered him to be a brave man, but it struck
me then that he was willing to lay down his life
for this cause.

Eventually he would do just that.

There was an irony to this scrap, only we didn't
know it at the time. The auction was held on Saturday, April 13, 1861. More than 1,000 miles away the
previous day, the fool Secessionists in Charleston,
South Carolina, had opened fire on Fort Sumter.
On Sunday, April 14th, while Mother read Bible
passages to us at home, refusing us to leave the
safety of our house and attend the camp meeting,
the Federal soldiers inside the fort would lower the
United States flag and surrender.

The Great Rebellion had begun.

CHAPTER FOUR

The heavily perspiring gent in the gray flannel suit sitting on my right said he had paid a scalper $50 to watch Game 1 of the 1946 World Series, what he called "a game for the ages, the Pollet-Hughson duel."

"That's a right smart of money," I said.

"Nothin' compared to what I'll have in my billfold when the Cardinals win the shebang," he responded. "Some fool bookie out there's givin' four-to-one odds. Must be dreamin' or plumb mad iffen he thinks the Red Sox can whip our boys."

After the national anthem, he lifted his program, shielding his face from me, and tried to sneak a drink from his flask. I guess he thought hospitality would force him to offer a sip if I saw him imbibing, although I hadn't swallowed a drop of intoxicating liquors since my seventy-eighth birthday. When the program lowered, he asked in a rye-scented voice: "How much did you pay, old-timer, for your ticket?"

"Nothing. I am a guest of honor."

"No foolin'. Who are you, Marty Marion's grandpa or somethin'?"

"No, sir, no relation to any player on either team. Truth of the matter is, I don't rightly know why they invited me, other than I am about as old as the game itself, and I used to be a ballist."

"A ballist! 'T'hell's a ballist?"

I laughed out loud, leaning forward as left-hander Howie Pollet got ready to make the game's first pitch. "I asked Mike Peabody that very same question in the summer of 'Sixty-One."

The gent didn't talk to me for the rest of the game. In fact, he never said another word until Rudy York sent Pollet's pitch in the tenth inning into a hot-dog stand in the left-field bleachers. Then he started cursing, which he kept up until Earl Johnson mowed down the Cardinals in the bottom half of the inning for a 3–2 Red Sox victory and sent the gent in the gray flannel suit cursing his way to Sportsman's Park's nearest exit.

"Look at you," I told Mike Peabody that sultry August afternoon when I saw him for the first time since leaving Rhode Island three years before.

Mike had filled out, shooting up to stand a towering three inches over me. His shoulders had broadened, and he even sported what amounted to peach fuzz over his upper lip, although the way he stroked it, he must have considered it a prize-winning tonsorial masterpiece.

I hadn't been marveling at my best friend's growth spurt, but rather his wardrobe. He wore athletic tie-ups, blue stockings, white jodhpurs with a wide belt, and a white shirt sporting a blue scripted **N** emblazoned over his heart. A white cap, slanted at a rakish angle over his red hair, topped his outfit.

"Hey, Win, I've become a first-rate ballist, am on Newport's first nine," he said excitedly, offering neither a handshake nor a Good to see you, been a long time. "We're playing some New Yorkers this afternoon. Thought you might want to watch. Hello, Missus MacNaughton."

"Hello, Michael," Mother's voice sounded behind me. "How are your mother and father?"

"Fine. I was inviting Win to watch our contest. You want to come, too? They got seats set up underneath parasols for the ladies."

"Thank you, no, Michael, as I have much to do here. But you run along, Winthrop."

I grabbed my hat, pulled the door shut behind me, and gave Mike Peabody a comical sneer. "A *ballist?*" I asked derisively. "What on earth is a *ballist?*"

"Don't josh me, you Texas milksop. I'm a baseball player, and a good one, too. You'll see, Win. The game's changed a mite since you took off for Texas. I still play first base, better than ever, and you should see me strike. Why, I reckon I've tallied two hundred times this season alone."

"If I remember right, Andy Turner was moving you to catcher when we moved to Texas," I said.

"Oh, that didn't take," Mike answered. "And Andy, he ain't played with us in . . . gosh, I ain't got no idea. No, sir, I'm playing first base. Big game today against the White Plains boys, but I think we'll win. So, how was Texas? I thought you might have become a Secesh yourself, living out there in the wild, whipping your chattel."

"Not likely," I said, and gave him an abbreviated report of my stay abroad as we walked briskly to Brenton Cove.

We were never assaulted by Pig Oliver or any of the men who had threatened Father after the auction. In fact, we had lived several more months in Jacksboro, although keeping to ourselves and the few other Abolitionist Unionists who called northwest Texas home. Mother, homesick and scared, turned paler each day, or so it seemed to me, but Father said he would not flee like a coward. It was not until after we received word of the crushing Union defeat at Bull Run, Virginia—Manassas, they called it in Texas—in July that we decided to return home.

"I am not running from these fools," Father had told us. "They shall never see my back. I aim to fight them on their level. I will join a Rhode Island unit and send these unholy traitors to perdition."

I never knew what became of the two slaves Father freed, whether they reached Kansas safely, or were killed or captured and returned to bondage. We departed Texas in late July and arrived home by early August, where Grandfather Easton put us up in one of the cottages he owned on Haliden Hill. Father kept his promise, too, enlisting in the 1st Rhode Island Light Battery even before Mother had us settled into our new home. He looked dashing in his uniform, almost as dashing as Mike Peabody looked in his.

"I almost didn't recognize you when you opened the door, Win," Mike said after I finished my story. "You've growed some, too, and you sound like a Rebel, not any Down-Easter no more."

"I do not!" I protested, remembering how in Jacksboro many children, back when they were speaking to me, often begged me to come over and "talk Yankee to them." My accent remained strikingly New England, or so I thought.

"You talk slow, Win. So your pa's joined the fight, eh?"

"Artillery," I said without enthusiasm. "How about your father?"

"Nah, he figures there's more money in selling John Barleycorn to soldiers than soldiering with them, 'specially after how them Rebs beat our boys down in Virginia last month. War won't last long, no how. Papa's still running the dram shop. That's where I saw your pa . . . him and his friends ordering brandy smashes and jawing on and on about freeing those damned darkies. Almost didn't recognize him, neither, in that tunic and kepi."

"Well, Mike," I said, "I barely recognized you."

Scarcely did I recognize the game they played that Saturday afternoon, either. Mouth agape, I sat among the men in the crowd and watched in shock, disbelief, at what these strangers called baseball.

My four-inch-wide, flat-faced bats were no longer allowed—too similar to those used in cricket, I heard—being replaced by rounded bats with two-and-a-half-inch diameters, a rule that came about in 1859. Whitewash now marked the foul lines, and an umpire, chosen by the two team captains, could suspend play and call balls fair or foul.

Yet these improved instructions I found picayune compared to what else I saw before me.

My square infield had been turned into a diamond, and canvas bags replaced tall wooden stakes as bases. The base paths were longer, too, stretching ninety feet, a good ten yards farther than on the fields on which I had played. Balls caught on the first bounce, which had led to that brawl during the first contest I watched in Newport three years earlier, were recorded as outs. Pitching seemed foreign, too, for I had been taught, and had taught others, to throw the ball overhand, but this, the elitists informed me, did not show the art of *pitching*. In dismay, I studied the White Plains pitcher send his right arm in a comical circular motion, like some erratic windmill, step forward, and deliver an underhanded toss that blurred as it rifled forty-five feet— instead of the thirty-five feet of my baseball game—to home plate. Mike Peabody, the striker, swung his bat-stick hard, rocketing the ball over the shortstop's head for a single that scored Mr. O'Quinn.

"It's the New York game," I said at last.

"Boys at the fort, most of them micks from Brooklyn, been insisting on it," a bystander remarked. "I must admit, though, that I like it better than the way your father played this contest, Master MacNaughton."

I stared at the face I should have recognized, but no name came to mind. Perhaps it was my shock, or rather my revulsion. *New Englanders, Rhode Islanders, shunning Massachusetts rules for the New York version!* They had bastardized my baseball, which I found as seditionist as anything being done in the South.

"Seems much more livelier, requires much prowess," the man went on.

"I don't know . . . ," I began, only to stop as the next Newport striker popped up a fly ball to the left fielder, ending the inning.

"Plus, it's a quicker game," the man said. "They play nine innings, instead of waiting around to see which club can reach one hundred tallies first. You plan on trying to make the first nine?"

"Well . . ." I had not really thought of it, or been invited.

Newport won, 33–29, and afterward I congratulated Mike on his fine athletic form, and Mr. O'Quinn, too.

"Welcome home, Winthrop," my former schoolmaster told me. "Would you like to try out for the Blue Stockings?"

Mr. O'Quinn wasn't the club captain or manager, merely the center fielder, but, when I shrugged, he motioned for me to follow him to the crowd of players—both Blue Stockings and members of the Elite Club of White Plains, New York—and a few fans gathering at home plate, which indeed was a plate of iron, about nine inches in diameter, painted white.

The team captain, who Mr. O'Quinn introduced as Conn Flannery, relinquished a bung starter he had been using to pound on a keg, and gripped my hand, pumping it vigorously. His green eyes blazed with a contagious friendliness. I had prepared myself to dislike this man, this baseball traitor, but I could not help but smile.

"Nothing like a keg of lager for gentlemanly

winners and losers to share after an exhilarating match, eh, Winnie? That's what Henry Chadwick espouses."

I mumbled something—"I guess so," probably—for I didn't know anything about lager or Henry Chadwick, although I would soon learn an ample amount about both. My smile flattened at the name Winnie, but the Newport captain did not notice. Flannery guided me away from the throng that erupted in cheers as soon as the beer started flowing from the spigot, and we relaxed underneath the shade trees.

"Mike and Kelan allowed how you might be desirous of joining our club," he said after stretching out on the lawn.

Moments passed before I understood Kelan to be the schoolmaster's Christian name. I had not formed an answer when the Irishman continued in his thick brogue. "They told me how you and your dad started this club before the unpleasantness began, and that's grand. Your dad joined the First Light Artillery, isn't that so, lad?"

"Yes, sir. About my father, I mean. And, well, about playing on the club . . ."

"What position is your strongest suit?"

"Uh, I played catcher when we first started playing here back in 'Fifty-Eight, but I was pitching in Texas, only, sir, well, the thing is we played a different way."

Conn Flannery nodded. "The Massachusetts game. Nothing wrong with that, but the future is in the New York version. Overhanded throwing isn't pitching at all, and . . . well, 'tis not the place to argue bloody politics or baseball. Catcher and pitcher, though, that's grand. Why the two most important positions on any team are catcher and pitcher. Cannot play without them. Here's me provision, Winnie me lad, do you know where Nammett's store is on Thames Street?"

I said I did.

"Good lad. For ten cents, you can purchase a copy of *Beadle's Dime Base-Ball Player*. Study the rules, and come to our practice on Wednesday. We have a solid first nine, but I see a fine cut about you. Second nine, at the least, and I dare say that it's much more refreshing enjoying lager wearing our blue stockings than broadcloth and gaiters. What say we go have a wee taste?"

I purchased Henry Chadwick's book, subtitled *A Compendium of the Game*, and tried to accept the changes to my beloved pastime. I practiced with Mike Peabody and Kelan O'Quinn on Monday and Tuesday afternoon, then again Wednesday morning before the club's practice session at the cove later that day.

Conn Flannery praised my enthusiasm, dedication, and my place in history for getting the Newport Base Ball Club moving forward. He didn't have much to say, however, about my ability.

Try as I might, and I tried hard, I could not master these new rules. Having grown up watching the modern version of baseball, you probably think that it's infinitely easier to hit a ball tossed underhanded than it is to make contact with a Harry Brecheen screwball, but I struggled dearly whenever I came up to strike. Nor did I prove to be anything but futile at the position of catcher. If hitting the ball seemed difficult, catching it became downright impossible.

I did not make the first nine that season, nor the next. Nor did I make the second nine. I served on the muffin nine, comprising the worst players, and even my status there, I believe, was more of a gift, a place of honor for Henry Wallace Mac-Naughton's only son.

Oh, I had persistence and determination, traits that helped my club and professional careers last longer than they should have. Whereas Father most likely would have given up, I would not be bested here, not in Newport, not where the Mac-Naughtons had pushed to form a baseball club. Mother and I lied in our letters to Father, saying how I kept improving. I went to school, practiced with the muffins, helped Mother around the house, and was conscripted by Grandfather Easton into working in his shipping line's office weekday afternoons during school days, weekday mornings during the summer.

The year 1861 dissolved into 1862 and '62 into '63. Mike Peabody's father had been badly mistaken in predicting a speedy outcome in the conflict, as had many in both North and South. On raged the war. Father wrote with joy, apologizing for the tears that stained his letter, when Lincoln's Emancipation Proclamation became law in January, and he wrote how proud he was upon hearing the news that the 54th Massachusetts of Negro volunteers had marched out of Boston to fight for the Union. West Virginia became the thirty-fifth state admitted into the United States, a general named Grant began to lay siege to some city in Mississippi, and Confederate forces dealt another crushing blow to the Federal cause in a battle at Chancellorsville, Virginia.

By the summer of 1863, I had grown from a mule-headed son of a daydreaming apothecary to a restless and bored sixteen-year-old who absolutely loathed working in the cramped, stuffy confines of a shipping office, learning, I was constantly reminded, to be a bookkeeper. I kept overhearing Grandfather Easton tell Mother that I would begin my apprenticeship soon.

Yet I had moved my way off the dreadful muffin nine of the Newport Blue Stockings. I had practiced catching until my hands turned black and blue, till my knuckles swelled, and my fingers resembled raw, pudgy digits, becoming the first substitute at catcher. Oh, I would love to place the reason as talent, but it had much more to do with attrition.

CHAPTER FIVE

Conn Flannery had departed Newport after Antietam in 1862, joining the Rhode Island 12th Regiment, and would fall in the slaughter at Fredericksburg that December. Shortstop Mickey Seber, left fielder Richard Feamster, and second-nine third baseman FitzGerald Kerry enlisted in other units, Seber never to return and Kerry to be invalided after losing both legs at Cold Harbor. Several players moved away, a couple joined other ball clubs, and fewer and fewer spectators—we didn't call them fans in those days—showed up at the cove to watch the Blue Stockings play.

We fielded a terrible team. Gone were the days of 33–29 victories, replaced by 41–9 losses to superior teams like the Gothams, Eckfords, and Athletics. Mr. O'Quinn had become our captain, and Mike Peabody the star, followed by catcher Jimmy Bliss. Although I had moved up to the second nine, I seldom played, although I got to start on a fabulous Friday afternoon at the Brenton

Cove Grounds because Jimmy Bliss had come down with the ague. July 3, 1863. It marked the last time I would play baseball in Rhode Island until a year after Appomattox.

Only a handful of Newport residents attended the game. They had lost interest in baseball games because of the war, and our horrible record, yet on that day the Blue Stockings would play with the skills and finesse of a professional Cincinnati club I watched in Troy, New York, in 1869. Well, maybe that's a stretcher from an old codger pushing the century mark, but we did play brilliantly, as did our opponent, the Fort Adams Unionists.

The last time I competed against our closest rivals, I acted like a muffin, fumbling the ball on defense, not coming close to hitting it on offense, and generally misleading my team to a 100–47 loss in 1857. Today I dominated, catching several pop fouls for outs, tagging out five fleet Unionists trying to score, and striking for hits nearly every chance I stepped to the plate, including the ninth inning.

Oh, that glorious ninth.

We trailed 19–18 heading into the last inning, and our pitcher, William Smith, Jr., oldest son of Newport's most popular dentist, if there can be such a thing, faced what a sportswriter would call today the power of the Fort Adams' line-up. A burly sergeant, who had hit three triples that afternoon, called for high pitches, boomed a shot down the rightfield line that just missed being fair, then made it count on Smith's second pitch, and easily reached second base.

Yet a tall corporal fouled out to me. Neither he

nor I could believe it for the soldier had struck solid doubles all day. That brought up another powerful hitter. He called low, and Smith threw him a beautiful pitch that he somehow muffed, popping up straight to that son of a dentist for what should have been an easy out. Only Smith's knees buckled and he went sprawling in the dirt. I raced forward to catch the ball, hearing Mr. O'Quinn's cries: "No, Winthrop! No! Protect the plate!"

I knew my mistake, for home plate now lay open, and everyone in the infield raced to catch the ball. The sergeant on third base, guessing the ball would drop for a hit, ran home. I lunged, stretched my right arm as far as it could go, felt my feet lifting off the ground, and sailed over the pitcher's body, snagging the ball just before it dropped, then crashed into the warm sand.

"Out!" claimed the umpire.

"Get back! Get back!" shouted the Fort Adams' players.

I did not hesitate, pulling myself to my knees, jumping to my feet, preparing to throw the ball to third baseman Eric Ross for a double play only to see Eric Ross gawking at me two feet away. The sergeant sprinted back toward third base. I tried to beat him. We both touched the bag at the same time, but the umpire shouted: "Out!"

Rules being rules and gentlemen being gentlemen in 1863, no one argued, and the soldiers took the field. They still led by one run, and facing William Smith, Kelan O'Quinn, and Win Mac-Naughton did not make them overly nervous.

Smith struck out on four pitches, but Mr. O'Quinn lined a base hit into center field. The

Fort Adams Unionists brought in their defense, ready for a double play. I had hit safely four times that day, but had not showed any hint of power.

Mike Peabody would later say that it must have surely come a strong gale, because he had never seen me strike the ball so far. I couldn't believe it myself, almost didn't even run when I belted a high outside pitch over the startled center fielder's head.

"Run, Win, run!" my teammates screamed.

I ran. Never known for much speed, I tore across the base paths, trying to block out everything around me. First base. Second base. Mr. O'Quinn scored. I had tied the game. Hold up at third base, I told myself. Let Mike Peabody drive you in for the winning run, but I didn't stop, couldn't stop, and now, as I raced the last ninety feet, I heard my friends and fellow Blue Stockings yell at me to hurry. I sensed, more than saw, the second baseman catch the center fielder's throw and relay it to the catcher, a bruising sergeant-major with a bristling black beard.

Running so hard, I tripped just a few rods from home, landing on my chest, churning earth like a plowshare, stretching my right hand forward to touch that white iron plate—performing history's first headfirst slide, I surmise, beating King Kelly by a decade or so, although I've heard accounts that a chap named Eddie Cuthbert of the Keystone Club of Philadelphia stole third base that same year with a headfirst slide against the Brooklyn Athletics. Anyway, the sergeant-major made the catch, swung down his arm, and slammed the ball against my head. My vision blurred, but I heard the umpire.

"He tallies. Newport wins."

Fort Adams protested the slide as illegal, but the umpire found no reference to it in Chadwick's rule book as lawful or unlawful, plus I had tripped, so the move wasn't deceitful, merely accidental. Although Bob Addy would later get credit for the first slide two years later when he was playing for the First City Club in Rockford, Illinois, and did it as a professional ballist when he was with the Cincinnati Red Stockings in 1877, I have heard stories of slides being performed as early as 1857, and Sharky the Seaman would later regale me with a story of a slide (feet first) he pulled off in Portland, Maine, in 1859. King Kelly made the slide popular, of course, as I well know for he stole a number of bases against me when I was catching for the Providence Grays.

Forgive my history lesson. Sometimes I get carried away. To get back to my story, my run was allowed.

Dizzy and nauseated—from the blow to the head or all that running, I could not tell—I forced a smile at the sound of cheering. My eyes opened, and Father's sooty, bloodied face smiled back at me, which paralyzed me since he was off with the Army of the Potomac, "trying to Abolitionize the entire Second Corps," Mr. O'Quinn once joked. I blinked away the illusion, and Mike Peabody's mug replaced Father's grin as Blue Stockings surrounding me cheered my name. Shrugging off the specter of my father, I allowed myself to be fêted. Mr. O'Quinn let me have the first taste of lager, too, after tapping the keg, and the Fort Adams Unionists shook my hand, calling me a first-class ballist.

"Bet your name will be all over the *Daily News*," Mike Peabody told me. "You won the day."

I pretended to be humble, but, inside, I couldn't wait to read the newspaper. The *Daily News* seldom cared much about our teams, especially since we began losing more than we won, but Mike had sound reasoning. After all, the umpire chosen for that game happened to be the assistant city editor of the *Daily News*.

No papers would be published that week-end because of the eighty-seventh anniversary of our nation's independence, so I had to wait until Monday to learn if I would be immortalized. We celebrated the 4th, Mother and me, listening to the bells ringing for a half hour at sunrise, noon, and sunset, and a salute fired from a ship in the harbor, then attending a concert by the Naval band at the Mall on Saturday. On Sunday, I attended church with Mother, had supper with my grandparents, and read the Bible with my mother that evening. Finally, Monday dawned. I dressed hurriedly, barely touched breakfast, and bought a copy of the *Daily News* on my way to Grandfather Easton's harbor office.

There was no mention of our baseball game. Instead, I read an item in the first column under the headline: THE BATTLE IN PENNSYLVANIA.

On Friday occurred a great battle in Pennsylvania, the story began, *the news of which reached here on the 4th and yesterday. It is cheering in its general results.*

So preoccupied with my baseball heroics, I had failed to pay attention to any talk about battles or defeats of the Rebel horde at some place called

Gettysburg. Mother never mentioned it, but she never spoke of the war these days. A chill overcame me at work, a foreboding, and I tallied numbers with less interest and more mistakes than normal until Grandfather's bookkeeper, Mr. Childs, sent me home at ten.

Mother sat in a rocking chair, reading her Bible. She didn't speak to me, didn't notice me, just waited.

It is cheering in its general results.

My God, how that sentence still saddens me.

They posted the first casualty list at the courthouse on Wednesday. Mike Peabody's dad called it "the butcher's bill."

Father had served in the 3rd Battery, now called Battery B, from the beginning, first seeing the elephant at Ball's Bluff. He had survived the carnage at Antietam, and had been creased by a Minié ball at Marye's Heights. The Rebels, as he had promised down in Texas, had never seen his back in a battle, and he had sent many to perdition.

Several more Confederates joined their dead brethren during the first two days at Gettysburg. On the third day, while I played a child's game called baseball, Father manned Battery B's fourth gun, as he had throughout the war. During the height of what history would call Pickett's Charge, Father swabbed the barrel and stepped to the side while another Rhode Islander inserted the powder charge. A Confederate shell struck the cannon, exploding, and my father, an inconspicuous and nebulous, but principled, druggist, died instantly.

The details of this I would learn later, from survivors of Battery B and my mother. On Wednesday, July 8th, I knew nothing . . . officially. Inside, I did know, remembering the smiling apparition at my baseball game, and I am sure Mother felt something, too. We did not receive word until Thursday, when more names were added to the butcher's bill.

Private H. W. MacNaughton,
1st Rhode Island Light Artillery, killed.

His remains lie somewhere in that hallowed graveyard in that revered Pennsylvania town, although Mother had a marker placed in the family plot at Newport.

Family, relatives, and friends gathered around us, and Grandfather Easton insisted that we leave the cottage on Haliden Hill and join him at his mansion. I stopped playing baseball. Mike Peabody and Mr. O'Quinn said they understood, expressing their condolences but reminding me that he died a hero, that the battle of Gettysburg would doom the Confederacy. Northern newspapers, including the *Daily News*, were already reporting that opinion as if fact.

Mother still donned black in September, and would continue wearing it until her death twenty-two years later. Two months after learning the tragic news, she and Grandfather Easton called me to the family parlor after dinner.

"It is time you began your apprenticeship to Mister Childs," Grandfather announced. "You are almost seventeen, a man in my eyes. Why, at seventeen, I had circumnavigated the globe. With your father's passing, you are the man of your house. Do you understand?"

"Yes, sir," I said without feeling.

He quoted First Corinthians. "'When I was a child, I spake as a child, I understood as a child, I thought as a child; but when I became a man, I put away childish things.'"

He was talking about baseball, and asked again if I understood.

"Yes, sir," I answered.

"Good. You will start on Monday the Twenty-First."

The war, I realized, meant nothing to him, as my father had meant nothing to him, but suddenly they meant everything to me, more than baseball. I owed Father that much, and the thought of spending the rest of my life ciphering profits and padding expenses for gyps like Robert Childs and Prentice Easton sickened me. I had already formulated a plan, only I lacked my father's bravery. I needed an accomplice, so that night I met Mike Peabody outside his father's groggery.

"Join the Army?" asked Mike, passing a pail of stale beer after swallowing a mouthful himself.

"They're enlisting in Providence," I said.

"Artillery? Win, I don't want to be blown to bits like your papa . . . I'm . . . uh, I'm sorry, Win, I . . ."

"I'm thinking cavalry, Mike."

"You ever ride a horse?"

"Yes. Often." A stretcher, I knew, but I had ridden some in Texas.

"Well, I ain't."

"It isn't hard, Mike."

"But you ain't of legal age. And I'm younger than you."

He rarely admitted that. "I'm practically seven-teen," I said. Or so my grandfather thought, al-though I had just turned sixteen that April. "And you're big for your age. You'll pass muster, and I don't think they'll be that particular."

"Is that why you want me along, 'cause I'm big."

"Because you're my best friend."

He stroked the reddish growth over his upper lip, shook his head, then gave me his biggest Mike Peabody grin.

"Ride a horse, shoot a musket, kill some Rebs . . . with my best friend, too. Sounds like a bully adventure to me, Win!"

Having packed my valise earlier that afternoon, I throw off my covers, still dressed in my britches, shirt, and stockings, and listen as the clock chimes twice. Satisfied, I pull on shoes and hat, rise, and open my bedroom door. Silence greets me, and I withdraw my bag from the armoire, and hurriedly, but quietly, head downstairs in the darkness. I'm through the parlor when a gas lamp is turned up, showering me with an orange glow, and I whirl, suddenly crying, when I see Mother rocking in her chair, an ambrotype of Father in her trembling hands.

"I know you must go, Winthrop," she says. " 'Tis Henry's wish. I pray for your safety. Carry this with you, along with your Bible."

She offers me the ambrotype, which Father had made at a studio on Thames shortly before leaving Newport.

I cannot move, though, and only stare at the hag-gard, weary permutation my mother has become, a skeleton, physically and emotionally.

It's just a dream, though. It didn't happen that way, although the war, or Father's absence and death, had aged Mother considerably. She was sleeping when I sneaked out that night to join Mike Peabody and steal our way to Providence. Or, rather, trying to. Her sobs followed me as I descended the stairs.

There were no teary good byes, just a note I left on a chest of drawers, and that was a deliberate lie to mislead any pursuers, saying I was going to Medway, Massachusetts, to join the Union Base Ball Club. I didn't take the Bible, although I would carry Father's ambrotype with me for much of the war. Regina Easton MacNaughton didn't offer it to me, though.

I stole it.

PART II

"Blessed shalt thou be in the city, and blessed shalt thou be in the field."

Deuteronomy 28:3

CHAPTER SIX

My first acquaintance with hell came in Louisiana.

I thought about that as I settled into my seat for Game 2 of the World Series at Sportsman's Park the following afternoon. October 7th conjures up images of fall, but St. Louis for the second consecutive day brought us temperatures in the high 80s and the Mississippi River city's omnipresent humidity. I didn't see how pitchers Harry The Cat Brecheen or Mickey Harris could last long in such stifling weather, but The Cat certainly shone that afternoon. For most of the game, hot as it was, I and close to 36,000 other fans marveled at Brecheen's ability as he made the Red Sox look ridiculous, leading the Cardinals to a 3–0 victory that tied the Series.

I remembered another baseball player nicknamed The Cat, a strapping young Irishman I got to know well after the calamitous Red River Campaign.

Although deep down I had feared, practically predicted, that we would be caught and sent

•

home, Mike Peabody and I encountered no trouble enlisting in the 3rd Rhode Island Cavalry. We cited our ages as twenty-three. I thought anything else might seem too obvious, and also had instructed Mike, if we were interrogated, not to waiver, give his real birth date—July 29—but change the year of his birth to 1840. I could just see him breaking into a sweat, swearing up and down that he was twenty-six but citing a birth year that would have made him forty-nine. Mike's math skills rated far below mine, but I prayed he could remember two numbers, 1840 and twenty-three.

As it turned out, no one bothered to question either of us.

Neither of us certainly looked older than sixteen, but after the carnage at Gettysburg—23,000 Federal casualties—the July riots in New York City over the draft, and reports coming in from Chickamauga of 16,000 Federals killed and wounded, Union officers didn't question anyone willing to sign an enlistment paper.

"When do we leave to fight?" I asked after being issued my uniform and equipment.

"Don't ye beat the Dutch," the quartermaster answered. "Ready to kill graybacks, is ye?"

Actually I just wanted to get out of New England, get away from Grandfather Easton. My deception would be uncovered soon, once Grandfather and Mother learned that I had not been seen anywhere near Medway, Massachusetts. My only prayer was that no one in Newport would think that Mike and I would join the Army, especially a cavalry regiment, rather than a baseball club.

The 3rd Rhode Island had been organized in

Providence on September 12, 1863, and, in my ig-
norance, I assumed we would be sent to fight immediately. Instead, we spent the next three
months in Rhode Island, drilling, drilling, and
drilling in weather too cold for baseball, and ill
suited, considering that we would be sent to New
Orleans on New Year's Eve.

Cavalry drill can be brutal. Even experienced
horsemen walked with stiffness after a few days.
Mike Peabody's size hurt him—tall and big as he
had become, he would have been better suited for
artillery or infantry—and, although he complained fiercely, although he cursed my scheme,
although I expected him to desert and return to
his father's saloon, he never shirked his duty, or
his loyalty to me. We tried to learn tactics, fared
better learning how to shoot carbines, struggled
miserably trying to wield sabers. For many new
recruits, the training caused days to blur into one
another. For me, fearing capture and Grandfather's punishment, those fall and winter months
passed with a never-ending nervous tedium until
we broke camp at year's end and moved south by
ship and rail.

In Louisiana, I thought I could relax. Our regiment had been attached to the Department of the
Gulf's defense of New Orleans, and I felt safe and
secure from the Eastons' clutches, but the boys of
2nd Squadron soon came to loathe our captain. Relax? Not hardly. Suddenly I found myself in an
occupied Southern state 1,500 miles from home.
The warmth of January surprised me. The dialect
of the natives bewildered me. The hostility of
those Louisianans disturbed me, although I soon
learned of the brutality of Benjamin The Beast

Butler, reviled by citizens and soldiers alike, who had been appointed military governor before being removed in 1862.

I served under Captain Conall McGee, riding until my chafed thighs and sore backside screamed in agony. The captain's cavalry drill bore little resemblance to the training we had endured in Rhode Island; it was far, far more miserable. Mike Peabody, no equestrian at all, fared worse than I did and soon cursed me even more than he had in New England for enticing him to join the regiment.

"Thought we'd be killing Secesh," he said. "Ain't killing nobody but myself, though I sure as certain would like to kill Capt'n McGee."

Before long, 2nd Squadron dubbed Conall McGee The Beast, too.

Till one balmy February evening when I saw another side to our commander. Off duty, I sat outside our Sibley tent, which housed seventeen Rhode Islanders, including Mike and me, and felt like a furnace day or night. Diligently I worked on an inspirational project. I had discovered a rubber ball in the Gallatin Street *banquettes*, afterward bought yarn from a peddler on Royal and hurried back to camp. After wrapping yarn around the ball, I began stitching a piece of leather around my creation. I felt quite certain that I would not get the circumference or weight close enough to the latest rule book, but it resembled a baseball. I hadn't touched one since Father's death.

After tying off the last stitch, a grin exploded on my face, and I hefted my masterpiece, hurled it skyward, and let it bounce off my boots when I noticed Captain McGee staring at me.

I jumped to attention, but to my surprise he bent, picked up the ball now at his feet, and tossed it back to me. The move startled me, and I cringed after making the catch, knowing I had not stayed at attention and that martinet would likely hang me from my thumbs for such a breach of military etiquette.

Instead, he said in a low whisper: "Baseball."

Silence followed. He stared straight at me, but I don't think he saw me. His thoughts seemed so far away. A long moment later, he sighed, and returned to the present.

"Do you play the sport, MacNaughton?" he asked.

He knows my name, I thought with wonder. To him and his *segundo,* Sergeant Champlin, I had always been Trooper, or some profane insult. "Some," I answered, adding in hindsight, "sir."

"Massachusetts or New York rules?"

I blinked again in dismay. The Beast, we all assumed, knew nothing that could not be found in Cooke's *Cavalry Tactics.* "I . . . uh . . . started with Massachusetts, but played the New York game before joining the Third, sir."

"Played with the Jersey City Hamiltons, did I," he remarked with pride. "First nine, left field. Before I moved to Providence in futile pursuit of a fine colleen." Stepping forward, he plucked the ball out of my hand, threw it high into the air, backed up, began whistling some Irish tune, and snagged the ball one-handed, a magical grab because baseballs, especially such homemade efforts as mine, could prove difficult to catch in days before gloves became standard. He threw the ball back to me.

"You made this yourself?"

"Yes, sir."

"Pretty good job, MacNaughton."

"Thank you, sir."

"What position did you play?"

"Catcher in—" I stopped. I had not given a false name when enlisting and suddenly feared that my fraud would be discovered. Not only that, but if I admitted that I had lived in Texas, they might think me a spy. Besides, McGee had not asked me where I had played, just what I had played. "Catcher and pitcher."

He measured me curiously, and I noticed the green sprig he had tucked inside his hatband. So he would be fighting under the green, I later understood, a true son of Erin. Conall McGee was a handsome man, tall, thin, with curly black hair and a light in his eyes that sparkled with humor, though those piercing blue-green eyes had often blazed with clear grit and Lucifer's wrath.

"Does anyone else play the game?" he asked. "In the Third?" he added.

"Mike played first base . . . er, Mike Peabody, I mean. I don't know anyone else, sir. I mean, when we joined, sir, it was getting too cold to play in Rhode Island, and we haven't had much time to get up a contest here."

I cringed. We hadn't had much free time because the officer in front of me had drilled us so roughly.

Yet again Captain McGee did not take offense.

"A word to you, then, MacNaughton. If you can find enough enlisted men for a game, a couple of bats I have to loan you. Ash bats, in me trunk.

Bases and home plate we'd have to make do with sacks or something, but that sha'n't be hard for a proven scavenger like yourself." He winked—I tell you, The Beast *winked*—at my ball. "Nothing like a game to boost the spirits of the lads, don't you think?"

Still stunned at this display of humanity, I could only nod.

"Trained hard have the lads," McGee continued, "and that will bonify us all when we move north with General Banks to fight the Rebs. But a sporting contest of baseball, me thinks, is sound military training. Round up two nines, Mac-Naughton, and report to Sergeant Champlin when you have them, if you have them, and remind the sergeant that I said 'tis important."

"I'll get them, sir," I said enthusiastically, and it quickly dawned on me to invite him. "Would you join us, Captain?"

His grin, and I had never seen him smile in Rhode Island or Louisiana, revealed straight white teeth, one capped gold. "Called me The Cat during me days with the Hamilton Base Ball Club, they did. Pounce on a ball hit anywhere near me, I could, and that's not County Wexford brag. Grand it would be to play again, Mac-Naughton, but, no, 'tis for you lads. And this man's Army frowns upon fraternization. You have your orders, MacNaughton."

Mike Peabody greeted me with anger—"Ain't in mood for none of your stretchers, Win!"—when I told him of my conversation with Captain McGee. "The Beast wants us to play a baseball contest? You're an almighty poor liar."

"God as my witness, it's true," I pleaded. "He even sounded human, said he played with a club in New Jersey, left field, said if we can get enough players for two teams, he'll give us bats, ash bats, for the game."

I must have convinced him, but he shook his head. "I don't know if I'd want to play in this oven."

February had turned muggy, although we would soon learn the true definition of Southern summers in the months to come.

"Would you rather drill some more under the captain's eye?" I had him, but I wanted to make my point. "Get hit by rotten fruit from some citizen while patrolling The Swamp? Ride forty miles, then care for your own horse before lancing your blisters?"

"You actually think you can find . . . ?" He tried to do the math, but couldn't. "You think there's enough people that know the game of baseball to put together two teams, Win?"

I grinned. "If it means a couple of hours without saber exercise, shoveling horse apples, or soaping saddles, yes, I do."

It turned out to be a little more difficult.

First, I had to find time between evening mess and tattoo to locate any interested soldiers, and most turned out to be too irritable, after drilling, to think about anything except food and sleep. Yet when our training ceased abruptly on March 3rd, I began to find cavalry troopers with baseball experience.

Rumors spread throughout camp that General Banks's great campaign would begin soon, that we would march north, all the way to Texas, and meet the enemy, 90,000 strong according to some, less than 100, the bulk women and children armed with slingshots and stones, according to others.

"We ain't gonna fight nobody," Mike Peabody told me. "We're just gonna sit around in this heat and rot."

He was wrong, but I didn't bother to point out the fact that more and more gunships had arrived in New Orleans, and news came that thousands of Major General William T. Sherman's troops were to meet us at Alexandria. There most certainly would be a campaign, and the 3rd Rhode Island would play a part of it, the reason for Captain McGee's strict discipline and unrelenting treatment. A battle satisfied me, even more than the prospects of a baseball game. I would follow in Father's footsteps and fight the men who had killed him, I told myself, although he had been killed by troops of the Army of Northern Virginia and I would be fighting Major General Richard Taylor's command and Tom Green's Texians. No matter, at least I would honor Private Henry Wallace MacNaughton.

But first, we had a game to play.

CHAPTER SEVEN

"Massachusetts rules?"

Immediately stopping shaving, Captain McGee folded his razor, which he tossed beside a tin wash basin. He turned to me, those blue-green eyes ablaze, half his face still lathered, black bangs pasted to his forehead by sweat. "Massachusetts rules?" he asked again.

I stood in his tent, having been escorted there after reporting to Sergeant Champlin, who stood impassively despite the heat, beads of sweat rolling into his thick blond mustache. As little as the sergeant understood baseball, we could have been speaking Gaelic.

McGee shook his head, toweled off his face, and pulled on his blouse, although he did not button it. "Massachusetts rules are an abomination to the essence of baseball," he told me sharply, spoken like a true New Jersey player.

Knowing better than to argue with him, I explained: "The men are from Rhode Island, sir.

Most of them only know the Massachusetts game."

"Told me yourself that you played under New York rules, MacNaughton."

"Yes, Captain, but . . . well, some of the clubs we played against considered Newport an abomination. The only reason we played that way was because a bunch of soldiers from Fort Adams insisted on it. We often had to bring down teams from New York to play us, or switch rules, play the Massachusetts game when we were playing over in New Bedford or Worcester, use New York rules when playing at Brenton Cove."

As the captain's face hardened, sweat began to pour down my face, caused more from fear than the stifling heat. I hadn't meant to mention Fort Adams or Newport, for although I had given my truthful name when I had enlisted, I had lied about my hometown, writing down Bristol Ferry only because I remembered I had an aunt living there. Conall McGee had no interest in from where I came.

"Squares instead of diamonds, sticks instead of bases, throwing instead of pitching . . . might as bloody well be playing town ball or rounders."

I waited in silence beside Sergeant Champlin while McGee shook his head, removed his blouse, furiously worked his brush in the tin can, and reapplied lather to his face. He whipped his razor angrily against the strop, and did not speak again until he had finished shaving and dressed. Then he spoke to Champlin, asking his opinion, telling him to speak freely.

"Sir," the sergeant answered in his usual

abrupt voice, "I care nary a whit for baseball, know nothing of it, don't want to."

McGee smiled. "That's a wee too freely, Champlin. Baseball was my passion before the Rebellion. Still is."

"Begging the captain's pardon, sir."

The captain's gaze lighted on me. "Massachusetts?"

"That's what I was told, sir. I had trouble finding enough soldiers who could play, and they said it had to be the Massachusetts game. In fairness, Captain, they don't know the New York rules, and we need a few practices before we could play a match. We'd need even longer if they all had to learn the New York way of playing. And that's if they would play that way, and they say they won't."

"Mutinous it is," McGee said, only he was smiling now. "A civil war over state's rights, over the question of slavery. And now a mutiny over a sporting contest." He shook his head, defeated. "What is your suggestion as to when the contest should be played?" he asked.

"I was thinking a week. . . ."

The shaking of McGee's head stopped me. "We haven't a week, MacNaughton. Tomorrow it must be, and pray it does not rain."

"Tomorrow, sir?"

"Tomorrow morning, before it's too hot. I'll issue orders, and those not playing will watch." His head shook sadly as he dismissed us. "Massachusetts. What a waste."

First baseman Mike Peabody captained what McGee designated The Saddle Club, while McGee appointed me, playing catcher, captain of The Spur Club. Sergeant Champlin was ordered—McGee's idea of punishment or a joke, I suspect—to umpire, and, although he had no inkling and little tolerance for the game, serious as he was, we presented him with an 1860 rule book.

In all the games I had played, never had I been struck with a case of the butterflies, but nerves on that morning turned my face pale, caused my hands to tremble. A sea of blue surrounded the square we had laid out, soldiers not only from the 3rd Rhode Island, but other regiments, even Union sailors from the gunboats docked on the Mississippi River levee. A hospital tent had been set up behind home plate, benches and seats brought in from the tents of officers, and ladies sat in their best poplin and velvet dresses, twirling fancy parasols. Beside that tent had been erected another one, and in this one sat Michael Hahn, Union governor of Louisiana, next to General Nathan Banks, Colonel Thomas Lucas, and Admiral David Porter. Later some swore that they saw General William T. Sherman as well, but I think they were mistaken. Black servants and blue-clad strikers brought the guests of honor chicory coffee, tea, gin-slings, and brandies. We players had a couple canteens of water, which we would need as the temperature had already climbed into the 80s. Ominous black clouds gathered over the Gulf, prompting one player on Mike's team to remark: "Let's try to score a hundred tallies before there comes a turd float."

Mike's team won the toss and elected to bat first. Rules requiring catchers to stand at all times, I found my place well behind the striker, and our pitcher, a 10th Squadron corporal from Warwick, delivered the first overhanded throw to Mike Peabody, who called for low placement.

The crowd applauded when Mike nailed the pitch for a double, and the game was on.

As captains, Mike and I had picked our respective teams, which worked out pretty well for we had opposite opinions on what constituted a winning club. To no surprise, Mike concentrated on offense, power, getting the players he thought could hit the ball the hardest, score the most runs. I always liked defense and pitching, although after watching the second Saddle Club striker double Mike home, I began to wonder if my pitcher was as good as I had been led to believe.

The Saddle Club tallied sixteen times in the first inning, but The Spur Club surprised everyone, including their young captain, by striking for fourteen scores before our side was out. After that, Corporal Al Young settled down, our center fielder made a diving catch that brought the ladies to their feet, and we held Mike's team to only six tallies.

Make no mistake about it. Mike Peabody had selected a potent offensive club, but, like Mike, they were slow-footed. I started our side with a hit up the middle for what should have been a single, but the ball kept rolling, almost to the commissary, and I scored what today would be called an "inside-the-park homer".

By the time our side was out, the score was tied at 22.

Admiral Porter was the first to leave, congratulating Captain McGee and offering the players his compliments. I expect he just didn't want to get caught in the downpour everyone knew was coming. General Banks, who looked about as interested in the game as Sergeant Champlin, left shortly thereafter, but Colonel Lucas, God bless him, stayed for the whole affair.

Three hours later, with the score 73-69 in favor of The Saddle Club, Mike Peabody slapped another hit and stopped at the stick in the ground designated first base. Sweat had pasted my shirt to my skin, and I stood behind the plate, panting, praying someone would hurry up and reach the 100-tally mark and end this torture. Much of the crowd had departed; I didn't blame them.

A brisk wind kicked in, bringing a much needed cooling relief, as a catcher from Providence came next to the plate, and sent a screaming drive down the first-base line that nobody, in 1946 or 1864, could have caught. Poor Mike Peabody couldn't get out of the way. He tried to turn, tried to duck, and braced himself for the ball's impact.

The sound sickened me, catching him as it did on the side of his face. Blood mushroomed, and Mike dropped like a falling timber.

I took a tentative step forward, not sure if I were dreaming, then broke into a sprint, screaming my best friend's name, fearing I would find him dead in a pool of his own blood, a death I had wrought. I slid beside his prone body, turned him over, and cradled him in my arms, tears cascading down my face.

As I looked up, as if to ask God why this was happening, or pray that this wasn't happening, the thunderheads burst open, and the torrent began.

Sheets of rain blasted us, washing the blood from Mike's face, and his eyes shot open, distant,

fluttering, unfocused, and then he began screaming.

"Gawd a'mighty, Gawd a'mighty! I'm kilt, Win,
I'm kilt!" Coughing, he spit out bits of teeth and
blood.

*Gawd a'mighty, Gawd a'mighty! I'm kilt, Win,
I'm kilt!*

I'd hear those words again, too soon, and have
heard them over the past eight decades in nightmares.

Mike Peabody didn't die. The deluge halted
the game that was never finished, and Captain
McGee ordered three of us to escort our injured
ballist to the brigade's medical wagon and surgeon, where we deposited the bawling young
trooper and returned to our tents. On the following afternoon, Mike returned to our Sibley tent. A
plaster bandage over his busted nose hid much of
the black and blue bruises, and he didn't talk
much, couldn't talk, although his jaw had not
been broken. He had lost a few teeth, had bitten
his tongue, and, according to the surgeon, had
the ball struck him higher, he probably would
have gone to Glory.

"Son," said one of the troopers sharing our
tent, a bespectacled man from Providence, "you
should have stayed where you was, invalided
yourself, shouldn't have reported back fit for
duty."

"Ain't no coffee boiler," Mike mumbled.
"Know we're 'bout to move out."

That was Wednesday, March 9, 1864. The Red
River Campaign began the next day, although we
did not leave until dawn, March 14th, bound for
Alexandria and Shreveport.

* * *

Twelve days later we reached Alexandria, on the Red River. We had not spotted any Confederates, had seen nothing but giant mosquitoes, huge snakes, and tree branches that popped us as we rode through makeshift roads, almost impassable because of mud. Weary, and brushwhipped, I stared in disbelief at sight of Admiral Porter's sailors loading cotton bales on their ships.

"Prize of war!" one seaman shouted gleefully at me. "You horse soldiers should have gotten here sooner."

Mike Peabody, mumbling a little more clearly now, shouted back something that caused the seaman's smile to vanish. The seaman recovered with an insult directed at Mike's mother.

"Shut your clam trap!" I yelled back.

"He's just a blower, lads." Captain McGee's words had a calming effect on me, or maybe he just frightened down my anger at those Naval plunderers. "Ride on, lads. Cotton is not what we trained to take. We're here to take Rebel lives."

Yet we still didn't see any enemy soldiers as we rode north, only frightened civilians, petrified slaves, and abandoned homes. The march turned into hell. Torrid heat one day, a numbing rain the next. Choking on dust on one road, churning through mud on another. We passed through Monett's Ferry, Cloutiersville, Natchitoches, and Campti. Mosquito bites peppered our faces and necks, sweat blinded us, and lice took root in our clothes and hair. We ate without relish, gaining nourishment from canned beef—"embalmed", we soon called it—and hardtack so rotten it served as castles for worms.

By the end of March, after we left Natchitoches, Mike Peabody had recovered enough that he could curse without mumbling, and he had removed his bandages. "Ain't no need in wearing them tarnal things," he said. "Sweat just washes them off my face anyhow."

Hell. It was hell.

Even in the South, you don't read or hear a whole lot about the Red River Campaign, for which I'm sure the descendants of Major General Nathan P. For Pisspot Banks are grateful. Captain McGee had trained 2nd Squadron relentlessly, but he had no control over the malaria and dysentery that waylaid much of his command. Nor could he counteract General Banks's incompetence.

Criticizing generals is sometimes deemed unpatriotic, but I think I earned my right.

The Federal objective was Shreveport, but Admiral Porter's fleet would have to first find a way to navigate the rapids above Alexandria, and Banks had grown impatient. According to Banks's plan, Porter's ships would provide artillery support and transports for the ground forces. So what did Banks decide to do? He left the river at Grand Ecore, sent us up the roads toward Pleasant Hill and Mansfield.

Sent us to slaughter.

We sat in silence one evening, sensing the foreboding, feeling Death's presence. No one told us we would engage the enemy, but the 3rd Rhode Island, 2nd Squadron, Conall McGee commanding, knew it was coming.

Leaning against a rotting tree, I wiped down the seven-pound Joslyn carbine with a rag, nervously fingered a .52-caliber cartridge, and wet my chapped lips. *How would I perform in battle? Would I honor Father? Would I die?* I felt sick, and it wasn't from embalmed beef and wormy hardtack.

Mike Peabody looked as anxious and pale as I did.

Somebody in the brush behind us started whistling a bawdy tune, and Mike snapped at him to shut up. The whistling stopped, and Conall McGee stepped into the light.

Both carbine and cartridge fell to the ground as I shot to attention. Mike cursed his stupidity, his bad luck, muttering an apology as he pulled himself to his feet.

Yet McGee focused on neither of us, but on a green leaf he wanted to stick into his hatband. When he was satisfied, he pulled on his black hat, gave us a salute, and asked pleasantly: "A touch of the fright?" I had expected him to act like The Beast, to court-martial Mike Peabody and maybe even me.

"No, sir!" Mike shouted. I didn't speak.

"Nothing to fear, troopers," McGee said. "Surely you've heard the infantry lads remark that they've never seen a dead cavalryman." His eyes bore through me, and I knew I had to answer.

"Yes, sir."

"Well, it's bogus. The sloughs will be filled with the dead soon, horse and foot soldiers alike, so just imagine yourselves dead and buried. No fear you'll have then, and your duty you will do."

He smiled at his humor, although Mike and I found nothing about it amusing, and started to leave. When he turned, however, his face had changed. Instead of looking like The Beast, he had become The Cat, a baseball player, a man of compassion.

"I meant to compliment you two," he said. "Back in New Orleans. Massachusetts rules be damned, but you two lads play a fine game of baseball. The saints be with you both."

CHAPTER EIGHT

It intrigues me how sounds, like smells, can catapult one's thoughts to another time. In the seventh inning of Game 2, Ted Williams fouled off one of Brecheen's screwballs, slicing a drive into the stands. Everyone tried to get out of its way, but a gangling teenager a few rows up and over from me turned too late, and the ball made a sickening sound as it smacked into his back. The kid cried out in agony. My eyelids snapped shut.

"Boy just had the wind knocked out of him," a voice said moments later. "He'll be all right. Bet ya even that Ted Williams signs that ball for him."

Yet I remained miles and years away. It wasn't the baseball game I remembered so vividly, the one where Mike Peabody got his face smashed in. It was Sabine Crossroads.

The rattle of infrequent fighting echoed on our flanks and ahead of us. We could hear the musketry, and our mounts became skittish, yet, as-

signed to guard the supply train, we could only
hear the skirmishing. We saw nothing.

Thus, April 7th passed without much incident,
and I began to think my fears, my premonition of
a major battle, were misguided. The next day
started to follow the same course, the sounds of
gunfire growing closer as we inched our way up
the narrow road toward the Mansfield-Pleasant
Hill pike.

"Skirmishers up ahead," Captain McGee announced. "Green's Texians, I hear."

Mike Peabody, riding behind me, whispered
my name, and my saddle creaked as I turned to
face him.

"Did you know this Green when you was in
Texas?"

Nerves got the better of me. "Jesus Christ,
Mike, do you know how big Texas is? I couldn't
know everybody!" I whirled around, fingering
reins nervously, staring ahead at the line of
horses, mules, and wagons stretching out in front
of me. Surrounded by woods that felt as if they
were closing in on me, crushing me, I tried to
concentrate on my duty. This is what I had
wanted, wasn't it? A battle? To meet the enemy,
avenge Father's death? So why had my hands
turned clammy?

Mike whispered again: "Ever think you might
face some friends of yours in battle?"

Groaning, I screwed shut my eyes. "Be quiet,
Mike," I snapped, although a few moments later I
added: "I didn't have that many friends, anyway." *Why did Mike have to bring up Texas?* My
stomach roiled, and all moisture left my mouth. I
hoped no one had heard us speak of Texas,

only . . . would I face schoolmates from Jack County?

We halted. Most of the mud-covered wagons had turned back that morning, to rest we were told, or to clear the road for fighting troops, and I wondered if we would be sent along to guard them. Orders, however, left us guarding the remaining wagons, only we did not advance. Gunfire became sporadic, dwindling to only an occasional shot, and finally nothing.

2nd Squadron, lined single file on both sides of the wagon train, waited.

"The Rebs are before us," a 96th Ohio Infantry volunteer said as he limped toward the rear, a bloody rag wrapped around his right thigh. "Just standing or sitting there. Sergeant Van Pelt don't think they want to fight."

As the hours stretched on, I began to think that perhaps it was General Banks who did not want to fight.

Battle lines formed in the clearings ahead of us, or so we were informed, and couriers raced back and forth as the day wore on. Noon passed without much notice. Our horses switched their tails and snorted, oblivious to the dangers ahead.

Another courier reined in his lathered mount in front of Captain McGee. They exchanged gauntleted salutes, and the trooper began speaking. I couldn't hear anything he said, but I expect half the soldiers in Banks's command understood McGee's response.

"Dismount and *rest?* For the love of God, mister, the Rebs are about to attack!"

"Begging the captain's pardon, sir, but those are the colonel's orders." I could hear the courier plainly now. "Save the horses for tomorrow. General Banks doesn't think the enemy will engage us today." He pointed to the sun. "Not much daylight left anyway, Captain."

Yet the Confederates did attack. That shrill Rebel cry unnerved us almost as soon as the courier had finished talking. He wheeled his horse around, stunned at that high-pitched screaming, followed by a bombardment of muskets and cannon. Spurring his horse wildly, the courier galloped to the sound of war.

"Steady, lads!" Captain McGee called out to 2nd Squadron. "Steady. Keep your horses steady, your nerves steady."

I lifted the Joslyn carbine, thumbed back the hammer, and braced the stock against my thigh.

We couldn't see the battle, the butchery before us, but soon caught the acrid scent of gunpowder. Minutes later, Minié balls whistled overhead, clipped branches off trees, thudded around us.

"Steady," McGee repeated.

The battle started at four o'clock, and Federals rushed down the slope to meet the charging Rebels. More Confederates massed forward to flank Banks's line of defense. It sounded so furious, so nightmarish, and we did nothing. When a cannon ball smashed the top of a tree across the road, my horse reared, and I almost dropped my carbine.

"Come on, Capt'n!" someone yelled while I tried to regain control of my mount. "They're killing our men up ahead!"

"We have our orders," McGee said calmly.

"Orders be damned, sir! Our orders were to dismount and *rest!*"

"Sappington!" Sergeant Champlin barked. "Get back in line!"

My horse settled down, at least as settled down as it could with the din of battle all around us. Mike Peabody complimented my horsemanship with a chuckle, saying he guessed that I had learned something after all from The Beast's relentless drills, but, finding no humor in his comment, I ignored him. Captain McGee's features tightened. He wanted to fight as much as Sappington, Champlin, Mike Peabody, me—all of us. A professional soldier, though, would never leave his post. We would guard the supply train.

Not that everyone proved brave souls that afternoon.

The private driving the wagon closest to me was the first to run. He leaped off his seat after a ricocheting ball splintered the lumber, footing it into the woods, leaning forward, sprinting toward Pleasant Hill.

Clouds of smoke drifted overhead, and sounds blended together, coming closer. Clashing metal, pounding hoofs, screams of horses and men. A riderless black stallion bolted out of the smoke, its eyes wide with fright, galloping down the lane— a scene straight out of a Washington Irving story—almost flattening soldiers standing in the road, and another teamster fled the train, chased and cursed by his sergeant.

The fear came from the waiting, from not knowing what was happening ahead of us. Trooper Wayne Hodge, in front of me, turned, his mouth crooked, tears streaming down his cheeks.

"Win," he said in a shaky voice, "I peed in my pants."

I didn't know what to say. Hodge and I weren't even close friends. Before I could formulate a response, he stiffened, slouched forward, and toppled over his horse, which stutter-stepped before smelling the blood, then bolted south.

The back of Hodge's head had been blown off.

Choking down bile, I mouthed Captain McGee's name, but no words came out. To my horror, men raced down the road, past us, littering the ground with their haversacks, belts, muskets. Somewhere ahead, a deep voice boomed: "Form a line! Form a line! I know you won't desert me!"

His pleadings went in vain. The trickle of men became a torrent, followed by the maëlstrom.

"Get the Yanks, boys! Send 'em to hell!"

Gray-clad cavalry lunged on our left flank like a cyclone, and bullets sang around me. I raised my carbine, fired, then followed Captain McGee to meet their charge, although that action seemed more of my mount's intention than my own. Somehow, I unsheathed my saber, and looked up to see a wild-eyed, toothless Reb reining in beside me. My horse stopped on my command, and I lifted the saber as that Reb slashed at me with a knife that reminded me of the pig-sticker Pig Oliver carried.

Our duel resembled nothing like the sword fights I had read about in the novels of Alexandre Dumas. My saber deflected his thrust, and the toothless Reb stared at me. I met his gaze, and we both froze, just for a second or two, although it felt like hours. Slowly the Reb's eyes lowered, and my gaze followed his. On the ground, I saw his hand, still clutching the knife, and half his forearm.

"You chopped off my arm, you bloody bastard!" the Reb cried out. I looked back at him, bracing for death, but the poor man's eyes rolled into the back of his head, and he pitched over his horse, beside his arm and knife.

Disarray. Chaos. Bedlam. Whatever your choice of noun. Another order was barked: "Fall back! Fall back!" There was no orderly retreat, however. All around us Federal soldiers fled, jumping over wagon tongues, dead mules, dead and dying soldiers. Guns and gear littered the ground. Rebel yells and Confederate canister soon drowned out voices begging for water, for mothers.

I left the unconscious Rebel soldier, trying to find Captain McGee, locate the battle, but the enemy cavalry had scattered, reminding me of the tales I heard in Jack County of how Comanches and Kiowas would divide up and vanish when pursued.

Wielding my saber, I rode in short circles, not knowing what to do or where to go. I didn't see Captain McGee again that day. Sergeant Champlin loped up beside me, told me we had to escort the wagon train back to Pleasant Grove, and I whirled my horse around, losing my saber this time. Most of the wagons had been abandoned, or the draft animals had been shot dead in their harness. When I turned back to Sergeant Champlin, he was gone.

A bullet smashed the stock of my carbine, and my horse bolted down the pike, following the flood of panicked troops.

"This way, Win! This way!"

I blinked away sweat, recognized Mike Peabody a few rods ahead of me, and spurred my mount wickedly, trying to catch up.

Cowardice. The thought sickened me. What was my father thinking? But what could I do when the entire Federal Army was running for its life?

"Full chisel! Full chisel! Ride hard, boys. Send them mudsills to hell!"

I looked back only once. Confederate cavalry and infantry chased after us, riding down those screaming Union soldiers who were too slow, hacking them with sabers, clubbing them with muskets, spearing them with bayonets. I pushed my horse harder.

Branches slapped my face, but I didn't care. I didn't remember when we had left the road, and I leaned forward, vaguely aware that Mike rode ahead of me. Blood trickled from my nose, my busted lips, and scratches all across my forehead and cheeks. We leaped over a ditch, into a field, Mike Peabody, the worst horseman of 2nd Squadron, now pulling away from me.

Then his horse went down, propelling Mike forward into the mud.

Ride on! a voice told me. *Ride to the woods. Run for your life! Save yourself!*

Yet I couldn't do that, no matter how frightened. I jerked the reins, leaping from my saddle before my horse had slid to a stop. My boots sank deeply in the mud, and I tripped, losing my hold of the reins. By the time I had pulled myself up to my knees, my horse had raced a quarter mile away, and Mike Peabody's had been crippled by a Reb caltrop, a cruel, four-pointed invention created to maim horses. No Texian, and certainly no one from Newport, I knew, would ever have invented such a horrible weapon.

Foot soldiers slogged through the mud past us. Cavalry troopers rode as fast as they could. No one stopped to help.

As I tried to get my bearings, Mike rolled over and sat up.

"You all right?" I shouted.

"Got the wind knocked out of. . . ." His eyes widened, and he scrambled to his feet.

"Run, Win! We . . . gotta run!"

He was pulling me to my feet when a ball shattered his right arm. That *smacking* noise, the impact of the bullet, the smashing of bone—I shall never shake it out of my memory.

"*Gawd a'mighty, Gawd a'mighty! I'm kilt, Win, I'm kilt!*"

I went to him, tugging frantically at his blood-soaked blouse while he screamed and writhed. His eyes focused on me briefly, and he barked an order through clenched teeth: "Get . . . out of here, Win! Rebs are . . . all over . . . us." Pain rocked him again, and he wailed again that he was dying. He cursed, spat, and cried.

Rebels overran us, as fast as they could in that bog. At first, none seemed interested in capturing prisoners, or killing us. I guess they had lost their blood lust after slaughtering our soldiers along the pike. Then one shoeless soldier wearing patched butternut britches slowed, lowering his bayonet, and slogged through the muck, cutting loose with a hoarse Rebel yell.

I leaped for the Joslyn carbine, remembering hours later that it was empty, rolled over, thumbing back the hammer, but I was too slow. The Reb thrust his bayonet against my chest, and, closing my eyes, I prepared to die.

"Up with ye, Yank!" he drawled. "And let that gun lie."

My eyes opened, and the pressure of the bayonet relaxed.

"Up with ye, or I spill your guts in this field!" the Rebel shouted, and I wearily rose, staring at him briefly until Mike Peabody screamed again.

"Win! They've kilt me, Win. Oh, God ... Mother!"

When I moved toward my friend, the Reb slammed the stock of his musket into the small of my back.

"He's done for! Leave him!"

I found my courage. "The hell I will."

The rest of that late afternoon, I don't remember much. Marching through the soupy mud, through brambles and weeds, carrying heavy Mike Peabody, half dragging him, prodded mercilessly by the Rebel's bayonet. I had wrapped my belt around Mike's upper arm, as a makeshift tourniquet, gave him a .52-caliber ball, and told him to bite it. Several times, we had stumbled to the ground, and each time the Reb told me to leave Peabody. Always I refused, pulling Mike to his feet, telling he had to come with me or he'd die.

"Over yonder." The Reb directed us toward the setting sun.

Union prisoners had been herded into a clearing, surrounded by men in butternut and gray. A sergeant lowered his jaw harp as we approached, and listened without interest as my guard reported that he had two prisoners to hand over.

Without comment, I started to take my place in the circle, but the sergeant held out a callused hand and shook his head.

"He don't go," he said dryly, tilting his head at half-conscious Mike. "Take him over to the dying tree." He motioned to a lone elm several rods away, where scores upon scores of Federal soldiers stretched out in the shade. Even from where I stood, in the dim gloaming, the stench of death was overwhelming.

"The hell . . ."

This time, I didn't get to finish. The Reb behind me slammed his musket against my skull. I didn't come to until dawn.

CHAPTER NINE

I found myself back in Newport, in my bed, Mother placing a cold compress to my forehead after I had taken sick with fever and chills, the salty smell of the air filling my bed chamber along with the scent of cinnamon tea and lilac soap, noise of the bustling city and port reverberating outside. Half awake, I reached out and felt her soft hand on my forehead, and gripped it tightly, never wanting to let go.

"Easy," my mother's voice said. "Go easy, lad."

Once my eyes fluttered open, the vision cleared, and the image of Regina Easton Mac-Naughton vanished. I lay on no downy comforter, but on trampled grass and mud, while Mother probably sat in her rocking chair, crying for Father and me, some 1,500 miles away. My lips were cracked, my brain addled, the back of my head pounding as Captain Conall McGee came weakly into focus. He lifted a wet, bloody rag off my head.

"How do you feel, MacNaughton?" he asked.

I shot up in a panic, but the world spun out of control, and down I went, rolled to my side, and vomited.

"Go easy there, trooper," McGee's voice said in a soothing Irish whisper. His hand grasped my shoulder as I gagged. "Tried to scramble your brains, someone did, cracked that skull of yours open, only your noggin must be harder than any of Admiral Porter's ironclads. But your face looks brush-whipped." He eased me onto my back, using the rag to wipe the vomit off my lips and face, then lifted my head, simultaneously bringing a flask to my mouth.

The liquor burned like molten lava, smelled like foul poison, and I coughed savagely, but McGee forced more down my throat.

" 'T'ain't the Irish, old boy, and three buttons from me tunic it cost, but this Rebel bark juice is all I could afford. Do you some good, it will. Come on, lad, give me just one more swallow. There. That's a fine fellow."

Light-headed, but not so dizzy, I sat up slowly, and looked around me. It seemed as if half of General Banks's command had been corralled into that cramped radius guarded by enemy troops. A few looked at me, but most just stared into the distance. Men from artillery, cavalry, and infantry regiments displayed a wide array of uniforms, from standard issue Union blue to colorful Zouaves, practically every one of them covered with mud, ripped, blackened by powder and dried blood. Men I had never seen before. I sought out friendly faces—Sappington's, Champlin's, Hodge's . . . no, Wayne Hodge was dead, killed by a stray bullet that blew out his brains. I wrestled away that horrific image, but another terrible sight replaced it. Mike. . . .

"Mike!" I shouted, trying to rise, but McGee's firm hand kept me seated. "Have you seen Mike Peabody?" I blurted out.

"You need rest," McGee said. "No. Peabody's not here, not that I've seen. There are a few blokes from Tenth Squadron on the far side of camp, one on detached duty over yonder, but none from our squadron that I've found. Of course, I dare say we shall meet up with a few more dear friends before the week is over. Don't think the two of us were the only unfortunate ones to be captured. Must be other camps scattered in these woods."

"Mike got shot, Captain. In the right arm. He was hurt bad, sir, bleeding something awful until I got my belt wrapped around his arm. I was trying to bring him in here, but they wouldn't let me. Told me to take him to the dying tree. That's all I remember."

That outburst left me exhausted, and I sank back onto the wet sod. My head rested on a pillow. Later, I discovered it was Captain McGee's slouch hat.

"Mike?" I yelled, repeating his name softer and softer, finally sobbing uncontrollably.

"There, there, MacNaughton. Fine work, that was, putting that belt on Trooper Peabody's arm. Slowed the bleeding. Likely saved his life. Grateful he'll be, when you see him next."

"But they were taking him to the dying tree, Captain," I wailed. "The *dying* tree."

" 'Tis all right, MacNaughton. The butternuts have set up a hospital over there, they have. Your pal Michael Peabody is in grand hands, I warrant. Not all of these Rebels are guttersnipes. A few are fine Christian gentlemen, including the doctors, me thinks." He looked toward the lone elm tree, every muscle in his dirty face taut.

"You think Mike might be all right?" I asked, needing reassurance, even a bald-faced lie.

McGee didn't answer. I don't think he heard me. The wails reached me for the first time, those unholy screams from the hospital set up beside the dying tree as surgeons worked their capital saws and raspators without the mercy of chloroform or morphine, not even turpentine or green persimmon juice.

"Mike," I whispered. "Oh, Mike. . . ."

Over the next couple of days, when I summoned enough strength to sit or stand, I would watch the activity around the elm tree and the hospital wagons, not talking, feeling helpless. Slaves carted off the dead for burial, and wheelbarrows filled with amputated arms and legs. I wondered if they had buried Mike Peabody already. Later, when I recognized the butternut soldier who had captured me, smoking a corncob pipe and laughing with another soldier beside a fire, I studied his feet. Barefooted when he had captured us, he now wore Union cavalry boots. I wondered if they were Mike's.

After cleaning my superficial cuts the best he could, Captain McGee wrapped the rag around his bloody left hand. I grimaced at his wound, but McGee smiled.

"No harm done, MacNaughton," he said. "A Navy ball through and through. Fingers are a wee stiff, but in a day or two I'll be swinging an ash bat the way I did during me Jersey City days." He took a pull of the Confederate liquor before capping the flask and sliding it inside his tunic.

"How were you captured?" I asked.

McGee's head shook. "Embarrassing it is, for a horse soldier named McGee. The ball went through me hand, it did, and into Mister O'Keeffe's brain." Mister O'Keeffe was his horse, a feisty blood bay stallion with three white stockings. "Down went that poor Tennessee Walker, on top of poor Conall McGee. Couldn't get me foot clear of the stirrup, so there I was, pinned down. Couldn't run. Couldn't fight, losing me revolver when I fell. 'Twas an Irishman who captured me, though, a strapping fine lieutenant named Burke from Dallas, Texas, so at least I can write me folks of that. No dishonor there, an Irishman capturing an Irishman. Might brevet Lieutenant Burke, though, to major in me letter home, so at least he outranks me, too. And yourself? How did the butternuts grab you?"

"Mike's horse stepped on a spike," I answered. "I stopped to help him, but my horse shied away, bolted after everyone else. Then Mike got shot, and . . ." I shook my head.

"Are you hungry, MacNaughton?"

I didn't answer. Truthfully I wasn't sure my stomach could hold down anything other than a few swallows of bark juice.

"Famished I am. Let me do a scout, see what kind of victuals one can find in these glorious accommodations."

He limped away, biting his bottom lip with

each step. More than his pride and left hand had been hurt when he had been taken prisoner.

Two days later, the Confederate guards made us stand, and a swarthy infantry captain spoke to us, although most of us found him almost impossible to understand, partly because of his Louisiana accent, partly because he kept twisting and smoothing his waxed black mustache, making it impossible to read his lips. We got the gist of it, anyway.

In two hours, we would begin marching west to Texas and a prison camp. If anyone tried to escape, he would be shot. Those who could not walk would be transported by wagon. The war, for us, had ended.

"Some of us are officers!" called out a New Hampshire cavalry lieutenant.

The Confederate officer bowed graciously, said something in French to his adjutant, then swept off his kepi. "*Monsieur*, my regrets. There are no separate facilities for officers and enlisted men."

"What about exchanges?" asked another prisoner.

Shaking his head, the officer twisted the ends of his mustache a final time. "That courtesy, as you well know, *monsieur*, has been revoked because of the ungentlemanly nature of your commanders." At least, that's what I think he said. "Your generals are not men of honor. They mistreat our men in their unholy prisons, do not honor our paroles, and they do not parole our soldiers."

"Bogus," Captain McGee whispered. "We've halted prisoner exchanges because the butternuts won't parole our Negro soldiers, and *their* soldiers won't honor *their* paroles."

The officer pulled on his kepi, saluted us, and smirked. "Enjoy your stay in the Confederate States of America. I do not think it will be long, for the way you and your generals showed yourselves in battle, it is my belief that the war shall end soon, the South shall have its liberty, and you shall return home."

"How old are you, Winthrop?"

McGee asked the question once we camped for the night after the first day's march. It startled me. He had never used my given name.

"I'm . . ." *What day is it?* My birthday had passed without notice. I was seventeen.

I almost told McGee the truth before remembering my lie. "I'm twenty-three," I said. "No, twenty-four now."

"No more falsehoods, Winthrop MacNaughton. Out with it now. How old are you? 'Tis too late to ship you back to your father for a stern lecture and sound paddling. How old?"

My chin fell against my chest. "Seventeen," I said weakly. "Turned seventeen on the second of this month. And my father's dead, killed at Gettysburg. That's why I enlisted."

"Seventeen?" McGee whistled. "You don't look anywhere near seventeen. Fourteen, maybe. And you're bloody small. 'Tis not a lie you're telling me, is it, MacNaughton?"

"Seventeen," I repeated. "I swear."

Pursing his lips, he studied me a moment before shrugging. "Is Winthrop MacNaughton your true name?"

"Yes, sir, though I'd rather be called Win, sir, if it's all the same with you."

"Gave your own name when you signed up? That could have got you caught."

"Maybe. I didn't really think about it. Well, no, that's not true, either, 'cause I did think about it. Thought long and hard. I wanted to fight under my own name, Captain, for Father's sake. Wanted to prove something to him, or for him, something like that. Didn't want him to have died for nothing."

It certainly seemed as if he had died in vain now. That Louisiana captain thought the tide had turned for the Confederacy after the Battle of Sabine Crossroads, that the war was lost for the Union, and I believed him. Father was dead. Mike Peabody was, in all likelihood, dead and buried in a shallow unmarked grave. I was on the road to Texas, a prisoner of war.

"Well, Win MacNaughton, how well do you know Texas?"

I eyed him again with a mix of curiosity and suspicion.

He grinned back at me. "Secrets never last long in this man's army, Win MacNaughton, especially when your secret is shared with a lad with a mouth like your good friend, Michael Peabody."

The way he said it, the truth of his statement, and the laughter in his eyes made me smile back until I thought again of poor Mike, his arm almost shot off, killed in a muddy field, trying to save me. And I had killed him. I had talked him into enlisting with me. Mike should be back in Rhode Island, stealing drinks of liquor from his father's saloon, playing baseball at the cove. Every now and then I would think I had cried my last tear over my old friend, and then the memo-

ries would come flooding back, followed by my
guilt. I brushed away a tear and kicked away a
squirrel-mangled pine cone.

"Texas?" McGee repeated with urgency, although his voice never rose above a whisper. "Do
you know where we're going, lad?"

"No, sir. I heard some grayback mention Kirbyville."

"That's a supply depot, northeast of Tyler.
Learned that much I have. Do you know Tyler,
lad?"

"No, sir. Sorry. We were in Jack County, and
that's a ways northwest of Fort Worth. We're
bound for East Texas, the piney woods. Never
been there. Like I told Mike, sir, it's a big state."

"Indeed, but not big enough to hold Conall
McGee."

All of our marching had not helped his left ankle. McGee now needed a crutch to walk. I had
recommended that he ride in one of the wagons,
but he would have nothing of that. "You
shouldn't try anything now, Captain," I whispered. "I mean with your leg, sir. You wouldn't
get far at all, and some of those guards brag how
they're itching to kill a Federal. They're mean, sir.
Spiteful mean and bloody killers, especially that
lieutenant in charge."

"Go to sleep, Win MacNaughton."

I collapsed beside him and closed my eyes.

"You're me guardian angel, aren't you, Win
MacNaughton?"

No answer came from me. *Guardian angel? Not
by a long shot. Ask Mike Peabody.*

"Don't worry, Win. Bide me time I will. And I'll

take you along with me. War's not over for us, lad. Not by God's grace."

Several minutes passed. I stared at the stars, exhausted, foot sore, but unable to sleep.

McGee's voice made me smile, although mine came with little mirth.

"A belated happy birthday to you, Trooper Win MacNaughton."

CHAPTER TEN

To my astonishment, Mr. J. G. Taylor Spink himself, publisher of The Sporting News, *called on me after Game 2 in my hotel room, where he presented me with a baseball signed by his newspaper staff, and gave me the option of returning home or staying in St. Louis in hopes that the World Series would return to Sportsman's Park. I could listen to the games from Fenway Park on the radio, Mr. Spink informed me, as if Civil War veterans couldn't possibly know about radios, even though I had told one of his reporters how Dizzy Dean's broadcasts of St. Louis Browns games often amused me so. If luck didn't shine on the Cardinals and they returned home in defeat, Mr. Spink had been told, they would love to have me visit with players and coaches at the train station. Of course, Mr. Spink let me know that* The Sporting News, *while the "Bible of Baseball", remained impartial. Boston players and executives would enjoy my company, too, if the World Series indeed returned to St. Louis. Everyone thought a great deal of me, he went on.*

But not enough to pay for a train ticket and hotel room in Boston, *I realized without any vindictiveness.* Guess they've forgotten that I am a Yankee by birth, a New Englander in fact.

"I know you have a lot to do, Mister Mac-Naughton," Mr. Spink concluded, *"so if you want to go back to Texas, we certainly understand."*

A lot to do. What does a fellow pushing 100 years old have to do?

"Be glad to stay," I said, and the sports journalist gave me a pithy grin and equally curt handshake.

After he left, I walked down to the corner café, grabbed a bite of breakfast, stopped at the Pelegrimas Five & Dime, bought another Big Chieftain tablet, and returned to my room. Tomorrow was a travel day for the teams, so I had all day to jot down my recollections.

When I chewed on a pencil, my conversation with Mr. Spink ran through my head.

"Keep this between us, sir, but I am confident in the Cardinals," Mr. Spink had said. *"Besides, six- and seven-game World Series are good for the sport, good for sporting publications like* The Sporting News. *In spite of the betting lines, I do not think the Cardinals will return to Saint Louis defeated. Hope they don't, anyway."*

"Me, too," I had agreed. *"I know that feeling."*

Defeated.

Cavalry boots are not meant for marches. With my socks worn to bare threads after several days on the road, broken blisters covered my sore feet. Captain McGee could barely walk, but County Wexford pride would not allow him to ride in the wagons, although eventually he leaned on me for support, an act that likely pained him as much as

his ankle. His endurance, the way he never complained, gave me strength, even pride that I had
served under him. Yet I feared he would wind up
like the Illinois infantryman who had walked until he dropped. The officer in charge of our escort,
Lieutenant Cy Burrows, had no tolerance, and,
instead of placing the young man in a wagon, he
looped a rope around the soldier's neck,
wrapped the other end around his saddle's horn,
and broke into a gallop for 600 yards. We buried
the soldier that evening.

"I will shoot stragglers," Lieutenant Burrows
announced, "as surely and as justly as I will shoot
anyone who attempts escape."

And I had once called Conall McGee *The Beast*.
We cursed Lieutenant Burrows's cruelty. So did
several Confederate guards.

Dejected, weary, broken, we broiled in the sun
or were drenched by thunderstorms. Mosquitoes
drained our blood. Wounds festered and stom-
achs shrank from the lack of food, yet, in fairness,
I concede that our Confederate guards had as little to eat as we were given. Every night, we buried
one or two prisoners who had died along the trail.
To lift our spirits, a handful of Wisconsin soldiers
entertained us with a song they made up to the
tune of "When Johnny Comes Marching Home".

In Eighteen Hundred and Sixty-Four,
  give thanks, give thanks;
In Eighteen Hundred and Sixty-Four,
  give thanks, give thanks;
In Eighteen Hundred and Sixty-Four,
  we drew our time from Gen'ral Banks,
And we'll never see that son-of-a-bitch again.

No one, to my knowledge, tried to escape. Maybe we felt too weak. Captain McGee no longer brought up the subject, and I never gave it any thought until I saw the stockade.

A palisade of logs, split in half, reached eighteen feet into the sky in the clearing surrounded by a dense pine forest. Perhaps a half-dozen structures had been built outside the prison, and just north lay a small graveyard that would grow for the duration of our stay. What struck me was the smell of rot. Lieutenant Burrows rode forward, saluting a lieutenant colonel who stepped out of a small cabin while someone barked for the gate to be opened.

Slowly the men ahead of us stumbled or staggered inside the compound walls.

"Home, sweet, home," came a bitter voice behind me.

Like a cannon ball, I bolted out of line, ignoring the pain shooting from the balls of my feet, up my calves. I can picture myself all these years later, a petrified teenager, fear masking my face and certainly clouding my judgment.

A cacophony of voices echoed behind me.

"No, Win, they'll kill you, lad!" . . . "Shoot that Yankee fool!" . . . "Escape! Escape!" . . . "Run, boy, run!" . . . "Hurrah! Hurrah! Hurrah for the Rhode Island horse soldier!" . . . "Don't let him reach the woods!"

The first Minié ball whistled overhead. The second tore through my blouse, burning my side, spilling blood. Horse hoofs thundered behind me. Tears blinded me. I had to get away. If I could just reach the woods beyond that spring. Another bullet dug up the sod at my feet, but then the shooting stopped as a horse drew closer. The Rebels couldn't shoot at me now for fear of hitting one of their own. Of course, the man riding me down could certainly kill me.

Make those woods, I thought, screaming at my legs to work faster. We had arrived, I had been told, on April 20th, which *The Farmer's Almanac* said would be a new moon. At least, that's what I had been told. If I could hide until sunset, I might have a chance, make my way back to New Orleans, find what was left of General Banks's command. Actually it turned out we reached Camp Ford on the 18th, although we hadn't seen the moon or any stars over the past few nights because of the clouds.

The patch of pine and scrub timber came no closer, but the pounding of that horse behind me did.

I had just neared the little spring when the horse flattened me. Air whooshed out of my lungs, and I landed hard. Every muscle stopped working, and I couldn't have stood up, run another step, but I tried. Fighting nausea and fear, I scrambled to my knees, crawling through mud and rotting leaves.

An explosion rocked through my head, and down I went, headfirst, into the spring's edge. I came up with a start, rolling over, coughing, spitting out water, clawing the thick slime from my face.

"That might be the foolest damn' thing I ever saw," a voice drawled. "Lucky I'm in a generous mood today. The hell was you thinkin', Yank?"

I tried to sit up, but my head throbbed, and

down I went, staring at the spinning sky and blurry Rebel above me.

The man came into focus soon after the dizziness passed. A giant hand clutched a Navy revolver, the barrel of which he used to push back a dirty black hat. A coarse beard hid much of his face, although only the huge mustache looked permanent, and his eyes burned with grim intensity.

My hand scooped water from the spring, and I washed the grime from my face before a spasm of pain reminded me of my wounded side. Instantly I stuck my hand inside my blouse, which proved a stupid move. The Reb jerked his revolver toward me, thumbing back the hammer and tightening his finger on the trigger.

"I'll kill you," he said evenly.

When I withdrew my hand, I showed him the blood.

"Hurt bad?" he asked without much interest. He wore a captain's shell jacket, gray wool with yellow trim, but the rest of his outfit looked more civilian than military, especially his stovepipe boots and large-rowel spurs. A tall man, vaguely familiar, he had not been part of the patrol that had escorted us from Sabine Crossroads, so I assumed he was stationed at the stockade.

"I don't think so," I answered, and returned my hand to stanch the bleeding. The bullet had carved a furrow beneath my ribs. It pained me greatly, but shouldn't be a nuisance unless it became infected.

"Then on your feet, Yank."

I didn't move. Other Rebels had caught up with us, and Lieutenant Burrows ripped his revolver from its holster, drawing a bead on my head with an oath.

"Lower that gun, Burrows," my captor ordered, and Burrows's eyes flared. "He ain't goin' nowheres but to the stockade."

When Burrows made no move to obey, the captain swung his Colt at the lieutenant. "Killin' men's a specialty of mine, and I don't give a damn if it's some Yank or a gonus like you."

Burrows's face and ears turned burning red, but the lieutenant holstered his pistol and spurred back to the compound without another word.

As my mind cleared, I recognized something in the captain's voice, and studied his features again, trying to place him while I caught my breath. Lowering his pistol, he looked at me, squinting, licking his lips.

"I know you . . . ," he began.

I recognized him then, my stomach teetering, a coil of fear strangling me.

"You're Pig Oliver," I said after finding my voice.

"Capt'n Oliver," he corrected, and gathered the reins to his horse, a blue roan gelding with a Union cavalry saddle and horsehair bridle.

"Jack County," he said after swinging onto his mount. "Ain't that right? You was that damnyankee pup with the nigger-lovin' daddy, went to school with Gene. MacNewton."

"MacNaughton. Win MacNaughton."

"Been playin' much baseball, boy?" He motioned for me to stand, and I obeyed, swaying at first, testing a knot forming on my head from where Oliver had clubbed me with his Colt.

"Not lately," I answered. "And you?"

He shook his head, jutting his jaw toward the stockade. I began walking back to the prison, Captain Pig Oliver riding behind me, followed by the remaining guards who had pursued me.

Cheers greeted me from the Union prisoners. Not to be outdone, the Rebel guards sang out Captain Oliver's name.

Oliver snorted. "Kinda like a baseball game, ain't it, MacNewton?"

I refused to answer, but Oliver was in a rare, talkative mood.

"What made you run like that?"

Why had I tried to escape? Wetting cracked lips, I remained silent as we slowly made our way back to the line of prisoners and guards. Before the cheers died down on both sides, I recognized Conall McGee, waving his slouch hat in salute, then making the sign of the cross before resuming his painful trek through the gate, helped by a 10th Squadron Rhode Islander named Ivins.

Perhaps, now that I think back on it decades later, my father prompted that ill-advised dash for freedom. When I saw the stockade, the gates swing open, it hit me. I wouldn't fight the Rebels again, wouldn't avenge Father's death. I had failed Henry Wallace MacNaughton. So, horrified, I ran.

"Almost got your head blowed off," Oliver commented. "You never was much for speed. I recollect that much about you from them baseball games.

"That was one good thing you Yanks done," Oliver went on. "I got a few fond memories about them contests we played. Have tried to get some of the boys stationed here interested, but I ain't the teacher you was, MacNewton, and most folks hereabouts ain't got interest in learnin' some damnyankee game."

When we reached the line, I started to take my place, but Oliver ordered me to stop. I held my breath as the lieutenant colonel strutted toward me. Tobacco juice had stained the corners of his gray beard, deep scars pocked his forehead, and his blue eyes looked translucent.

"Take him to the Wolf Pen," the commander ordered in a nasal Southern accent. "Give him a month."

"Hold on there," Oliver said smoothly. "Boy's got a hole in his side. Ought to see that ol' sawbones first."

"After a month in the Wolf Pen," the colonel said stubbornly. Behind him, I caught Lieutenant Burrows's grin.

"Month in that pigpen, and that bullet hole will mortify," Oliver added. "The boy deserves a fightin' chance."

"Pig's generous today," another Rebel said lightly. "He saw Miss Jane earlier."

The colonel tried to stare down Oliver, and, although he couldn't match that gaze, he spaced his words with an icy unfriendliness. "Captain Oliver, I have grown sick and tired at your questioning my orders in front of the men. Insubordination I will not abide, mister. Now take him to the Wolf Pen."

"Colonel Sweet." My head snapped toward the new voice. So did the colonel's. So did Pig Oliver's. In fact, the Union soldiers still outside the compound craned their necks for just a glimpse at that soft, feminine drawl that blended grits with afternoon tea.

"Miss Bartholomew." With an awkward bow, Lieutenant Colonel Sweet removed his straw hat. "I did not know you were present, ma'am. Your father is well, I hope. And you?"

Underneath my breath, I cursed Sweet and Burrows for blocking my view of this angel.

"This is not a proper place for ladies," Sweet said. "Allow Mister Burrows to escort you to my quarters. There I . . ."

"With pleasure, Colonel. But on a similar note, I am sure your Wolf Pen is not a proper place for even a wounded Yankee."

Brown hair—curly—a glimpse of a yellow print dress. I swayed back and forth.

"Captain Oliver," Sweet said without turning around. "Escort the Yankee to the hospital. When he is released from Major Rose's care, give him a month in the pen. Perhaps that shall break him of his habit of running."

"Sure thing, Colonel."

Silently I cursed Pig Oliver, too, for his blue roan gelding shielded this Bartholomew angel from me as we walked to the log cabin that served as a prison hospital.

"Who was that?" I asked.

"Jane Anne Bartholomew," Oliver replied. "Don't go to fancy her. Her daddy wouldn't cotton to the idea of some mudsill sparkin' his only daughter. Wouldn't care for it myself, neither."

I didn't realize we had stopped at the hospital until Pig Oliver addressed a potbellied, fat-jowl man in a dirty stable frock as Doc. This Doc

grunted and tore off a large chunk of chewing tobacco with long yellow teeth. Yes, a barn served
as the Camp Ford hospital. One of those dogtrot
style barns, seed and feed crib on one side, tool
crib on the other, a few stalls and a corral in the
back. Actually, at that time, only the tool room
had been designated for the one-man medical
corps. No floor, and the chinking had fallen out
between the heavy log walls, if indeed there had
ever been any chinking.

In no hurry to become a patient, I suddenly felt
like conversing with Pig Oliver. I started with a
weak thanks.

"Don't thank me, MacNewton. Still good odds
you'll die. And if you ever run again, I'll kill you
myself." He had worked a wad of tobacco into his
mouth, and now spit on my boots.

"Why in hell would you up and join that
tyrant's Army, boy?"

"For my father," I said. "He died at Gettysburg."

Oliver's expression changed, and briefly he
stared at the gray clouds overhead. "Reckon we
got something else in common. They buried
Brother Gene there, too."

CHAPTER ELEVEN

Major Jon Rose, post surgeon at Camp Ford, did not exactly inspire confidence in his patients, at least not me. The fact that the tool crib in a decrepit barn had been made his office and hospital did not help matters. A pale gentleman of ancient age and rotund proportions, gray hair thinning on a rectangular head, Major Rose sported several flabby chins, and spoke in a highly agitated Southern mumble. There was no Texas drawl. The good doctor shot out words faster than a Colt revolving pistol propelled lead, although he admitted that he preferred simple statements such as yes . . . no . . . dead . . . and, as he told me after stitching up my side: "You'll live."

I spit out the .56-caliber bullet I had practically flattened while he used a saddle stitch on my wound, cleansing the gash with turpentine, and gasped for breath as Major Rose wrapped torn linen over my waist. When Rose offered a sip from a green bottle, I took it without thanks and pulled long and hard. The raw liquor tasted and smelled much worse than the how-come-you-so Captain McGee had procured back in Louisiana, but, after surviving Texas Confederate medical practices, I certainly needed a drink, even that.

"Pig Oliver was doing me no favor," I complained underneath my breath, "sending me here."

Major Rose said something, but I couldn't make out any of his words. Offering him a confused shrug, I leaned forward as he fired off another sentence. The bulge of chewing tobacco in his left cheek did not help matters. Again, I shook my head. So did Major Rose, putting both hands on his fat waist and spitting tobacco juice that splattered against the hard-packed earthen floor.

"I said," Rose began, spacing his words deliberately, "take off them boots."

"Why?"

" 'Cause you was a-limpin', and I ain't no idjit. Seen bluebellies die of foot rot. Now, off . . ." The rest of his command befogged my weary ears, but I understood and, with a shout of pain, pried off the worn leather that had once, under Captain McGee's watchful command, gleamed from spit and polish. The shape of the soles, worn thin and filled with holes, surprised me as I tossed the pair to the floor. My spurs were gone, and I tried to remember what had happened to them.

"Wonder they let you keep them boots," Rose mumbled, looking up at me and asking loudly: "Did you understand that, Yank?"

"There were enough Federal dead, I guess," I said bitterly. "And they stole my spurs!"

Rose's eyes watered as he removed my thread-bare socks.

"Stay here," he ordered.

"What?"

"Stay here! Or run. Ruben Sweet loves a-siccin' his bloodhounds on bluebellies. Burrows, that trash, enjoys a-cuttin' throats. Oliver, he's the worst of the lot. Go. And be damned." He kicked open the door, wiping his hands with a red bandanna. "Understand that, Yank?"

When the door slammed after him, I collapsed on the cot and stared at the ceiling. It wouldn't hold a thimble of rain. A horrible stench, above the odors of turpentine, saddle leather, hay, and dung, gagged me, and I looked to my left and right, searching for that malodorous soldier sharing the makeshift hospital with me. Yet I found myself alone, except for a couple of rats. Cringing, I slowly lifted my head and looked down my body. I couldn't see my feet. Nor did I want to.

My head landed with a *thump*, and my eyes located a saw hanging from a rusty nail on the nearest wall. Flies swarmed around the tool—indeed, they filled the room, as flies are prone to do around barns in the spring. Yet the pests didn't concern me, for I couldn't escape memories of screaming soldiers around the dying tree at Sabine Crossroads. I pictured myself a convalescent, hobbling along Newport's sidewalks, garnering stares from children. God, I couldn't play baseball again.

That image remained with me when Major Rose returned. I heard his voice before he opened the door, talking, not to me for he had resumed his vocal canter, but an octave lower. In shock, I lay there, unmoving, not blinking, convinced my feet would be amputated, then recognized the heavenly voice of Jane Anne Bartholomew.

"Why, Mister Jon, this is no trouble a-tall. You've rescued me from Lieutenant Burrows, and that's the Gospel. Just don't tell the ladies at church. You know how they frown upon women doin' anything other than curtseyin' or pourin' afternoon tea in the parlor."

"Yes'm." Both rinsed their hands in a wash basin resting on a rickety table. With a nod in my direction, Major Rose told Jane Anne: "Hold down that feller's lower limbs."

I shot up, screaming, but Major Rose moved remarkably fast for such a leviathan. His weight all but crushed my rib cage, knocking me down, and he spoke forcefully, spraying my face, only inches from his, with saliva and bits of tobacco leaf and stem.

"Your feet's a bloody mess."

"You're not cutting them off!" I shouted.

"Not yet. But soon enough if you keep a-wrasslin' me."

I lacked strength to fight. My side burned from the movement, spasms shot through my feet up my legs, and the weight of the day, my attempted escape, and near death drained my last bit of energy. Closing my eyes, I blurted out a few choked cries, trying not to burst into tears, and then I felt a cool hand on my forehead. I looked up, and there she was.

My eyes must have played tricks on me, outside, when I first glimpsed Jane Anne Bartholomew.

Her hair seemed more auburn than brown, and not so curly, and she wore a peach dress, the hem and cuffs frayed, not yellow. I can't say she was beautiful. Truth of the matter is, now that I think back, Lucy Covey probably had grown into a more striking woman, but there was a gentleness in Jane Anne's light brown eyes. Her nose seemed too big, her lips too thin, while wrinkles knotted her forehead and bags lined her eyes. This close to her, she looked old, tired, although I later learned she was only a year my senior. Yet I found her attractive, just worn down from years of war and hardship. Jane Anne Bartholomew remained an angel, my angel.

Her voice sounded sweetly musical, silkily Southern, as she stroked my cheeks and forehead.

"You poor, poor Yankee. You poor, poor Yankee. Why, Mister Jon, he's just a boy."

"I'm seventeen!" I argued.

She didn't believe me. I read that in her eyes.

Major Rose had cut away part of my ragged trousers with a pair of scissors. He mumbled something, but I never took my eyes off Jane Anne Bartholomew.

"Understand that, Yank?" Rose's voice boomed with impatience.

I shook my head.

"First, Mister Jon's goin' to cleanse your feet," Jane Anne translated for me. "It'll burn a mite."

Smiling, she glanced at her arm, and I realized I had gripped it tightly. Frightened, I couldn't let go, though, wouldn't let go.

"Damn' site more'n that," Rose corrected.

Jane Anne and I smiled at each other. I had no

idea why, for Rose's comment hadn't been funny. "After that, he'll have to drain the infection," she continued. "To prevent gangrene."

"What about baseball?" I asked softly.

She knotted her brow, not understanding, but Rose snorted, punctuating his contempt by soaking my kneecaps with tobacco juice. "Baseball? Lord A'mighty, Yank." Suddenly he laughed, a bellowing burst that rocked the tack room and caused the horses stabled outside to kick their stalls. "Ain't seen a baseball contest since Galveston in 'Sixty-One. Baseball." His tone abruptly turned stern. "You can forget about baseball, about a-swimmin', about Spanish Monte, and about a-fornicatin' iffen if I don't get to work."

Jane Anne blushed. "Why, Mister Jon?" she said. "Such language."

Rose grunted something I took as an apology, but the light in Jane Anne's eyes made me think she didn't really mind his impolite talk.

"Well, he can forget about a-livin'. Miss Jane?"

Gently Jane Anne Bartholomew pried my fingers from her arm, and slowly moved toward my fetid feet and that scowling Confederate surgeon. Her face paled when she glanced down, and her eyes shot back up, locking with mine, never letting go. Swallowing hard, she grabbed my ankles.

"She shouldn't be here, Doc!" I demanded. "What kind of a man are you? This is no place . . . ."

He shut me up by dousing my feet with turpentine, and I shrieked. If I were trying to sound manly for Jane Anne, I failed horribly. Shrieked . . . like a girl.

"She's a-done it before, Yank," Major Rose told

me. "Some soldier-boy would break your ankles, brittle as they are, and I'd have to start a-sawin'."

Then, with a contemptuous smirk, he emptied the jug of turpentine on my feet.

"Understand that, Yank?"

For the next week, under Major Rose's care, I lay on that cot, my feet and side heavily bandaged. When I finally walked, it was at my insistence for I felt eager to get out of the stifling crib, and empty my own chamber pot. Perhaps I just didn't want Jane Anne Bartholomew to see me laid up, to think of me as a Yankee who couldn't even go to the privy on my own. She never returned to the hospital, though.

No longer did I have private chambers. A few Rebels reported in every now and then, claiming some ailment or the other, usually asking for a shot of whiskey as the cure-all, but Major Rose would chase them off. Union prisoners, however, showed up with real problems, and Major Rose had no assistant surgeon, no help since Jane Anne had returned to her plantation, unless you counted the two slaves who buried the dead.

In early May, I relinquished my cot to a feverish Ohioan, and took my place on the dirt beside several others. Within a week, the hospital had overtaken the feed and seed crib, the shelter between the two rooms, and all around the barn.

"We need a real hospital," I told Major Rose.

"*Umph*," he said.

The first prisoners had arrived at Camp Ford in the summer of 1863. Now known as The Old Seventy-Two, they had built the log prison themselves during their first year of imprisonment.

Others had been interred here, but nothing like what happened after the tortuous Red River Campaign. Almost 1,700 had been captured after the battle of Sabine Crossroads and other skirmishes, arriving in April. Of those, fifteen had tried to escape, but Pig Oliver's patrol had returned all but two. Oliver said he had killed the two others, but we couldn't be sure he was telling the truth.

Major Rose's biggest battle came against typhus flux that swept through the prison, bringing on fevers and horrible rashes that covered men's entire bodies except for their soles, palms, and faces. Every morning, Major Rose pleaded his case with Lieutenant Colonel Sweet. Every evening, he wrote a letter to a minister or a Confederate or even Union official, anyone, begging for quinine, morphine, and other medicines. Sighing heavily he remarked to no one in particular one afternoon that he would sell his soul for just one bottle of calomel. One box did arrive, from a Cumberland Presbyterian church in Marshall, but it didn't contain calomel. Major Rose opened a jar and laughed.

"Grape jelly." He tossed the jar to a wide-eyed Vermont artillery corporal. "Well, they mean well."

"It's good," announced the corporal, scooping out more with his dirty fingers. My stomach growled, and the jealousy I felt shamed me, but I wanted to taste grape jelly. Major Rose handed the box to another patient, and told him to pass the jars to the boys in the next crib. I couldn't hide my disappointment, but I said nothing.

As more soldiers suffering from typhus flux

filled the seed and feed crib, I decided I was just taking up space, so I asked to be discharged and returned to my command, to take my home inside what the guards called The Corral.

"Go," Major Rose ordered.

Carrying my boots, I left the hospital and hobbled toward the gate, escorted by an old man in patched britches, but Lieutenant Colonel Sweet, standing in the shaded porch of his office, ordered me to halt.

"You're forgetting something, aren't you, boy?" he asked when I turned to face him.

Instead of answering, I just stared at him. Truthfully I had forgotten about the colonel's sentence of one month in the Wolf Pen. The old guard prodded me gently with his musket and led me to the Wolf Pen.

A fairly accurate name, Wolf Pen. Thin logs laced together with baling wire covered a twelve-foot pit that stank of mud. Two other Rebels lifted the pine ceiling, and my escort pointed to a ladder. Awkwardly I climbed down, each step hurting. A few rungs from the bottom, I stepped on a protruding nail and fell, my outstretched arms and the thick gumbo breaking my fall. Blood leaked from the puncture, darkening my bandaged right foot, and I stared at the nail. It reminded me of the caltrop that had crippled Mike Peabody's horse. That nail had been hammered through the bottom of the rung deliberately. A cruel trap. Ignoring the pain in my right foot, I looked at the guards above me and cursed them.

The faces of those guards disappeared after they hauled up the ladder, but a pockmarked boy scarcely my age returned moments later.

"We'll lower a bucket in the morn by rope," he said. "That's for you to do your business. We'll haul that bucket out at dusk and give you another one. That's your supper. All you'll get till the next evenin'."

They'll probably use the same bucket, I thought bitterly.

A canteen dropped into the mud near my boots.

"When that's empty, stick it in your grub bucket, and we'll refill it," the boy explained. "Just remember, it's gotta last you all day."

"Thanks," I said sarcastically, and bit back pain from my throbbing foot.

The guard glanced over his shoulder, then whispered urgently: "Don't eat the cornmeal."

"What?"

"Don't eat the cornmeal. Meat ain't too rancid, but the cornmeal ain't kernels, just the cob all ground up. Lieutenant Burrows does it. Put that nail in the ladder, too."

That figured.

All that Major Rose had done to save my feet . . . and I'll probably get lockjaw, or the foot will be amputated.

"If you eat that meal, it'll play hell with your innards," the guard continued. "Bring on the trots. Don't eat the cornmeal. You hear?"

I nodded. "Thanks," I said, only this time I meant it.

"What's your name, Yank?"

"Win MacNaughton. And yours?"

"Andy Griggs. I'm from Tyler, just up the road."

"I'm from Newport."

He shook his head.

"Rhode Island."

Still no recognition. Andy Griggs reminded me again to pour out the cornmeal before he stepped away and ordered the log roof lowered into place.

I gathered my boots and canteen before the ceiling blocked out all but streams of sunlight.

CHAPTER TWELVE

Three days later, I welcomed my first cellmate to the Wolf Pen.

All I ever knew him as was Sharky the Seaman. A master's mate, Sharky had served on the gunboat *Diana*, which had been shelled relentlessly by Confederate artillery when the captain foolishly steamed her into Rebel-held Pattersonville in March of '63. He looked like a Navy man, swarthy, stocky, with curly hair, thick arms, and a sailor's cap, the only thing left of his uniform. Sharky had no shoes, not even socks, and he often eyed my worn-out boots with unconcealed envy. His britches had deteriorated into mere rags, and no sleeves or buttons remained on his filthy shirt, yet his spirit remained as bright as the gold St. Christopher medallion hanging from his neck.

"Do you snore, Win?" he asked after we had made our introductions.

"No, sir."

"That's too bad, because I sound like a sawmill. And don't *sir* me. I've been a prisoner too long to be sirred. Though I am old enough to be your daddy, bunkies in the Wolf Pen don't sir each other. How long you been here? And how long you staying?"

When I answered, he whistled. "Sweet isn't sweet on you."

I rolled my eyes at the feeble pun.

"Well, you're missing all the doings at Ford City."

"Ford City?"

"Yeah, don't you know where we live?"

I explained that I had yet to set foot inside the prison stockade. My familiarity with Camp Ford had been limited to the hospital and Wolf Pen.

Sharky sniggered. "Well, we call it Ford City. We got streets and a park square, a bakery, even got a newspaper, *The Old Flag*, five dollars subscription per annum, published by Captain William May, when he gets around to it. Win, we live in a veritable metropolis." When I laughed, he shook a finger at me. "I'm serious. Ford City. Serious about *The Old Flag*, too. That said, I will admit that Captain May's handwriting is not a thing of beauty. Nor are the streets and businesses of this fine borough. Still, we ought to invest in property, Win. Population's growing by leaps and bounds. A regular boodle of true Union men. Twelve hundred arrived yesterday."

"Twelve hundred!" I couldn't fathom such a mass of humanity in the prison's cramped quarters.

"Part of General Steel's command, up in

Arkansas. War's not going well for the Union, at least not in these parts. And I put the blame on you landlubbers. Four thousand or more of you Army boys, a regular boodle. Only a couple hundred of we men of Odysseus's ilk."

"Four thousand?" I couldn't picture that many men.

"Give or take one or two. They're expanding the city limits of home, sweet, home, so be glad. That's why I'm here. My father did not sire me to be a carpenter. I thought I might get conscripted into digging trenches or sawing logs, so I hit one of Sweet's Secesh with a dirt clod."

They might have shot him, Sharky explained, but he had considered the risk worth taking. After being hauled out of the stockade for punishment, Sharky had slipped one of Sweet's guards a plug of Star Navy tobacco to put him in the Wolf Pen, instead of hanging him by his thumbs.

"We're not the only ones serving out sentences, Win," Sharky explained. "Couple dozen are out by the guard shacks, bucked and gagged. I figure a week in the Wolf Pen is like a thirty-day furlough compared to that."

"A week, maybe," I said sullenly. "I have three more weeks down here."

Sharky whistled again. "Like I told you, Win, Colonel Sweet sure ain't sweet on you."

During the week Sharky bunked with me, I learned a lot more about Ford City. I told him how I was captured, about General Banks's blundering, but when I asked him how he landed in Camp Ford, he shook his head, saying he preferred talking about more recent events. From

Sharky, I learned that Ruben Sweet commanded Sweet's Guards, a partisan group of old men, young boys, and Confederate Army misfits and miscreants. "They weren't fit to fight, so they sent them here," Sharky said. "Although Sweet can be sweet. Some officers, Naval and Army, requested permission to build a real hospital, to get our boys out of that damned barn, and Sweet agreed. Prisoners are putting it up now, outside The Corral." He pointed toward the ceiling.

"That's what that noise is," I said, and Sharky smiled.

"Going up right beside the Wolf Pen, though it won't be as big as this fine boarding house."

Sharky knew just about everything. Despite what we had been told in Louisiana, Secesh and Federal prisoners, Sharky insisted, were being exchanged in the Western regions. That gave me, and everyone else confined at Ford City, hope. He told me the layout of Ford City, which guards I could trust, which would kill me (Burrows, Oliver—no surprise to me—and some slim-jim sergeant named Ward Keener). Sharky even knew not to eat the cornmeal. He could recite the names of The Old Seventy-Two, how far it was to Kirbyville, Gladewater, and Tyler, and exactly how many guards Sweet commanded. The one bit of information he lacked pertained to Jane Anne Bartholomew; he had never seen her.

I slapped my head. *Of course, he wouldn't know her. Jane Anne would never have been inside Ford City.*

"Tell me about her, Win," Sharky pleaded.

I was happy to oblige.

After I painted a portrait of my angel, Sharky sighed. We sat there in the mud silently, lost in thoughts of women, the buzzing of saws, and the shouts of prisoners above us as they constructed the hospital. When that noise died down, we knew dusk was approaching.

Overhead, a few grunts told us the guards had arrived to raise the roof, remove the slop buckets, and bring us supper. We sat on our haunches, watching the bustle of activity, warming our faces in the fading sunlight, filling our lungs with fresher air. Andy Griggs peered over the edge at Sharky.

"Let's make that trade," Griggs said, and, with a grunt, Sharky unfastened his St. Christopher medallion as he rose to make his way to his bucket of supper. I followed to get my own food, watching with curiosity as Sharky removed a piece of boiled beef, and dropped the St. Christopher on the cornmeal, which he left untouched. I stuffed the beef in my mouth before pouring my allotment of ground corn cob into a rising pile in the corner. As the Rebs withdrew our buckets, Sharky the Seaman waited beside me, the two of us chewing unpalatable meat.

After fingering the St. Christopher gently, Griggs nodded with approval, and tossed down an object—at first, I couldn't make it out—that Sharky caught with ease. He hefted the brown leather ball, his head bobbing up and down, a smile stretching across his face.

"A baseball?" I blinked away my amazement.

Sharky's expression revealed similar surprise. "You know the sport, Win?"

"Know it? I love it. I was a catcher, second nine, for the Newport Base Ball Club in Rhode Island."

"Great Scot! I caught for the Atlantics on Long Island." He tossed the ball to me.

"Got an uncle who played in New Orleans before the war!" Andy Griggs called out before the roof replaced the sky.

"I didn't know Secesh played baseball," Sharky said in the darkness. His statement had been directed at me, for he spoke too softly for Griggs to have heard.

I thought of Pig Oliver, of our games in Jacksboro.

"Some do," I allowed.

"Not as good as us, I'm sure. Come daylight, when we can see a little better, we'll toss the ball to each other. Time passes quicker when you have a baseball."

When Sharky finished his week-long sentence, he left me the baseball. I protested, knowing it had cost him his St. Christopher, but he wouldn't take it back. "When you return to the city limits, we'll make a trade. Till then, the ball is yours."

The loneliness I felt that night after Sharky had been freed rendered me to tears. That's what solitary confinement is meant to do, of course, but I did not remain alone. The Wolf Pen wasn't made for solitary, just as Camp Ford wasn't built to hold 4,000 prisoners. For the rest of my punishment, I had company, just one man to begin with, later two more, and finally what Sharky would have called "a regular boodle". By the time Andy Griggs ordered me to climb up the ladder and return to The Corral, I had at least a dozen cellmates.

Once I walked through the stockade's one gate,

sally port, the Texians called it, I tried to find
Captain McGee and Sharky the Seaman, which
proved daunting.

Sharky had not exaggerated too much about
our prison being a city. A small trench had been
dug about ten feet from the walls; I knew from
Sharky not to step over that ditch. It was the
deadline, and Sweet's Guards had orders to shoot
any prisoner who crossed it. The prison had been
expanded from the two-and-a-half acre enclosure
I had first seen, to at least twice that size. A piece
of warped plank had been nailed to a stake in the
dirt just beyond the deadline, and carved into it:

WELCOME TO FORD CITY
Pop. ~~72~~, ~~563~~, ~~65~~, ~~64~~, ~~97~~, ~~146~~, ~~132~~, ~~892~~, ~~2238~~,
~~2223~~, ~~2236~~, ~~3436~~, ENUF!

Front Street paralleled the wall, and I quickly
stepped out of the path of a squadron of Iowa in-
fantrymen marching down the small street,
drilled by a foul-mouthed, red-bearded sergeant.
In front of me, between what someone had designated Park Front and Park Row, stretched Park
Square, in which a group of red-capped Zouaves,
from the 165th New York I later learned, performed a marching drill for spectators. Other
men tossed baseballs, but I did not see Sharky or
Captain McGee among the group. A street ven-
dor, a small Ohioan, offered cornbread for sale to
not only Union prisoners, but Confederate guards
patrolling a catwalk along the log palisade.

"Sure, Yank!" one of the guards called out. "I'll
give you five dollars for that bread. Just bring it on
over."

The Ohioan smiled. "You know I can't do that, boss. You come and get it."

"You think I'd shoot you, Yank?"

"I know you'd shoot me, Reb, if I cross that deadline."

"Ten dollars then, Yank. Ten dollars in Confederate yellowbacks. But you gotta bring it to me."

Shaking his head, the soldier laughed. "Not for five hundred dollars, Reb, which wouldn't buy much no how." He moved on, calling out: "Cornbread! Fresh cornbread! Come buy some good cornbread. Reasonable prices."

As he moved into the park, the aroma of boiling coffee and frying bacon, besides the cornbread, knotted my stomach, and I wished I had bought a loaf of his bread.

"Ford City," I said, shaking my head.

Men built makeshift houses, others sang, and an Irishman pointed past Park Row and told me I'd find Captain May behind Finigan's Alley.

"What about Captain McGee?" I asked. "Third Rhode Island Cavalry?"

He shrugged. "Mac, do I look like I know every hoss in this corral? All I know is that Captain May wants new prisoners to report to him, so he can keep a tally in *The Old Flag.*" So Sharky hadn't been joking about the prison newspaper. "Besides," the Irishman said, "the spring's down that way. Look like you could use some water."

I thanked him, then thought to ask: "How about Sharky the Seaman? Do you know him? From the *Diana*?"

"Everybody knows Sharky," he replied kindly. "Far corner of Park Row and Fifth Avenue." He pointed south. "But tell Captain May first." He took a few steps toward the Zouaves, then abruptly turned on his heel, swearing at himself as he took me by the shoulder and steered me down Front Street.

"A poor host I'd be turning a boy loose in this wilderness," he said. "I'll take you to see Captain May meself. I'm Fergal O'Hara, Forty-Second Massachusetts."

"Win MacNaughton, Third Rhode Island."

"Second Rhode Island has its officers quarters on Fifth Avenue, across from Soap Street. They can probably help you find your captain."

Of course, Soap Street was as foreign to me as the other street names, but I said nothing to O'Hara. He took me to Captain May's quarters, a ten-by-twelve hut of wood and mud with a small clay chimney, where the gaunt, gray-headed officer welcomed me to Ford City.

"You're the boy who tried to escape, right?" Smiling, May offered me a cup of "Lincoln's coffee", and I accepted.

"About that escape attempt?" May gently prodded after I had taken a few swallows of the scalding drink that didn't taste much like coffee.

"It wasn't much of an escape attempt," I said. "I just ran, made it to the spring before Captain Oliver grazed my side with a pistol shot, then buffaloed me."

"Well, I'll mention your heroics in the next newspaper."

"I wasn't heroic," I protested. "Just scared."

He smiled, and let it go. "There are a few Rhode Islanders, cavalry troopers, toward the northeast corner. You'll probably find your captain and any other men from your regiment there."

After finishing my coffee, I saluted Captain May and went on with my search. O'Hara had gone, so I slaked my thirst in the flowing spring, waiting ten minutes in line as others before me drank, checked my feet—they had all but healed—and resumed my hunt.

I ducked in and out of masses of soldiers before discovering a clearing near the stockade's southern corner. Looking up, trying to get my bearings, I found an artillery corporal working in a fenced garden, or what would pass as a "fence" and a "garden" in a prison camp. The farmer stared at his feet as he walked up and down narrow rows of fledgling cornstalks, holding his trousers up at his hips. Dirt fell from the inside of his pants legs as he moved around.

A hand gripped my shoulder, and I jumped. The corporal's head jerked up, and he almost dropped his trousers. Spinning around, I faced an elderly man with long, unkempt silver hair, a full but shaggy beard, and wire spectacles that pinched the bridge of his nose. One lens was cracked along the bottom; the other was missing altogether. His insignia told me that he was a Navy lieutenant.

"It is impolite to stare," he said dryly.

"Yes, sir. Sorry, Lieutenant." I offered a feeble salute.

"Don't call me lieutenant. In here, I'm known as Professor Blevins. You just arrive?"

I explained my imprisonment in the Wolf Pen, and he nodded without much interest. The corporal had left the garden and now stood behind me, breathing heavily. I began sweating nervously.

"You're one of The Old Seventy-Two," I said, trying to convince Blevins of the truth of my statement. "Sharky the Seaman told me that."

"Told you when and where?"

"A few weeks back, in the Wolf Pen. Passing time. He'd try to name all the original prisoners, The Old Seventy-Two."

"Did he do it correctly?"

I shrugged. "I wouldn't really know, sir . . . Professor. He'd mention seventy-two names, eventually. It's harder than you'd think. You forget, repeat names, and . . ." I didn't need to explain. "But he did mention you, Professor Blevins, from a ship, I can't recall the name."

"*Queen of the West.*"

"I think so. Not sure. But I do remember you were always the first person he'd name, and he never repeated your name twice."

"Did he name himself?"

Silence. *Sharky was one of the first prisoners?* It had never occurred to me, but certainly he could have cited his own name and I wouldn't have known. To me, he was simply Sharky the Seaman.

Blevins did not wait for my reply. "There are rules, soldier, rules of prisoners, rules of camp, rules of war, rules of men," the professor began his lecture, never blinking. "You don't see things. You don't speak of things. Some prisoners remain true to the Union. Some become turncoat razorbacks and will sell you out for a sack of pipe tobacco."

I chose my words carefully. Inexperienced as I was, I knew what the corporal had been doing.

Somewhere a tunnel was being dug, and the prisoner was hiding excavated dirt in this garden.

"I'm no traitor," I said softly but forcefully. "And I haven't seen anything."

Professor Blevins pursed his lips as he stared, considering me. At last he dismissed me, and stepped in front of the corporal. "If a damned kid can see what you're doing, Scheid, a Rebel guard can certainly figure it out."

"Sorry, Professor."

"Sorry gets men killed. Now pull up your britches and get out of my garden."

CHAPTER THIRTEEN

Tarnation, sometimes I feel like I've lived a hundred hard years. One of Mr. Spink's The Sporting News *boys brought a radio to my hotel room so I could listen to Game 3 in Boston, and I did, or tried to anyway, but fell asleep. Had to go downstairs when I woke up and ask the desk clerk what had happened. When I got there, the clerk was engaged in an animated conversation with a boot black about Terry Moore, the St. Louis center fielder troubled by bum legs, and they gave me the evil eye for interrupting their talk with such an ignorant question.*

"Red Sox," the clerk said with a sigh. "Four to nothin'. Ferris held us to four lousy hits. You gotta think if Moore was healthy, if that calf muscle and. . . ."

"He's a gimp," the boot black shot out. "The war done it to him."

Dismissing me, they resumed their discussion about the Cardinals, Terry Moore and his bad legs. I guess they didn't recognize me as such a V.I.P. Also, guess

they didn't expect any big tips from an old codger
wearing slippers and a moth-eaten robe.

Terry Moore, the Cardinals' team captain, had been
one of the St. Louis stars before entering the Army and
missing the 1943, 1944, and 1945 seasons. He had been
discharged in January, and, while maybe he ran a little
slower, he still played well enough in my eyes. I thought
about Conall McGee and his bum left leg as I climbed
the stairs, returned to my room, and went to bed.

Captain McGee sat on the floor of his shebang,
illuminated only by a tallow candle burning in a
tin sconce hanging on the wall. His left boot, in
as poor condition as my own, lay beside him,
sockless foot propped up on a pine stump. He
started to rise when I knocked on the makeshift
doorjamb, but collapsed and shook his head,
smiling despite pain while motioning me to step
inside.

"Laddie, laddie, laddie, me spirits it does bully
good to see you up and about. You look fit, Win.
Jesus, Mary, and Joseph, has it been a month?"

"Yes, sir. They hauled me out of the Wolf Pen a
couple of hours ago. I've been looking for you. A
lieutenant with the Second Rhode Island told me
where to find you."

"Good boys they are. Have you seen the others?"

"Others?"

"Sergeant Champlin and troopers Leslie, Brett,
and Wessler from Second Squadron." I held my
breath, hoping to hear him call out Mike Peabody's
name, but that didn't happen, wouldn't happen, I
thought, couldn't happen. "We're not alone, you
and me, Win, not any more. Scores of Rhode Is-

landers from the Third there are, plus the Second, even one from the First. I'm the Third's ranking officer. Let me take you over to your shebang."

I protested, saying I could find it myself, even in the darkness, but he wouldn't hear of that. McGee struggled to his feet, refusing my help, and stumbled into a chair made out of grapevines. After pulling on his boot, he rose and blew out the candle, but not before pounding my shoulders and frowning. "Don't give me that look," McGee said as he put on his slouch hat. "Remind me of me mother, you do. I'm coming around. And you're looking fitter than you did when last I saw you. Not sure, I was, that you'd live."

"That Rebel doctor, Major Rose, knows what he's doing," I said. "He fixed my side and feet. You might . . ."

"Bosh. I'll fix me own leg without having to thank some grayback pill roller." He guided me through the door, needing my support but using the pretense of leading me to my quarters.

"Watch your step. Snakes get hauled in with the wood, mostly bull snakes, but Sergeant Champlin killed a copperhead the other morn outside his shebang. You'll bunk there."

Great.

Champlin's shebang resembled the huts that dominated Ford City—mud and wood structures with poorly constructed roofs, inviting nests for centipedes, scorpions, mice, and snakes. Located near the east wall, 2nd Squadron's enlisted men's shebang was a little larger than Captain May's or Captain McGee's quarters, but it had few amenities and only one window, with a snakeskin, the slain copperhead's I presumed, decorating the sill. On the other hand, I had seen prisoners living in burrows, others in brush arbors, and several whose only shelter came from tents made from saddle blankets.

Captain McGee leaned against the wall near the window. "Do you think you have room for this old boy, Sergeant?"

The sergeant had been stoking the fireplace when we entered. He leaned the blackened poker, made of wood, not iron, in the corner, and turned with a grunt, looking as glum as I remembered him, but his expression quickly changed. I had never seen Champlin smile until then. "MacNaughton will do, sir, but that will just about fill us up."

"Anybody else will bunk with Fifth Squadron." McGee lowered his voice to a near whisper that I could barely hear above the crackling fire. "We don't need too many lips."

"No, sir."

After glancing out the window, McGee lowered his voice even more. "Win, we're going to dig our way out of this pigsty."

"Good!"

"Quiet now," both McGee and Champlin admonished.

"While you were in the Wolf Pen," the captain explained, "fifteen men dug their way out, not far from here. Rebs brought back thirteen, killed two others, and those that did return were bucked and gagged for a week."

"Damned butternuts pissed on them while they were tied up like that, too." Champlin spit with contempt.

"Sharky the Seaman told me about the escape and capture," I said.

"Aye, and did he tell you how the boys were caught?" McGee asked.

"No, sir."

"Sold down the river, laddie, by some turncoat razorback." McGee's head shook in the darkness.

"Judas Iscariot." Champlin spit into the flames.

"Aye," McGee said. "We'll fix that scoundrel's flint if ever we learn who got paid those thirty pieces of silver. So, not a soul you tell of what we're doing. The only ones who know are me, Sergeant Champlin, and the men in this shebang." The conversation reminded me of Professor Blevins's lecture. "Anyone else, you keep your mouth shut, and I don't care if it's the bloody pope or your fa . . ." His eyes dropped as he remembered. "Sorry, Win, I . . ."

"I understand, Captain. I'll keep quiet, and I'm ready to dig."

They laughed, and I stared at them, puzzled, waiting. Finally McGee explained: "That's the spirit, me boy, but we have to get permission from Professor Blevins before we can dig. Blevins is . . ."

Blevins? Why did we need to ask that Navy man I thought might be a little touched? "I've met him," I began.

"All right," McGee continued. "Then let me correct meself. No one knows what's going on in anyone's shebang except the men in that shebang, *and* Professor Blevins. Though I guess the old sailor reports to Chauncey Perdue, commanding officer among all prisoners. Once Professor Blevins approves our plan, we dig. Fight our way back to New Orleans, drive these Rebs into the bloody sea."

"Understood," I said eagerly. "What's our plan? When does it get approved? What can I do?"

In the fading light, McGee fingered the snake-skin and Champlin chewed on a hangnail while I waited, wondering, impatient.

"Well, that's a wee little problem, Win," McGee said. "We haven't figured out a plan just yet, at least nothing that's gotten past Professor Blevins."

Sitting in a chair in Park Square, Lieutenant Zachary Blevins withdrew a handkerchief from a mule-ear pocket and began wiping the remaining cracked lens in his glasses. Captain McGee had just laid out a plan for his consideration, but, when he eventually spoke, he shouted at some artillery gunner playing baseball. "Catch the damned ball, Norris! Your hands are like rocks." He pointed at the player, but now addressed us. "Sit down, gentlemen, and pay attention to the game. Don't look at me. Rebs are watching."

This was our second meeting with the professor. The first, in which my idea had been proposed, had taken place a few days earlier. Blevins had rejected it as sternly as he had just scolded Private Norris.

"A gopher can dig a hole in the ground," Blevins had said after hearing my plot. "But how do you propose getting rid of the dirt? That's the key element. You have to tunnel deep enough to get underneath the walls, and those logs are set three feet deep. Then you have to dig several rods to get near the woods. Else you'll be shot dead. Most likely, you'll be shot dead anyway, or ripped apart by bloodhounds. The Rebs expect tunnels.

You hear that?" A gunshot had sounded dully somewhere behind us. "Them lop-ears have nothing better to do, so they fire their muskets into the ground, in case someone's digging underneath them. Got as much chance of hitting someone as Norris has of catching the damned baseball, but that's no matter. The options for tunneling are limited. Can't go north, that's where the Reb compound is. Can't go south because of the spring, Colonel Sweet's house, and more men. West is hilly, but not much timber except for some scrubs, ash and oak. So that leaves the east, where you boys live. But that's still a heap of digging. So, how does your dirt disappear?"

My plan had been contrived after thinking about the soldier Professor Blevins had scolded in his garden. Instead of in a garden, however, I had suggested we take the dirt outside the compound when we were allowed, under escort, to gather firewood. Captain McGee had proudly related this information to the professor in his shebang, but Blevins had rejected it immediately.

"There's a lean sergeant with long blond hair outside the gate named Keener," Blevins had said, shaking his head. "Good set of eyes, Sergeant Keener has. He'd spot you in a minute. Dirt needs to stay inside the city limits. Outside, it's just too risky. You'd have a better chance just running from the Rebs while collecting your wood, and that's no chance. No, your idea is hopeless. Come back with another one, and try to think this one through."

Now we were back—McGee, Champlin, and me. I don't know why the captain kept bringing me along, except I think he had adopted me after

Sabine Crossroads. I didn't like the idea of having to get permission from this crazy old-timer anyway, but Captain McGee said it made sense. This might be a prison camp, but it was still this man's army, and you followed the chain of command.

"Look at it this way," McGee had told me. "We might dig into another tunnel, might try to escape the night before some other blokes were going out, cause all sorts of problems. Someone has to know, and at Ford City that someone is the professor."

I studied Blevins as we gathered around him on a late spring afternoon. His face appeared comical to me, and his Boston accent made him sound silly. When he began explaining baseball rules, I considered him to be insulting my intelligence. I didn't care much for Lieutenant Zachary Blevins, although, deep down, maybe I just resented how he had gunned down my escape plan, even though he had been absolutely right in doing so.

"This is baseball," Professor Blevins said mildly. "Not town ball, not rounders, but the Massachusetts game of baseball."

"Aye," McGee said. "I played for the Jersey City Hamiltons, only we played the New York game. And this young trooper"—he nudged me—"caught for the Newport Base Ball Club. Pitched some, too."

"Is that so?" Blevins fitted the wire spectacles over his ears and nose, leaped from his chair to swear vilely at one of the players who had tripped over second base.

"And you, Sergeant?" he asked moments later after settling into his seat.

"Game's stupid if you ask me," Champlin replied. "Waste of time."

Blevins's laugh sounded musical. "Pretty smart for a cavalry sergeant," he said. "But baseball is an obsession to many. I played first base for a club in Boston. I was playing probably before"—he acknowledged me with a tilt of his head—"you were out of diapers. My late wife, God rest her soul, I once told her that if I had to choose between carnal pleasures and baseball, I'm not sure what I'd pick." He snorted. "Kate chose for me." Suddenly he leaped from his seat, ripping the glasses off his nose and bombarding one of the players with a litany of curses I had never heard.

"Norris! Get a hold on that bat, boy. Grip it like you would a whore's tit, not a stinging lizard!" He sat down, wrapped the handkerchief around his glasses, and slid them in his trousers pocket. "I can't watch this display any more!" he screamed at Private Norris. "You're a disgrace. Get the hell off Park Square."

Behind us came laughter from the Confederate guards spying on us.

"Let's hear your plan, Captain," Blevins said quietly. "I hope it's better than your last one."

"Sergeant," McGee commanded, and Champlin leaned closer to the professor.

"We dig in our shebang, at night," Champlin whispered, his eyes staring at the baseball contest going on in front of him. "Get near the woods, come up and run. I figure we'll have about six hours before the butternuts beat out roll call. Of course, you'll have to approve the night we try it."

"That was your plan last time," Blevins said.

"The dirt, boys, the dirt. Where do you put your diggings?"

"Our chimney."

Blevins stared blankly, then scratched his chin. "You have a twelve-by-fourteen-foot shebang, Sergeant." He spoke as if he were addressing a child, and my dislike for him intensified. "More than one chimney isn't needed."

"No, sir. We'll be rebuilding our one chimney. I was a master stonemason in Providence. Professor, I know how to build chimneys that will last centuries. Likewise, I know how to build chimneys that will collapse every time you burn a fire too hot."

That had astonished me when Champlin revealed his plan to Captain McGee and our bunkmates. For some reason, I had always assumed that Champlin had been a soldier all his life. It never occurred to me that he had some other, civilian trade.

"Besides," Champlin continued, "the butternuts won't be poking around our shebang while we're rebuilding a chimney every day after it collapses while cooking breakfast."

Professor Blevins frowned, and I thought he would reject the proposal. "That's a lot of work to ask of your men. Rebuilding a chimney during the day, digging a tunnel at night, committing arson each morn."

"True, but the Rebs won't suspect us of trying to escape. They think we're all lazy bastards, anyway, couldn't get a job until President Lincoln hired us. And as for being worn out, well, you ask any of the men from the Third Rhode Island, and they'll tell you that Second Squadron claimed no malingerers."

Blevins clapped, cupped his hands over his mouth, and screamed encouragement, instead of insults, at another ball player. "Don't you think you'll arouse suspicion, though, as often as you'll have to rebuild your chimney?" he asked Champlin.

"It's a chance, Professor. But I think we'll just be the laughingstock of Sweet's Guards."

We watched the game for several minutes, the professor's inquisition over. I tried not to look at Blevins, but failed. It had taken him seconds to reject our first plan, and I preferred that instantaneous decision rather than this waiting, this anxiety.

"Try not to burn down all of Ford City, boys," the professor said at last. "Best of luck to you."

CHAPTER FOURTEEN

We dug.

Shoring up our tunnel with pieces of wood scraps, the residents of the 2nd Squadron shebang worked at a murderous pace at night, digging down and east, hiding our dirt underneath blankets and a slop bucket until Sergeant Champlin decided it was time. Two or three times a week, Champlin built a roaring fire, and within hours we were prodding, poking, and slamming the clay chimney outside to save our quarters from going up in flames.

After two weeks of that, our neighbors, some rough-hewn boys from the 12th Michigan Infantry, dismantled their shebang and moved to more inviting climes. Rebel guards started calling us fire flies.

As soon as the collapsed chimney cooled off, we went back to work, repairing the chimney, collecting wood and water. The small entrance to the tunnel required even a small boy like me to wig-

gle like a worm to get in and out, and we covered
it with a chair made from woven grapevines,
much like the one I had seen in Captain McGee's
shelter. We worked tirelessly, probably too exhausted to complain about our food. Each morning after roll call, Confederate guards issued a
pint of meal per prisoner and somewhere between a quarter-pound to a pound of beef, maybe
bacon, some of it condemned as unfit to eat. That
said, the prisoners at Ford City had it better than
other Southern dungeons. This wasn't Anderson-
ville, Florence, or Salisbury by any means. By the
same token, I must admit, Rebel prisoners in
Northern camps such as Camp Chase, Rock Island, and Elmira also starved, rotted, and died in
horrific numbers.

At Camp Ford, however, we could supplement
our rations, even trade with the Rebs. Along
Ray's Creek, which ran north of camp, we gathered wild onions, and Lieutenant Colonel Sweet
allowed prisoners to keep a vegetable garden,
much larger and better maintained than Professor
Blevins's patch near Water Street. Breakfast at the
2nd Squadron shebang usually consisted of corn
mush, bacon burned to a crisp, and rye coffee, but
Champlin surprised us every now and then with
a plate of cornmeal pancakes and pine syrup or
what he called panola, cornmeal browned in bacon grease with sugar mixed into it.

"The sugar," he told us, "came with Captain
McGee's compliments."

We took our meals outside, our quarters too hot
after Champlin's conflagration. Sometimes, when
our sergeant proved too capable with his fires and

we wound up losing our breakfast as well as our chimney—and once our entire shebang—we would wander over to the center of Ford City. New Yorkers at the Fifth Avenue Bakery sold doughnuts for ten cents, grape pies for a dollar. Bacon cost two dollars a pound, and coffee (burned rye) came in one-pound bags for eight dollars. Those were Union script prices. If you wanted to trade in Confederate currency, which Sweet's Guards used, the cost of items shot up astronomically. Naturally you could always barter.

Socks were priceless, and good footwear out of most men's budgets. Buttons moved like golden nuggets, and practically everyone wanted tobacco, especially Confederate-cured plugs. My friend from 2nd Squadron, Frankie Wessler, once traded a letter he had received from his girlfriend back in Saundersville for two dozen doughnuts, and he got the lone page back as soon as the baker had finished reading it. Why, I bet a copy of *Harper's Weekly* would have fetched a week's worth of steak suppers.

Frankie Wessler also got the honor of being granted permission to go fishing in a stock tank past the pigpens north of camp. He excitedly brought back a huge, slimy creature that looked like some prehistoric dinosaur. It must have weighed ten or twelve pounds.

"What is it?" asked Jay Leslie.

"Rebs called it a mudfish. Said it's mighty good eating."

"Gee whillikens!" Quinton Brett exclaimed. "Look at the teeth on that thing!"

We snapped to attention as Captain McGee entered the shelter. He studied Wessler's trophy silently, slowing hefting the string holding the mudfish, his eyes twinkling. "The Rebs . . . did they happen to tell you how to cook this whale?" McGee asked.

"Said to stuff it, Captain."

"Aye." McGee dropped the mudfish on dirt. "You stuff it with shit, laddies, bake it for an hour, then eat the shit and throw the mudfish away. Nobody eats mudfish, not even Secesh."

But we did. Didn't stuff it the way Conall McGee said, but we filleted it that afternoon and cooked it that evening, inviting all fifty-something prisoners from the 3rd Rhode Island to partake. Forty-three took us up on the offer, and nobody complained about the hard-on-the-palate supper.

"Well," commented one corporal from 7th Squadron, "it's diff'rent."

We even played baseball, sometimes Massachusetts but more often New York rules, and those afternoon games at Park Square attracted legions of fans. Guards watched us with curiosity. A few even cheered a good catch or hard hit.

I competed in some of those games. Mind you, we weren't digging, collecting materials we would need in the tunnel, or hiding our excavations by building another clay chimney all the time. Lest we arouse suspicion, Champlin insisted that we pull regular routines, and engage in friendly social activities such as concerts, plays—an officer from the 13th Illinois Cavalry gave stirring weekly recitations from Shakespeare—and, even though he disliked the sport, baseball games.

Most days passed slowly, blending into a murky sameness, although one day in late June stood out for me.

I had wood detail, which meant that early in the afternoon I would be escorted along with a dozen or so other prisoners out of The Corral to gather firewood. No one envied this job, for working in the broiling sun had left some prisoners with sunstroke. At least two had been bitten by snakes, and I always pictured that copperhead skin on the sill of our shebang. Before we marched out, I requested permission from Andy Griggs, one of the Rebel escorts, to pick a handful of wild onions.

"Gonna stuff that in the next mudfish you fire flies catch?" asked a bucktoothed private with silver hair.

I didn't respond, just looked at Griggs, waiting for his answer. "Not many," I told Griggs, "just a few that I can stick in my pockets."

Griggs tossed a baseball from hand to hand, never taking his eyes off me. The ball had been made locally, for I could not recall ever seeing a baseball in New England with leather of that color, brindled with a small patch of white. After flipping the ball to the dirt, Griggs shrugged.

"Don't try nothin', Yank. And just a few onions."

We walked through the sally port, past the new hospital and Wolf Pen, and then the guards' quarters. Ray's Creek flowed unevenly at that time of year, never seemed high enough for fishing, and the onion crop had all but played out, yet a buckboard had been parked on the edge, and, as we drew near, a head popped above the high embankment.

My heart caught in my throat at sight of Jane Anne Bartholomew. Stupidly I stepped out of line, lifting my right hand in a friendly greeting. Almost at that instant, a stunning blast in my back knocked the breath out of me and sent me face first to the ground. I couldn't break my fall, and I felt the cartilage give way in my nose when I hit the hard-packed path.

Soldiers from the 47th Pennsylvania and 114th New York helped me sit up, tilted my head up as blood poured from both nostrils. Dully I made out Andy Griggs's voice.

"I told him he could pull up some onions, Sergeant. He wasn't tryin' nothin'."

"Who gave you authority to give anyone permission, Griggs?"

"He wasn't tryin' to escape, Sergeant."

"I know that. If he was, I would have hit him with something harder than this."

Pain exploded in my groin. The next thing I knew, I lay curled up in a ball, whimpering, wanting to die, but finally the agony passed enough that I could sit up again. That's the first time I remember seeing Sergeant Ward Keener.

Hair, the color of corn silk and just as stringy, fell past his shoulders, and he sported translucent blue eyes and a face beaten mercilessly by the wind and sun. Thin but tall, he didn't seem to have an ounce of muscle on him, and I wondered how he could have hit me so hard with the baseball on the dirt beside me, the same ball I had seen Andy Griggs playing with just a few minutes earlier.

"You got a pretty good arm there, Sergeant

Keener." I recognized that voice, and spotted Captain Pig Oliver a few yards away, mounted on his blue roan gelding.

"Thank you, Capt'n. Been watchin' them blue-coats play a mite." He splattered the baseball with tobacco juice. " 'Course, I reckon I can teach them a thing or two myself."

Oliver grinned. "We could 'a' used you in our games at Jacksboro, right MacNewton?"

I just stared, and tried to stop my nose from bleeding.

"What happened?" Oliver asked.

"Reb stepped out of line," Keener said. "Griggs said he give him permission to pick onions, but looked to me like he had another interest. And we ain't grantin' Yanks permission to mingle with our lady folk."

"No, Sergeant, we ain't. And seein' how Miss Bartholomew is pickin' our onions, don't seem we should spare any for the enemy. Can you walk?"

Despite the pain, I made myself stand. I wouldn't give these men the satisfaction.

"Figured you could. Walk yourself back to the Wolf Pen. Couple days there might teach you some manners." He straightened in his saddle and called out: "And from now on, onions are not to be picked by you damned mudsills! If you want onions, plant 'em in your damnyankee garden!"

That evening, I sat in the Wolf Pen. My nose had stopped bleeding, and my testicles hadn't been ruptured when Sergeant Keener nailed me with that baseball, but my back felt badly bruised. The guards lifted the roof, and lowered my bucket of cornmeal and beef. Gingerly I made my way to my supper, and stared in surprise at the contents.

Beside the beef, atop the ground cob, I found a handful of wild onions, plus a bag of goober peas, along with a note.

"Hurry up, Yank!" Andy Griggs shouted, and I withdrew the beef, onions, and note, then poured the meal onto the dirt. I hurriedly read the brief note before the Rebels closed the roof.

> Sir:
> I am sorry to have caused you any harm. I did not mean to get you into trouble. Forgive me. I hope you like boiled peanuts.
>   Kindest regards,
>   Jane Anne Bartholomew

I cherished that note more than I did the onions I ate for supper. Regarding the boiled peanuts, or goober peas, though, I labeled them the most repulsive things I had ever tasted.

Frankie Wessler and Jay Leslie joked that I just wanted to get out of masonry work after the Rebs let me out of the Wolf Pen.

"I can't argue with that logic," I said as I plastered another layer on the still warm ruins of our chimney.

"Keener hit you in your balls with a baseball?" Leslie asked.

"After he nailed me in the back with it," I said.

"Sergeant Keener does not know the rules." Professor Blevins's voice made me whirl. "In rounders, a striker is out if he is hit with the ball, but not in baseball. Never, never is the ball to be thrown at the runner."

"I don't think," I said, "that Sergeant Keener cares much for rules."

"Perhaps." Blevins shifted his feet. "Tomorrow is the Fourth of July, and, to celebrate our Union's independence, we are featuring a baseball contest at Park Square beginning at one o'clock." He kept his focus on me.

"Well," I said uncomfortably, "if Sergeant Champlin doesn't try to burn down our shebang tomorrow, I'm sure we'll be happy to attend."

The professor's small head shook. "No, no, troopers, attendance is mandatory, by orders of Major Chauncey Perdue. I am here to invite you, Trooper MacNaughton, to catch for the Union Club, to represent the Third Rhode Island Regiment of Cavalry."

My bucket of mud dropped to the ground. "Sir, uh, Professor, I. . . ."

"The contest is to be competed under New York rules, much as I detest them," Blevins said. "I understand you have experience playing both versions of the game."

"Yes, sir, but, well, Professor, I mean, if someone's going to represent the Third Rhode Island, it should be Captain McGee."

"My first choice," Blevins said icily, "but he declined, because of his left ankle, recommending that I pick you. I've seen you play a time or two. You speed is ludicrous, your hitting suspect, but you know the game, and you stand your ground. You would be a fine representation for Union loyalty. Besides, your opponent, catching for the Fed-

eral Club, is your pal Sharky the Seaman, a former
catcher for the Atlantic Club in Jamaica, Long Island. I imagine just watching him might improve
your ability. You are to report at Park Square at
eleven. Carry on, soldiers."

Although he had experience as a first baseman
and could have played, Professor Blevins served
as umpire. As one of The Old Seventy-Two,
Blevins held the respect of most of the prisoners,
so the choice seemed appropriate. Second baseman, Hans Jurgen, of the 160th New York, captained my club. Major Chauncey Perdue, a
second baseman from the 173rd New York Infantry and ranking officer at Ford City, led the
Federals.

I hadn't played before a crowd this size since
New Orleans on the eve of the Red River expedition, but nerves did not affect me. I felt calm before the game. Fergal O'Hara of the 42nd
Massachusetts, one of the first men I had met inside Ford City, played shortstop for my club. An
ensign from the *John Warner* was our pitcher.

Our two best players were center fielder Ole
Hendrickson, a horse soldier from Iowa, and Jurgen, but the Federals had us outclassed. Powered
by left fielder Bruce Few, a gunner from the 1st
Wisconsin Battery, third baseman Conrad Turner
of the 47th Pennsylvania, and Sharky the Seaman,
the Federals hammered our pitching and chased
down our fly balls. Major Perdue was no slouch,
either. A short, stocky man in his forties, he
amazed me with his speed. Sharky the Seaman
had a cannon for an arm, and his big hands rarely
dropped the ball, no matter how hard pitcher

Sergeant Major Paul Golden, 5th U.S. Artillery, Battery G, threw it.

Rebel guards lined the catwalk to watch us play. I spied Pig Oliver and Sergeant Keener among the group, along with Andy Griggs. Mostly they insulted us, but a few would send out shrill whistles after a hard hit, more often performed by the Federals than the Unions.

I held my own, scoring several runs and striking a few hits, and our team played valiantly only to lose in the ninth inning. Major Chauncey Perdue scored the winning run for the Federals, trampling me as he charged home while I awaited the throw from Ole Hendrickson, which sailed over my head after Perdue knocked me off my feet.

"Contest!" Blevins yelled. "Federal Club wins, thirty to twenty-nine."

As I shook the cobwebs out of my head, a rough hand jerked me to my feet. "That's the spirit, trooper!" Major Chauncey Perdue brushed the dirt and grass off my back. "Never say quit. You held your ground, defended home base. I'd have you on my team any day."

"Thanks," I began. My hands throbbed from hours of catching, and a knot had started to form on the side of my head, but, when I looked up, I realized my protecting home plate had injured our commander. Blood trickled from Perdue's nose into his graying mustache. "Did I do that, Major? My apologies. . . ."

"Son, this is a badge of honor. Besides, I'm the hero of the Federals."

Clapping his hands, he stepped away from me, raising his voice. "It is customary for a keg of libations to be shared among all contestants after a fine sporting contest of baseball. However, since we have no ale, let us sing." And he broke out into a fine baritone version of "Battle Cry of Freedom." Other prisoners, players, and spectators joined him.

I found Sharky the Seaman soaking his swollen, bruised hands in a bucket of water, and complimented him on his game. "You should soak your own hands," he told me, then stopped, staring at the north walls. Most of the guards, I noticed, had gone, but those that remained now leveled their muskets at the crowd of prisoners.

"Prisoners!" came a Rebel command. "Stand easy. You have company!"

The singing and chatter died as the gate opened, and a dozen men in dirty rags walked through the sally port. Captain May, ever the newspaper editor, withdrew pad and pencil from his pocket, and approached the newcomers. No one else moved, until I recognized the red hair of Mike Peabody.

Alive! All this time, I thought him dead, but there he stood, huddled between a few other men with pale faces and vacant stares. Forgetting all of my aches, I shot out of the crowd, yelling Mike Peabody's name. He looked confused, his eyes darting left and right, finally finding me. His face hardened, and I stopped beside Captain May, dropping my gaze.

"What's the matter, Win?" Peabody said bitterly. "Never seen no damned cripple before? Look at it, damn you. Look at me! Look at what you done."

"I . . ." The right sleeve of my best friend's blouse was pinned up at his shoulder. Swallowing the rising bile, I made myself look up. "I'm sorry, Mike."

"You lousy son-of-a-bitch." Mike Peabody stormed away.

CHAPTER FIFTEEN

"Quick, Win!" I looked up barely in time to see the baseball heading toward me, Captain McGee standing in the entrance to our shebang, grinning. My hand went up too slowly, and the ball bounced off my fingers, thudded against the wall, and rolled back to McGee, whose grin vanished.

He bent to pick up the ball, then leaned against the wall. "Still blaming yourself for your pal Peabody's misfortunes?" McGee asked.

I started to reply, but only sighed. Words came hard now, and I didn't really have to answer for Conall McGee could read my face. Certainly I blamed myself. I had talked Mike into running away with me to join the cavalry. Mike had been trying to save my life when the Rebel ball shattered his arm. I couldn't blame my best friend for hating my guts. Right then, I hated myself.

" 'Tis not your fault, Win," McGee said gently. "Men lose limbs in war. Men die in war. And if I remember right, Michael Peabody would be buried in Louisiana if you had not carried him off that muddy field. Thanking you for his life he should be."

"He wishes he were dead," I blurted out. "I don't blame him." Living with only one arm, left arm at that. How worthless, useless, would I feel, having to learn to use my left hand for everything, feeling the stares from everyone, the way I had gawked at Mike Peabody. I remembered praying when Major Rose worked on my feet, praying that God would take my life, instead of my feet.

"If Trooper Peabody wishes to blame someone for the loss of his arm, he should see me. 'Twas my command. You didn't hoodwink Peabody into this man's army. He came of his own volition. Bitter he may be now, but that too shall pass. In due time, Win, your friend will come to understand that what happened was the will of our Lord." This wasn't the first time McGee or Champlin had tried to lift my spirits, but those words never comforted me. "You saved his life, and I'd rather have one arm than no life. Anyway, that's not why I am here. The Second New York Cavalry has challenged the Third Rhode Island to a go at baseball, day after tomorrow, at Park Square. You're to catch for us."

"I don't think so."

"But I do. These New Yorkers are more than proficient, and we need your help. New York rules, thank His Holiness. Fergal O'Hara of the Forty-Second Massachusetts to umpire. I'm playing, too. Me ankle, I've decided to test, see if I'm still The Cat out in left field. Got some good sportsmen from Eleventh Squadron and a couple from Fifth Squadron."

My heart ached. Mike Peabody was bunking in the 5th Squadron shebang.

"I wouldn't be much good to you, Captain."

"You'll play, Trooper MacNaughton." The politeness had left McGee's voice. "And that's an order."

After the game, a 32–18 loss in which I had struck out four times, I wandered up Broadway Street toward the *Diana* mess, where I found Sharky the Seaman cutting a sailor's hair with a pair of makeshift scissors. I had thought about buying something from one of the nearby bakers, maybe a pie, but that wouldn't work. The day after Mike Peabody had arrived at Camp Ford, I had bought him a dozen doughnuts with the last of my Union script. Mike had dumped them on the ground, cursed me, told me to get out of his sight.

Sharky dusted off the sailor's shoulders and proudly announced: "I've given the vermin parole. Be gone with you, O'Dell."

"I feel ten pounds lighter, Sharky," the sailor said after tossing Sharky a coin.

Pocketing the silver, Sharky motioned me over. "Care for a trim, Win?"

I could use a haircut, plus a scalding bath to rid my body of lice, but I shook my head. Sharky told me to sit down anyway, and I did, and he began combing and clipping my bangs. I had a gift for Sharky, but before I could present it, or even feel like giving it to him, he began talking.

"Your hands are bruised and cut," Sharky said above the noise. "Play a game today?"

"We lost," I said without much interest.

"Lose your boots, too?"

I stared at my bare feet, but couldn't answer.

"Ah. Barbers have no secrets, Win. We're like priests and mothers. Out with it, son. What is it that ails ye?"

So I told him about Sabine Crossroads, about Mike Peabody, about Newport, Rhode Island, and my father. For the first time in days, the words came spewing out, not easily, mind you, but I felt the need to tell everything, even about my father's death. I hadn't talked this much in my life. Sharky never interrupted, just combed and clipped, until I finished, when my shoulders slumped and my head fell forward, expended.

"Keep your head up, Win," Sharky said. I thought he was speaking as a barber, but later I understood what he really meant.

"Did I ever tell you what happened on the *Diana*?" he asked.

"No. You wouldn't at the Wolf Pen, but I've heard stories."

"Stories!" Sharky snorted, and tilted my head back. "Son, you're starting to sprout whiskers. Might as well give you your first shave while you're here. Can't lather you up, but I don't think I'll slit your throat too badly."

He spoke as he ran a straight razor against a leather belt, then pressed his fingers against my cheek, pulled back the skin, and began shaving. I listened to take my mind off his shaking hands and the razor's sharp but chipped edge.

"We were in Berwick Bay in March of 'Sixty-Three when T. L. Peterson, our acting master, got the orders. Proceed into Grand Lake and steam down the Atchafalaya to the mouth of Bayou Teche. On a scout, more or less, not to engage the enemy, though on the *Diana* we always believed in carrying the fight to the Rebs. We knew the butternuts held Pattersonville, knew the safe thing to do was to turn around, but Master Peterson asked me, master's mate, what I thought we should do. 'Give the Rebs hell,' said I, and that youngster, only knee high to a bantam, concurred. 'Let's see what they got,' he agreed.

"Well, we saw. God help me, I still see. Shore batteries opened up on us, and you've never seen such fire. First, they cut our tiller ropes. Then we lost all power, just drifting on the river, fires everywhere. The *Diana* became a burning wreck, a bloody coffin. For two hours, the Rebs kept at it. Peterson got blown apart. My friend, Jim Godich, burned to death before my very eyes. That smell, it stays with a man. Finally we raised the white flag. Rebs captured the *Diana*, salvaged her, sent we survivors off to Camp Ford."

Sharky pocketed the razor, and dabbed my nicks with some homemade talcum powder, shaking his head. "'Give the Rebs hell,' I said, me, some cock-of-the-walk master's mate. Maybe if I had said turn this bloody bucket around, Godich and Master Peterson would be alive, and the *Diana* wouldn't be flying a Confederate flag today. And here's what really galls me, Win. I say I'd trade places with Jim, with Master Peterson, but I don't mean it. Truth is, I'm grateful to be alive, though I'd sell my soul to be out of this pit."

The melancholy disturbed me. Never had I seen Sharky the Seaman anything but confident, full of vigor. "I blamed myself for what happened aboard the *Diana* for months, Win. But it wasn't my fault, and I know that now. It was war. You can't blame yourself for what happened to your buddy. If you want to do something about that, get out of this place, get back to our troops, live to fight again. That's what I'd do."

The words came out before I knew what I had said. "We're digging a tunnel . . . almost done. . . ." My face pleaded with Sharky, who closed his eyes tightly.

"Win, you shouldn't have told me that. For all you know, I'm a tunnel traitor. You know what happened to those New Yorkers?"

Almost a week earlier, Rebel guards had marched into the hut of the 114th Infantry, discovered a tunnel, which they collapsed before beating and dragging the Irish soldiers outside for punishment. That had given the 2nd Squadron a bit of a fright, but the Rebs didn't search our shebang.

"Keep your mouth shut about such things," Sharky admonished.

"But . . . I . . . you just said . . ."

"The hell with what I said. I said 'Give the Rebs hell.' I said I'd trade places with Master Peterson and Jim Godich. Didn't mean none of it. I'm nothing but a coward, Win. Go on. Back to your shebang, boy, but not before you pay me what you owe me. Five dollars a haircut and a dollar a shave."

I reached into my pocket, and withdrew the St. Christopher medallion, which I placed in his callused hands. During the ball game, I had noticed the medallion around the neck of the 2nd New York's first baseman. It cost me my boots, which were beyond repair, but I felt I owed Sharky the Seaman something. No, that wasn't it, not really. My first thought was to trade the medallion for something else, for someone else, maybe a cake, or a pie, or some clothes for Mike Peabody. But once I saw Sharky, I knew I owed him. Sharky and I had never made that promised trade after he left the Wolf Pen back in May, leaving me his baseball. Besides, a St. Christopher couldn't buy Mike Peabody a new arm, and, if I gave him the medallion, he would just throw it in the dirt.

At first, Sharky just stared at the St. Christopher. Slowly he sank to his chair, and, as I pushed my way through the throngs of prisoners, he began sobbing.

Two days later, I found Mike Peabody outside, stirring a pot of hish and hash, sweating in the July heat, a bottle of Rebel bark juice at his side. His malevolent stare did not alter my course, and I squatted in front of him.

"Mike . . ."

"What?" he snapped. "You bring me some more doughnuts? How many doughnuts do you think will make up for my right arm? Christ, MacNaughton, leave me alone."

"I have an idea," I whispered.

"The last idea of yours was for us to run away from home. Remember? I wasn't half a man back then."

The anger surprised me, shocked Mike Peabody, too, for he dropped his spoon and stared, his mouth agape as I cursed him with an anger that boiled out of me. Rebels had shot him in the arm, and a Rebel surgeon had sawed off

GET
4 FREE BOOKS!

You can have the best Westerns delivered to your door for less than what you'd pay in a bookstore or online. Sign up for one of our book clubs today, and we'll send you **4 FREE* BOOKS**, worth $23.96, just for trying it out...with **no obligation to buy, ever!**

Authors include classic writers such as
LOUIS L'AMOUR, MAX BRAND, ZANE GREY
and more; PLUS new authors such as
COTTON SMITH, TIM CHAMPLIN, JOHNNY D. BOGGS
and others.

As a book club member you also receive the following special benefits:
- **30% OFF all orders through our website & telecenter!**
- **Exclusive access to special discounts!**
- **Convenient home delivery and 10 days to return any books you don't want to keep.**

There is no minimum number of books to buy,
and you may cancel membership at any time.
See back to sign up!

*Please include $2.00 for shipping and handling.

YES! ☐

Sign me up for the Leisure Western Book Club
and send my FOUR FREE BOOKS! If I choose to stay
in the club, I will pay only $14.00* each month,
a savings of $9.96!

NAME: _____

ADDRESS: _____

_____

TELEPHONE: _____

E-MAIL: _____

☐ **I WANT TO PAY BY CREDIT CARD.**

☐ VISA   ☐ MasterCard.   ☐ DISCOVER

ACCOUNT #: _____

EXPIRATION DATE: _____

SIGNATURE: _____

Send this card along with $2.00 shipping & handling to:

**Leisure Western Book Club
1 Mechanic Street
Norwalk, CT 06850-3431**

Or fax (must include credit card information!) to: 610.995.9274.
You can also sign up online at www.dorchesterpub.com.

*Plus $2.00 for shipping. Offer open to residents of the U.S. and Canada only.
Canadian residents please call 1.800.481.9191 for pricing information.
If under 18, a parent or guardian must sign. Terms, prices and conditions subject to change. Subscription subject
to acceptance. Dorchester Publishing reserves the right to reject any order or cancel any subscription.

JOIN NOW!

that mass of broken bone and severed veins. A Confederate guard had told me to leave him, but I had carried him for miles. I had wrapped a belt around his arm to slow the bleeding. I had saved his life.

"What life?" he shouted back at me. "The life of an invalid! I can't throw a ball any more. Can't swing a bat or hold a musket. If I hadn't listened to you, I'd be back home. I don't give a damn about niggers or the South, so why should I fight for Lincoln? I don't even like that high and mighty President, and I sure as hell don't give a damn about you."

"I'd like to help you," I said.

"How? Give me your own right arm?" He took a pull of liquor.

"Get out of Ford City," I whispered after forcing myself to calm down. Mike Peabody resumed stirring the pot.

I didn't care about those warnings, what Sharky the Seaman had said, or Captain McGee, Professor Blevins, and Sergeant Champlin. More than fifty men of the 3rd Rhode Island were incarcerated at Camp Ford, but only the ones living in the 2nd Squadron quarters and Captain McGee would use that tunnel. What sense did that make? Fifty-five men, but only six escape? Mike Peabody had ridden with 2nd Squadron, and he had paid a price dearer than anyone else held here. He deserved a chance to get out. I owed him that much.

"We're digging a tunnel, Mike," I told him after making sure no one was close enough to overhear. "That's why we've been rebuilding our chimney so often. To hide the dirt. Professor

Blevins granted approval, so we'll dig out tonight, around midnight. Make our way back to New Orleans."

With a snort, Mike shook his head, no longer looking at me. "And then what? Fight again? Be hard for me to saddle a horse, don't you think?"

"About midnight," I repeated. "Don't tell anyone."

He just stirred the pot.

My eyes shot open in the darkness, and a hand covered my mouth.

"Easy, lad, go easy," Captain McGee said, and I tried to stop shivering. It wasn't cold. Nights in East Texas did not cool off in July. I sat up and caught my breath.

"It's time," McGee said.

As my eyes grew accustomed to the darkness, I detected the forms of familiar figures: Sergeant Champlin, Frankie Wessler, Troopers Brett and Leslie, the latter halfway into the tunnel. I didn't see Sharky the Seaman or Mike Peabody. Oh, I guess I hadn't expected either to show up, and maybe I felt relief now that they hadn't. That would have required some explaining to Champlin and McGee.

"You all right, Win?" McGee asked.

I gave a feeble nod. "Just us?" Immediately I regretted my question.

Frowning sternly, McGee leaned closer and whispered in my ear: "Win, you haven't told anyone, have you?"

"No, sir," I lied.

"Good lad." He believed me, or, at least, he wanted to. "I hate to say it, but not every Rhode

Islander here can I trust." He straightened, repeated our orders, and motioned me to enter the tunnel next.

During all the hours I spent in that narrow hole, I had never felt scared, not even after a section caved in on me and Champlin had pulled me out. On that night, though, the walls closed in, and I broke into a chilling sweat. I could smell my own stench, hear the echoes of my breathing and pounding of my heart. Desperately I crawled after Jay Leslie and tried to put as much distance from Frankie Wessler, just behind me.

I felt a blast of fresh air, and stopped, realizing that Leslie had pushed through the earth. "See you in New Orleans," he whispered, and climbed out of the hole.

For a few seconds, I froze, waiting for that rifle shot, but I heard only the faint sounds of a banjo coming from the Rebel barracks. I didn't even hear Leslie's footfalls as he raced to the woods.

"Hurry up, Win," Wessler said behind me.

I pulled myself halfway out of the hole, making out the stockade walls in the distance. We hadn't dug as far as we thought we had, and I turned around, trying to find the woods. The moon, in its last quarter, peeked behind a cloud, bathing the grounds in more light than I desired. I should run now, before the moon totally cleared the cloud, so I crawled onto my belly, found my feet, and ran, leaning forward, watching the shadows of the trees grow nearer.

Once I made the woods, I slowed down, trying to catch my breath, but came to an instant stop when my bare foot snapped a branch. It sounded like a rifle shot, and I froze, panic masking my face. The noise faded almost as suddenly as it had popped, the banjo played, and the wind rustled the trees. No one had heard. We were in the clear. I couldn't see Jay Leslie ahead of me, but I heard Frankie Wessler sprinting toward the pines.

Stupidly I thought: *We made it*.

Shouts of Confederate guards surrounded me, followed by rifle blasts, and, moments later, Frankie Wessler's piercing screams.

"To the woods, laddies! To the woods! Don't let them catch you!" It was Conall McGee, but a volley of musketry drowned out his cries.

A bullet thudded in the tree next to me, showering me with bits of bark. I ducked and ran, while a new sound frightened me in the darkness—the baying of Ruben Sweet's vicious bloodhounds.

CHAPTER SIXTEEN

Screaming lungs, burning feet, and cramping leg muscles forced me to stop, hugging a tall pine for support. Behind me came footfalls, and I waited for a Rebel ball to end my life. Angry barks, shouts, and gunshots sounded throughout the woods, and a firm hand jerked me from my precarious hold on the tree.

"Move," Captain McGee gasped. A shove sent me stumbling through the brambles, my bare feet bleeding from briars and pine cones, McGee right behind me. Suddenly we stepped out of the cover of trees and onto a narrow road.

"Which way?" I asked.

I didn't hear the wagon, but McGee did, for he pulled me out of the road, and we flattened ourselves against a carpet of pine needles. The *clop-clop-clopping* of hoofs drew closer, pounding the earth at a rapid pace, and, despite our heavy breathing and poor hiding spot, I thought we might not be detected, not in the darkness, not as fast as this night traveler kept pushing those horses, not with the commotion behind us.

The driver pulled the two-horse team to a stop just a few rods past us. "Get in," the voice said urgently.

My head shot up.

Alone in the driver's box sat Jane Anne Bartholomew. "Get in," she repeated, "if you want to live."

A bullet thudded into a pine, probably not as close as it sounded, but unnerving nonetheless. The horses pulling the rickety buckboard stamped their feet impatiently.

"Damn it," Jane Anne began, with no trace of that soft, sweet accent I had heard at Camp Ford. "Get in here. Now!"

For the first time since I had known him, Captain Conall McGee turned indecisive. My face pleaded with him in the darkness, but he glanced back, swearing underneath his breath. The dogs sounded closer, and at last he bolted to his feet, pulling me with him, and we leaped into the back of the wagon as Jane Anne Bartholomew lashed the horses with a whip, screaming at them to run.

McGee said nothing during the long ride down that tree-lined road. He just stared down the shadowy road, expecting Rebels to appear at any minute. My head turned from him to her, wondering what she was doing out at this time of night, why she just happened by, why Jane Anne, a Texas belle, would risk her life to help two fleeing prisoners of war. Her face, grim with determination, revealed nothing, and the only words she said were—"Hang on!"—moments before she made a sharp turn that almost catapulted us to Glory.

The buckboard righted itself, though, and the lathered horses maintained that murderous pace. We left the woods road, bounded over a few small hills, crossed a wooden bridge, and passed shriveled cotton plants before she halted the weary team in front of a towering three-story home.

After setting the brake, Jane Anne leaped from her seat and ran up the steps. "Hurry!" she called from the porch, before rushing inside. "We haven't much time."

This time, I led Conall McGee. We stumbled inside the house that echoed with an emptiness. Some homes, even in the darkness, possess warm feelings, a sense of familiarity, but this mansion made me shudder. To the left of the hallway, in the family parlor, Jane Anne turned up a lantern, and the captain and I collapsed onto an overstuffed sofa. In the flaring light, I watched my angel, who looked nothing like a heavenly creature. Her face glistened with sweat, her hair was disheveled, and her blouse mis-buttoned. As she worked furiously, tossing me cold biscuits and Captain McGee a pewter flask, her lips trembled.

"Why are you doing this?" I finally asked.

"Don't get romantic notions," she answered in an edgy voice. "You're just two of Mister Lincoln's hirelings to me, but you're my ticket out of this. . . ." Her head shook violently.

"Any weapons here?" asked Captain McGee, sniffing the flask suspiciously.

"No."

"Where's your father?" McGee began.

A callous curse followed a mirthless laugh.

"Slaves? Family?" McGee continued his inquisition.

"Sold, dead, or gone," Jane Anne answered.

"What were you doing out?"

She whirled, cursing us, but I didn't see anger in her eyes, just terror. Moments later, she disappeared upstairs.

Captain McGee capped the flask without drinking, and shook his head when I offered him a biscuit. They tasted stale, but, unlike Conall McGee, I didn't think Jane Anne had carried us this far from harm's way to poison us. Slowly McGee stood, tiptoed to the staircase, and looked up, listening. Since meeting in the woods, McGee had scarcely said a half dozen words to me, and, whenever he considered me, his eyes held no friendliness. My stomach knotted upon realization that he likely suspected me of betraying 2nd Squadron. Which I had.

After making myself stand, I limped to the nearest window, pulled back a dusty curtain, and peered outside. The farm looked abandoned, dead, and even the trees stood still as the wind died. When the clock chimed thrice, I jumped, knocking over picture frames and a tea set resting on a table.

"Don't wake the dead," McGee snapped. He lit a candle and began looking around the house.

Moments later, Jane Anne Bartholomew raced downstairs and into the parlor, holding a grip but spilling several items in her hands onto the floor. Berating her clumsiness, she pitched the grip across the room, almost to the front door, and picked up the fallen items, tossing a pair of socks and boots at Captain McGee, and another pair of socks and worn shoes at me.

"Try those on," she said. "My . . . father's. Might fit you," she told McGee, but added that the shoes were too big for my small feet. "Still," she said, "it beats runnin' around barefoot. Put them on. We don't have much time." Without waiting, she ran to the front door, and had it pulled halfway open when McGee, moving like The Cat, intercepted her and slammed it shut.

"And where the bloody hell do you think you're going?" he snapped.

"Soldiers will look here soon enough," she replied testily.

"Why?" I asked. No one had seen us. I didn't think anyone had heard us. Why would Rebs search a respected plantation miles from the prison compound? They'd be scouring the woods, creek beds, and fields close to Camp Ford. I wondered if anyone else had made it out of those woods. I wondered if Frankie Wessler were still alive.

"Never mind the why," Jane Anne barked. "I'm gonna change the team. Those two flea-bitten grays won't carry us far. We need fresh horses. Now, if . . ."

"*We?*" McGee said with a sneer.

"I'm going with y-all."

Immediately I began shaking my head, and McGee said: "Like hell you are."

"Like hell I am," she said.

"Lass." A sigh stopped McGee, and he released his hold of the door, stepped back, and spoke in measured tones. "Your help, 'tis truly appreciated, but you cannot be coming with us."

"It's too dangerous," I interjected.

She tilted her head back and laughed. "Dangerous? Listen, you two Yankees don't know which way to go. I know the roads. I know this country. I can get you to New Orleans."

"You'll get yourself killed," I argued.

Her eyes closed. "That's better than stayin' here." The words came out as a sigh. While I tried to comprehend her reasoning, she opened the door and was gone. McGee didn't try to stop her, and began putting on the socks and boots, but I remained her protector.

"She can't come, Captain," I said. "Those Rebs . . ."

"Shut up." McGee crossed the hallway into the formal parlor. "There's got to be some guns in this place."

Yet he found none, and what I discovered surprised me.

I expected Jane Anne Bartholomew to reside in some glorious mansion, full of servants, brandy decanters, and mint juleps, but the paint was peeling, and dust covered much of the furniture. Even in the darkness, after pulling the socks and shoes over my bloody feet, I could tell that the fences were falling and the rose bushes surrounding the house needed pruning, although those roses provided the only pleasant aroma to the Bartholomew plantation.

In the moonlight, Jane Anne Bartholomew led the team of horses into a rawhide barn. Moments later, she returned leading a pair of white-faced bays, more bones than muscle but in better condition that the two worn-down horses that had carried us from the road to her home.

"What's she doing?" McGee asked from the bottom of the stairs.

"Harnessing the team."

As if he didn't trust me, and perhaps he didn't, McGee peered out another window, then dropped to his knees and opened the piece of battered luggage Jane Anne had left behind.

"Hey," I protested, "that's her stuff."

"Shut up!" He scattered her unmentionables, a muslin dress, a leather-bound book, and a photo across the floor. "No gun," he said sourly, exhaled, and picked up the book, flipping through the pages. I realized this was Jane Anne's journal, where she kept her most personal thoughts, and stepped forward.

"You've got no right . . ."

"Damn you, boy, get back to that window, keep your eyes peeled!"

I obeyed, but, when I looked out, I blinked, stared, and said: "She's gone."

Muttering an oath, McGee pulled himself up, still clutching Jane Anne's diary. He looked outside to verify my report, but only found the buckboard and a fresh pair of horses.

"We could run now, Captain," I offered. "While she's gone. Get in the wagon, head east for Louisiana. Still got a few hours maybe till daylight." It might save Jane Anne's life, I thought, stealing the wagon, leaving her behind. Captain McGee thought differently.

"Ambuscade." McGee kicked the wall. "A bloody trap it is, set up by that bitch."

"She's not!"

"The hell she's not! The second we step onto

the porch, boy, the damned butternuts will cut us down. Probably hiding in the barn."

A back door slammed, and McGee limped toward the fireplace, found a poker, and hobbled back toward the parlor entrance, lifting the weapon in his right hand, absently still holding the journal in his left, when Jane Anne raced inside.

"Don't!" I yelled, and both briefly froze.

"Who's out there?" McGee lifted the poker higher.

"No one," she said. "Yet."

For several seconds, no one moved. "If you plan on killin' me, Captain, make it quick, sir," she spoke. "Take the wagon, and be gone. I'll see you in hell soon enough."

The poker dropped on the floor, and I let out a breath. Then McGee tossed the diary at Jane Anne's feet.

"Why should I trust a whore?"

Anger coursed through my veins, flushing my face, reddening my ears. "You take that back, you son-of-a-bitch!" I rushed forward to strike my commander, but Jane Anne's calm words brought me to a stop.

"I am. . . ." She struggled, looking at me, trying to remember, and finally smiled. "Winthrop."

"Win," I corrected.

"I like Winthrop. It sounds nice, sweet." So did her voice, until she turned toward McGee. "And what a gentleman you are, readin' a lady's diary. I suppose Colonel Sweet and the others are right about you tyrannical bastards. Your father must be proud of you, your manners."

McGee pointed at the journal. "And your father must be proud of you."

She started to laugh, hysterically at first, but the laughs turned into choked cries, and suddenly she stood there, sobbing, her body shaking. "My father . . . it was that . . . his . . . idea. My . . . *lovin'* . . . father." I ran to her, not really understanding, and she collapsed in my arms. We sank onto the floor, leaning against the wall, her face buried in my shoulder, crying, shaking all over.

"Sold his crops . . . sold our slaves . . . sold his soul to the bottle, then, sold me. To keep up appearances, you see." I stroked her hair, tried to think of something to say, but what could you say?

"You looked like you enjoyed it," McGee said bitterly. "Quick with a smile back at Camp Ford."

When she looked up, wrath filled her eyes, a malevolence I had never seen. "Oh, I can be a great actress, Captain. When I have to be. My daddy would do anything to maintain his respectability, even if it meant being a . . . what is it they are called? . . . a procurer. We're starvin'. Failed crops. No hands, but Mister J. Lyman Bartholomew, oh . . ." She wiped her eyes. "Yes, I can be an actress, and I can be a devoted daughter. That's the way I was raised."

She pushed herself away from me and snatched the diary, which she hurled into the empty fireplace before hurrying across the room, gathering her belongings, stuffing them into the grip in front of the door. "You can come with me, or not. I do not give a damn."

At that moment, as the clock chimed, the front door flew open, thudding against Jane Anne's skull, sending her backward. At least two figures filled the doorway, and Captain McGee turned to run. I just sat on the floor, confused.

"Another step, gimp, and you're dead," a voice commanded, and McGee stopped, lifting his hands toward the ceiling. Lieutenant Cy Burrows had us trapped. He stepped into the light, holding a Navy revolver in his right hand. Another soldier stepped in behind him while a third came out of the darkness and filled the back entrance to the parlor. With his left hand, Cy Burrows removed his hat, and affected a bow in Jane Anne's direction.

"Why, Miss Jane, I pray I did not hurt that pretty little head of yours." Sarcasm laced his voice, but his next sentence came out with a fury. "The way you almost stoved in my head on the creekbed."

She spit at him, and he kicked her in the ribs.

When I shot to my feet, a bullet clipped my collar and whined off the fireplace mantel.

I didn't dare breathe, but somehow managed to raise my hands.

"Let's have some coffee," Burrows suggested. He reached down and savagely jerked Jane Anne to her feet. "Before we decide what to do with our two prisoners, and Miss Bartholomew. Luke."

A jaundice-faced private holstered a revolver and nodded with a widening grin when Burrows ordered him to take Jane Anne to the summer kitchen and bring back coffee. Only one man remained with Burrows when they left us in the family parlor, and they motioned us into the corner while they lit more lamps and candles.

Two men. How much longer would we have before the third guard returned with Jane Anne? What kind of chance did we have anyway? One guard bit off a wedge of tobacco, tucking the stock of his musket in his armpit. The clock in the corner continued to tick away the minutes, while I worked up courage to . . . what? Die? What chance did I have with Burrows holding a Navy .36?

"That was quite a ruction," Burrows said as he settled into a chair, keeping his revolver aimed in our direction. "I thought it might be fun, having Miss Bartholomew for some horizontal refreshments while waitin' for you boys to make your play. Only that strumpet put a knot on the back of my head the size of a walnut."

McGee said nothing, but I shot out angrily: "You sick bastard!"

The bullet burned my ear before it broke the window behind me, and I jumped. Lieutenant Burrows thumbed back the hammer. "I'll not be insulted by the likes of Northern trash. Take it back, boy, or the next one goes in your gut."

Somehow I made myself stand up straight.

"Take it back." Burrows leveled the revolver.

"Why?" I stepped forward. "What difference does it make? You're going to kill me anyway."

When the front door slammed open, and Burrows shot a glance, I thought to make my move, but it passed too quickly, and Burrows was standing, his attention back on McGee and me as Jane Anne entered, holding an enamel pot with a thick pot holder.

"You took long enough, madam," said Burrows, turning to her with a wry grin. He didn't seem to notice, or care, that that private named Luke wasn't with her.

It seemed to happen so slowly, as if I could make out every detail. Jane Anne flung the coffee pot, the lid fell open and boiling water crashed

into Cy Burrows's face. As he screamed, his
hands covering his scarred flesh, Captain McGee
broke into a run and dived through the closest
window. I just watched, frozen, as the coffee pot
clanged against the floor and Jane Anne reached
behind her apron. The other guard tried to level
his musket, fumbling with the hammer. Jane
Anne withdrew a brass-framed revolver and shot
the man in the chest. Blood and tobacco juice
dribbled from the corners of his lips as he slid
down the wall, candle light reflecting in his eyes
as he died.

My ears rang from the gunshot, but I could still
make out Burrows's cries of agony as he crawled
out of the parlor toward the front door. Jane Anne
lowered the pistol, thumbed back the hammer,
and slowly followed him. As Burrows crossed the
threshold, the gun popped, and Burrows
grunted, and rolled over.

"I won't . . . ," Jane Anne began, and pulled the
trigger, the bullet driving back the Rebel officer,
"feel your grubby hands . . ."—she fired again—
"pawing my body . . ." Another shot. "Ever again."

By the time my legs would move and the ringing died in my ears, the only thing I heard was
the metallic noise as Jane Anne cocked and fired,
cocked and fired, although all the chambers were
empty. I stepped onto the porch. I must have understood that the other guard, the one who had
escorted Jane Anne to the detached kitchen, was
dead, too, for I didn't worry about him. The man-
gled, lifeless body of Cy Burrows straddled the
steps as I slowly took the Spiller & Burr from Jane
Anne Bartholomew's shaking hands.

CHAPTER SEVENTEEN

The radio announcer talked about Enos Country Slaughter during the broadcast of Game 4 from Fenway Park. The St. Louis outfielder started the pounding in the second inning by sending a line drive over the right-field fence, and, from what the announcer said, that ball flew out of the park before anyone could blink. The Cardinals continued slugging all afternoon in a 12–3 victory that tied the World Series at two games apiece, and young catcher, Joe Garagiola, got four hits, but the announcer just talked and joked about Slaughter.

"That home-run ball traveled a whole lot faster than Country Slaughter talks."

Tobacco-spitting, tobacco-farming Enos Slaughter, a thirty-year-old left-handed hitter, hailed from North Carolina and spoke in a twang but, contrary to that announcer's opinion, never did anything slow. That boy ran to first base on a walk, hustled every time he stepped on the field, but, because he came from the South, he was Country, just a backward bumpkin.

It's a stereotype, of course, and I, a Down-Easter, have been guilty of spreading that myth. Too often we think of Southerners as hillbillies, easy-go-lucky, slow-to-rile hayseeds full of corn pone and fatback, or charming members of the landed gentry who sip iced tea on verandahs and talk about their Revolutionary War ancestors. There's a gentleness to the South, to Southerners, a grace and charm. Yes, but underneath that charm, grace, and gentleness, often lies inhumane violence. I know.

After escorting Jane Anne into a porch swing, I sat beside her, still dizzy by what I had witnessed. I didn't even think about Captain McGee until he stepped onto the porch, his shirt, face, and hands ripped by glass from the window and thorns from the rose bushes. All I thought about was Jane Anne Bartholomew, what she had been through.

"It's all right," I whispered. "Everything will be all right."

McGee didn't speak as he climbed the steps, glancing at the body of Cy Burrows before sticking his head in the door, spotting the other dead guard, and turning to us.

"Ma'am?" he said.

Slowly Jane Anne lifted her head. "That third guard?" McGee asked.

Her chin pointed toward the kitchen.

"Drag the bodies in there," McGee directed me. "Ma'am, you'll be coming with us now." He held out his hand. "I want you to come with me to the formal parlor, sketch us out a map." What he really wanted, I know, was to lead her away from the carnage.

I gagged when I grabbed Cy Burrows's arms, but didn't make the mistake of looking at the lieutenant's face again, struggling to drag him across the yard, the horses harnessed to the buckboard snorting at the smell of blood. After kicking open the door to the kitchen, I backed inside, tripping over another body.

This time, when I saw the dead man, I vomited.

After I finished retching, I pulled Burrows's corpse beside the guard Jane Anne Bartholomew had killed in the kitchen, stood up, and turned down the lantern they had lighted so I wouldn't see that gore when I returned with the third dead man. Three Confederate soldiers killed, all by Jane Anne's hand.

Back in New Orleans, I had bought a small little pamphlet called *The Soldier's Prayer Book*, which I had carried with me during the Red River Campaign, along with the picture of my father, both long gone from my possession, but, as I walked back to the Bartholomew mansion, I tried to recite one of the prayers listed.

Oh, God our Father! Wash us from all our sins in the Savior's blood, and we shall be whiter than snow. Create in us a clean heart. . . .

I couldn't remember the rest.

Inside the house, McGee's soothing voice reassured Jane Anne that everything would be all right, that she had done nothing wrong. The family parlor reeked of death, and heavy gunsmoke burned my eyes. I leaned the dead man's musket against the wall, grabbed his feet, and pulled him away, a trail of blood smearing the floor. After I deposited him inside the kitchen, I stepped out, closed the door, and felt a crushing blow behind my left ear.

The void that swallowed me came with welcomed relief.

They said Captain McGee ran out of the house and sprinted for the fields, that he refused to listen when Andy Griggs yelled at him to stop. "Like a madman," they said. A sergeant named Harry Pate roped McGee with a lariat just as he reached the crops, and dragged him, screaming, clawing the dirt, back to the main house.

I thought they would have killed him, but Sergeant Pate and Andy Griggs seemed decent men, although they left him down in the dirt, near the buckboard and team, hog-tied and gagged.

Dawn had broken by the time I came to, resting on the parlor sofa, watching red-eyed Jane Anne Bartholomew wash the bloody wound behind my ear. Captain Pig Oliver towered behind her, thumbs hooked in his rust-colored belt, spitting tobacco juice into a brass cuspidor beside the sofa. Andy Griggs and Sergeant Pate stood near the window.

"Captain McGee?" I asked weakly.

"He's alive," Jane Anne answered. "Tied up outside."

I stared at Pig Oliver. "And the others?"

"They're all dead, boy." Tobacco juice rang inside the cuspidor.

Pain stabbed my heart, and I sank into the padded sofa, closing my eyes for a few seconds.

Dead. Because of me. My big mouth. My trust of . . . of whom? Sharky the Seaman? Mike Peabody? Cy Burrows said they had been waiting for us, so some traitor had sold us out. But who? It couldn't be Mike, I told myself, nor did I want to picture Sharky as a turncoat.

Oliver wiped his mouth with his shirt sleeve. He held his hat in his left hand and shifted his feet uncomfortably. "Miss Jane," he began, "now that the boy's come to, you mind clearin' up a few details?"

Her lips began to tremble, but I shot out a confession before she could speak. "We grabbed her on the road. Made her take us here. She wasn't a party to any of this. We forced her."

I couldn't read her eyes as she stared at me.

"Did they harm you in any way, Miss Jane?" Oliver asked.

"They. . . ." Her voice sounded distant, unsure. "They were perfect gentlemen."

Andy Griggs shifted his musket, butting the stock against the hardwood floor. "Weren't no gentlemen to the lieutenant, scaldin' his face and shootin' him to pieces. Or Luke Shane, buryin' that meat cleaver in his head."

"Yeah," Sergeant Pate added, "but ain't nobody gonna be sheddin' tears over the passin' of them three."

"The colonel might see things diff'rent," Griggs said.

Jane Anne cleared her throat. "I . . ."

"I killed them!" I shouted. "I killed them all. It's war. That's all."

"No," Jane Anne began, her voice beginning to crack, "I won't let you . . ."

"It's a soldier's duty to try to escape," I reminded my captors.

"Maybe so." Pig Oliver drew his own revolver. "But I done told you, MacNewton, that I'd kill you myself if you ever run again."

When he leveled the pistol barrel at my head, Jane Anne stood. "Ulysses," she pleaded. "Please . . . for my sake."

Ulysses? Well, at least I'd know his real name before I died.

Oliver shot her a quick look, and his expression changed. As his jaw began working the tobacco in his cheek, he glanced at Jane Anne's grip, at the coffee pot on the floor. He knew what had really happened, who had killed Burrows, Shane, and the third soldier, but it dawned on me that he was in love with Jane Anne Bartholomew. I had never thought Pig Oliver capable of loving anyone, but his eyes betrayed him. He must not have known of the revolting arrangement her father had made, what Cy Burrows had done and . . . I shook that thought from my head, and it struck me that I loved Jane Anne, too.

"Miss Jane, where is your pa?" Oliver asked.

Her face hardening, she looked back at me. "Gladewater, I think," she answered.

"Anybody else here?"

"No."

Oliver spit again. "Miss Jane . . ." He holstered the revolver. "Even if I let this boy live, there's no way the others back at Camp Ford will allow what happened to go unpunished. The colonel, he'll hang these two Yanks. Burrows, Shane, and Jones didn't have many friends, but Colonel Sweet liked 'em."

"Please," Jane Anne said, "I'm begging you."

For a long while, Oliver stared at Jane Anne. He shot me a hard glance before turning to face his men. "Pate, Griggs, go bury them bodies."

"Capt'n . . . ," Pate began, but Oliver cut him off.

"Bury 'em, I said. Bury 'em deep. We ain't seen Burrows, Jones, or Shane, you hear? Far as we know, them three deserted." For emphasis, he rested his palm on the butt of his revolver.

They hauled us back to Camp Ford in the Bartholomew buckboard, where they stopped in front of Lieutenant Colonel Sweet's cabin. Sweet looked pleased when he spotted us, and offered his compliments to Captain Pig Oliver.

"That accounts for them all," Sweet said. "Throw them in with the rest. A couple of months in the Wolf Pen might cure them of their foolishness."

The rest? Relief swept over me. Oliver had lied. The others, at least some of them, hadn't been gunned down in the escape attempt. I breathed a little easier.

"Not him." Oliver pointed a long finger at me.

"What do you have in mind?" Sweet asked with amusement.

He didn't answer, didn't grin, just sat on that gelding, working tobacco with his jaws.

"Have you seen Lieutenant Burrows?" Sweet asked, his tone no longer amused. "He and privates Shane and Jones are missing."

Still glaring at me, Oliver answered with a lie. "No. Likely deserted. Burrows had been jawin' 'bout tryin' his luck with cards and strumpets up in Jefferson."

I couldn't see Andy Griggs's face, for he was driving the buckboard, but I studied Harry Pate's reaction, wanting to see if he would let Oliver's lie stand. He just sat in his saddle, gripping the horn, his face void of any emotion. Either he feared Pig Oliver or, as he had said back at Jane Anne's home, he didn't care a whit for those three dead men.

What Pig Oliver had in mind for me turned out worse than the Wolf Pen. He locked me in the stocks the Rebs had put up earlier to punish the Irishmen whose tunnel had been discovered. Now the New Yorkers were back inside The Corral while I baked for two weeks in the summer sun. Mosquitoes feasted on my face, arms, and back, the only relief coming when the sun disappeared behind the clouds. It didn't rain, not while I stood out there, but guards brought me water regularly, let me visit the privy once a day, and fed me Confederate cush, cornmeal, and bacon boiled together into a tasteless mush, for breakfast and supper. A corporal named Coker swore that the meal used wouldn't make me sick, giving me his word as a soldier, gentleman, and a fan of the baseball games he had watched from the catwalk.

Major Jon Rose checked me out every couple of days, too, to make sure I hadn't died. He'd also force some salt into my mouth, and relate the latest news.

"New rule in that sport you love," Rose told me on his first visit. "Read about it. Runner must touch all bases. Reckon he just had to get in the vicinity before."

"What?"

Rose clucked his tongue, and repeated his information in a slower, more coherent voice that I could decipher.

"Oh," I said. Baseball didn't interest me at that moment.

"How are the others?" I couldn't continue until Rose lifted a ladle of water to my lips. I drank greedily, one ladle, then another, and, as Rose began wiping my sunburned forehead with a wet bandanna, I explained: "The ones who tried to escape with me. What happened to them?"

"West took a ball through his body."

"West? Oh, Wessler."

"Luckiest Yank I ever saw. Didn't hit no vitals. He'll live. 'Nother one tried to double back, but they caught him at the creek. Dogs treed your sergeant, tore up the arms and legs of, think his name was . . . Leslie."

"He's all right, though?" I pleaded.

Major Rose's fat jowls shook as he laughed. "Better'n most. Him and West is a-gettin' paroled. Plus another thousand. If you hadn't a-run, you might 'a' gotten out, too. Understand that, Yank?"

The next day I watched as 1,000 prisoners, the bulk of them old, wounded, or crippled, walk out of Camp Ford under escort and begin the march to Shreveport. From inside the log walls came that rich voice of Major Chauncey Perdue:

Salvation! O the joyful sound,
Glad tidings to our ears;
A sov'reign balm for every wound,
A cordial for our fears.

Glory, honor, praise, and power,
Be unto the Lamb forever.
Jesus Christ is our Redeemer.
Hallelujah, praise the Lord!
Salvation! buried once in sin,
At hell's dark door we lay;
But now we rise by grace divine,
And see a heavenly day.
Glory, honor, praise, and power,
Be unto the Lamb forever.
Jesus Christ is our Redeemer.
Hallelujah, praise the Lord!

I wanted to cry, from disappointment, it
shames me to write, instead of joy for my freed
comrades. I wanted to cry, but couldn't, dehy-
drated as I was that afternoon. All I could do was
listen to Major Perdue's haunting vocal as those
weary prisoners trod past the graveyard and to
the main road leading to Louisiana.

Salvation! let the echo fly
The spacious earth around;
While all the armies of the sky
Conspire to raise the sound.

CHAPTER EIGHTEEN

She brought me a rose the day before I was to be freed from the stocks. Believing I must be delirious when I caught the fragrance, I opened my eyes to see Jane Anne Bartholomew. She rested the long-stemmed flower atop the stocks before bathing my face with a wet rag.

"You foolish, foolish boy," she began. "What were you thinkin'?"

I mouthed the words: *Of you.*

Tears slowly rolled down her cheeks. "Look at your face," she said, trying to change the subject.

"Gallinippers."

"What's that?"

"Gallinippers. What . . . Corporal . . . Coker"—my mouth and throat turned to sawdust, and I wasn't sure Jane Anne heard me—"calls your . . . mosquitoes. Big as . . . gulls."

She must have heard, because she laughed, dabbing tears with the sleeve of her blouse. "Why, Winthrop, those are nothin'." Her voice had that musical tone about it, sweet, confident, coaxing. "Why just the other day, I was comin' home from Tyler, and I looked up at a tree limb and saw these two mosquitoes, big as ravens they were, starin' down at me. And one said . . . 'Should we eat her now or take her home?' And the other said . . . 'Best eat her now. If we take her home, our big brothers will take her from us.' "

I wanted to laugh, but couldn't. I couldn't say anything until Jane Anne squeezed her rag over my mouth, and the cool water fell on my swollen tongue. She continued that for several minutes, dipping the rag in a bucket of water, slaking my thirst.

"Ulysses is gonna put you in solitary confinement for six more weeks," she said, her tone serious. "I wanted to see you, to thank you."

"I should . . . thank you. You . . . saved my life. Burrows . . ." I fell silent. *Don't remind her of that night.*

"Well, you saved mine." She leaned forward and kissed my sun-baked head. "I guess . . . I guess you're not just one of Mister Lincoln's hirelings to me, Win."

She hurried away.

She was there again at the end of August when they let me out of solitary. Not waiting for me, *per se*, but she dropped by the hospital, where Major Rose had to examine me before I could be returned to The Corral.

"Seen better," Major Rose said, "seen worse. Reckon you're fit."

I looked past him at Jane Anne Bartholomew. Major Rose noticed where my attention was directed and almost grinned. "Miss Jane, if you'd be so kind as to rub some salve over this Yank's forehead, I'd be indebted. Need to check that ol' boy over yonder, see if his fever's broke."

She smiled as she applied the balm. "You look like a ragamuffin," she said.

"You don't. That dress looks real pretty on you."

"It's older than dirt, Winthrop. A dress like this would cost almost a thousand dollars in Tyler. That's why...." Her gaze dropped, and, when she pulled her hand away from my head, I reached up and grasped it, squeezing it softly.

Trembling, she made herself look up. "Win . . . Win, you and Ulysses think I'm some virginal goddess. I'm not. I'm . . ."

"I think you're lovely, Jane Anne Bartholomew."

"Two hundred dollars," she said. "That's what I cost. Sounds like a lot, but it's not, not in Confederate yellow-backs." She wanted me to look away, or let go. That's why she told me this, but I refused, and squeezed her hand tighter.

"I'll take you away," I said, "far from your father."

"Win . . ." She brought my hand up to her face, pressed it against her lips. "You are so foolish."

"I love you."

She dropped my hand, her face stunned. It took a minute or more for her to speak. "You shouldn't think that, shouldn't say that."

"I can't help it."

"You don't even know me."

A tear rolled down my face. I just stared at my lovely angel.

"Miss Jane!" Major Rose called from across from the room. "A moment of your time, ma'am?"

"Certainly, Mister Jon." She placed my hand on my chest, looked back to make sure Major Rose wasn't looking, then leaned forward and kissed me on the lips. Awkwardly I returned the kiss as best I could. After wiping her face, she left my cot. My eyes closed as I savored the taste of Jane Anne's lips. Seventeen years old, and I had never kissed a girl before, and certainly had never been kissed by one.

"Out with you, Yank!" Major Rose yelled. "Get back to The Corral. Guards!"

"Hey, there, Billy Yank!"

My escort stopped, nodding his permission, and I turned toward the man who had shouted at me. Staring with disbelief, I found Confederate soldiers between the spring and hospital where they had laid out a baseball field. I guess the word is *surreal*. Eighteen men in butternut and ragged gray, muskets stacked behind home plate, a makeshift collection of bases, bats, and balls, much like the equipment used inside The Corral at Ford City's Park Square.

One Rebel, wearing a corporal's chevrons, ran toward me, bat in hand. Smiling, he held out his right hand and introduced himself as Bobby Logan.

"Seen you play some," Corporal Logan said. "Figured you could solve a riddle for us."

Confused, I shook his hand, told him my name, and waited for his question.

"Sometimes you Yanks call a batter out, if the ball is caught on the first bounce," Corporal Logan said. "Sometimes he's only out if it's caught in the air. Which is it?"

"Well, it depends." I looked past him to consider the field. "You're playing under the New York rules," I continued, "so if the ball is caught on the first bound, it counts as an out. If you were playing under Massachusetts rules, stakes for bases instead of bags, a square field instead of a diamond, then the ball must be caught on the fly for an out."

"I was gonna ask you about that, too. Don't think we'll call them New York rules, though. Maybe Tyler rules. Anyway, about that out rule. Fair or foul?"

"Either. Fair or foul, if the ball is caught on the bounce, it's an out. Lot of players for New York clubs, though, prefer that outs be recorded only if the ball is caught in the air. Wouldn't be surprised if they change that rule in the next few years."

"I'm learning to play third base," Corporal Logan said. "Watching y'all play. Thanks, Billy Yank." He pivoted and raced back to the field, shouting out the rule on fly balls.

My escort prodded me gently, and I walked to the gate, waiting for other Rebs to open it and send me back to Ford City.

The tunnel inside the 2nd Squadron shebang had been collapsed, and the shelter burned to the ground, replaced by a new row of privies. As punishment, the new quarters for 2nd Squadron and Captain Conall McGee were put up just behind the latrines. I walked inside my new malodorous home, surprised to see Mike Peabody sitting on the floor, leaning against the wall. Leslie and Wessler were gone, exchanged by now, maybe back home in Rhode Island, but Sergeant Champlin, Captain McGee, and Trooper Brett stood, anticipating my return.

I didn't expect what happened next.

Champlin buried his fist in my gut, and I doubled over, unable to breathe. Another punch belted my kidneys, and the next thing I knew I sailed into the wall, collapsing in a ball on the floor.

"You fool," Champlin said savagely. "You could have gotten us all killed."

When he drew back his right foot, I covered my face with my arms to protect myself from the kick that never came.

"Nicholas," Captain McGee said calmly, "that'll be enough."

Ever so gently Conall McGee rolled me over, waiting for the pain to lessen, for my lungs to work properly.

"Little bastard," Champlin said.

"Sarg. . . ."

"No," I interrupted our captain. That one word caused my chest to ache, and I cringed. Biting back the pain, I continued. "He's right. I broke my vow, told about the tunnel."

"Who did you tell, lad?" A weary sadness accented McGee's words.

Mike Peabody and I stared at each other, not speaking, and McGee lifted me to a seated position. I leaned against the wall, still studying my former best friend.

"What's he doing here?" I asked.

"He's bunking with us now, Peabody being a Second Squadron trooper and all. Out with it lad, who did you tell?"

"Sharky the Seaman," I confessed, still staring at Mike Peabody. "The afternoon of the ball game, a few days before we dug out. He was so melancholy, heartbroken. I'd never seen him like that, so I told him we were. . . ." I shook my head, remembering, and tears cascaded down my cheeks.

"Sharky." Sergeant Champlin sighed.

"Been here a long time," Quinton Brett said. "Wonder how many others he betrayed."

Captain McGee rose, pulling down his battered hat firmly. "Sergeant, Trooper Brett, let us pay a social call on that old pounder. Peabody, wait here, you and MacNaughton. We'll have a little parley with Mister Sharky in a short while."

I kept my eyes trained on Peabody even after they left; he never looked away from me. At last, he said hoarsely: "Well, you ain't no Judas."

My eyes bore through him, and he sighed.

"I was coming," he began, "making my way for the tunnel when the shooting commenced. Nothing I could do but head back to the Fifth Squadron shebang. I ain't no turncoat razor-back."

I held up my hand, and he stood, gripped it with his one hand, and jerked me to my feet. I hit him hard in the jaw, the force of the blow jamming my knuckles, and down he went, crashing hard.

"You son-of-a-bitch!" I shouted, and jumped on him, pinning him down with my arms, screaming for Captain McGee. They filled the entrance to the shebang quickly, rushed inside, pulled us apart. Peabody broke free from Champlin's grasp, and swung at me, but I ducked and, although held by the captain, kicked Peabody in the kneecap.

Cursing, McGee hurled me across the cramped quarters. I crashed against the wall, but kept my feet, pointing at the writhing figure on the dirt floor.

"I told Mike, too," I said. "Told him that day I told Sharky."

Champlin swore at me. "You told two people. Damn you, MacNaughton, damn you for being such a loud-mouthed fool."

"Quiet!" McGee barked, then roughly rolled Peabody on his back.

"'Tis a conundrum we have," McGee said. "Sharky the Seaman or Michael Peabody?" McGee reached inside his blouse and withdrew a Barlow knife. He opened the blade, broken but sharp, and looked at me.

"What makes you think it was your pard?" he asked.

"I've known Mike all my life, Captain. I'd know when he's lying, see it in his eyes, hear it in his voice, and he sure was lying to me just now. I only told Sharky we were digging a tunnel. I didn't tell him when we were busting out. I did tell Mike that."

"You bas—," Peabody began, but McGee punched him in the temple, silencing him, took off his dirty bandanna, and wadded it into a ball.

"Wessler!" Peabody screamed. "Him or Jay Leslie could—"

His words were cut off when the captain rammed the gag inside his mouth. McGee's cold eyes scanned the door and window, but in Ford

City what happened in a shebang was the business of the residents of that shebang. Still, he asked Brett to look outside, and the trooper stepped outside briefly, then came back in.

"Guards ain't interested in us, Captain. Concert is being held on the Park Square."

McGee studied me. "Rebs could have been waiting, not knowing which night," he said. "And Peabody's right. Wessler and Leslie could have told someone."

My head shook. "It was Mike, sir."

"What makes you so damned certain?" Champlin asked.

Reservations shattered my nerves. "Promise me you won't kill him. It's my fault. I . . ."

"Answer the sergeant," McGee ordered.

I stared at Mike Peabody until I couldn't see him for the tears, then shook my head. If I learned one thing living in Jacksboro, Texas, it was that out West friendship was a bond. You didn't betray your pals, no matter what. I grappled with this, remembering all the good times we had shared, and the bad. Mike Peabody had been with me through thick and thin, up until Sabine Crossroads. Why was I so damned certain he had been the turncoat, and not Sharky the Seaman? Lord help me, why had I told either of them?

Peabody moved suddenly, punching McGee in his face, almost breaking the captain's nose, and hurled himself to his feet, barreling toward the door blocked by Brett. I dived across the room, wrapping my arms around Mike's legs, bringing him crashing to the floor as he spit out the gag and screamed.

"I didn't do it, Win! We were friends!"

"Frankie Wessler was my friend, too!" I said through clenched teeth, pinning his arm behind his back, holding him tight. Frankie Wessler. That sealed it. I had to tell the truth, even if it meant sacrificing Mike Peabody. This was war, and that red-headed louse had disgraced his uniform, betrayed the Union cause, almost gotten us killed.

Brett helped hold the wild animal Michael Peabody had become, Champlin grabbed the legs, and McGee, his nose pouring blood, clasped his left hand over Peabody's mouth and pressed the ragged knife blade against Peabody's throat. My friend's eyes glazed over with fear, and he quit squirming.

"We've got to be sure, Win," McGee said.

"They paroled one thousand prisoners last month," I said, "for exchange."

"Aye? What does that have . . . ?"

"Invalids, mostly," I said. "Badly wounded, old-timers. Why didn't they parole Mike? War's over for him."

When McGee lifted the blade, he shook his head. "We've got to be certain of this," he said softly, and Peabody twisted in a desperate attempt to free himself, almost crushing me with the weight of his body. The lining of his blouse ripped, and a handful of Confederate notes spilled onto the floor.

He fought harder at the sight of the money.

"Miserable Judas Iscariot." Champlin spit tobacco juice on Peabody's britches.

"Win! Let me ex—" McGee clamped his hand

over Peabody's mouth again, and forced the Barlow knife against his throat, drawing blood.

"Don't kill him," I pleaded.

"Neither murderer nor executioner am I," McGee said, "but, on me mother's Bible, I am no informer." Deftly he lifted the blade and carved a deep T on Mike Peabody's face, the top stretching across his forehead to his hairline, and the stem coming down onto his nose.

As Mike Peabody shrieked in agony, we held him tighter. Next, Captain McGee tossed the knife aside and had Champlin spit tobacco juice into his hand. Once this was done, McGee rubbed the juice over the wound, Peabody's howls piercing our eardrums.

After McGee wiped the mess with the bandanna, he stood. "Tobacco juice is a mordant, tanning agent," McGee said softly. "That'll brand Michael Peabody forever as a traitor, scar him till in his grave he lies." He wiped his hands on his britches, then brought that filthy rag to his own bloody nose.

I released my hold, and broke down, sobbing hysterically as they shoved Mike Peabody, my best friend, through the door, tossed out his meager belongings behind him. Wrapping my arms around my knees, I rocked back and forth, back and forth, feeling sick, angry, ashamed.

Captain McGee sank onto the floor beside me, still pressing that blood- and tobacco-soaked rag against his nose.

"It's my fault," I managed. "You should have tattooed that T on my face."

"No, lad. Michael Peabody didn't play the rat

to get revenge on you." He pointed a bloody finger at the Louisiana and Texas notes littering our floor. "He did it for that. Sergeant, throw that Judas money out of our home."

CHAPTER NINETEEN

*Didn't feel much like listening to Game 5 on the radio,
Mike Peabody haunting my memories, so I walked the
streets of St. Louis the afternoon of October 11, 1946,
finally disappearing into a little tavern not far from
the Mississippi River.*

*When I ordered coffee, the barkeep chewed on his
matchstick furiously, at last decided I wasn't worth
chastising, and poured a cup of potent black tar.*

*The way inebriated patrons kept cursing Howie Pol-
let and Al Brazle, I figured the Red Sox had won.
(They had, I later confirmed, taking a 6–3 victory behind Joe Dobson's complete game and a sixth-inning
homer by Leon Culberson.)*

*Oddly enough, it was some bigoted Cardinals fan in
overalls who took my mind off Mike Peabody. This fellow wasn't interested in the World Series; he just kept
mouthing off about Jackie Robinson.*

*"The Dodgers, I hear, are talkin' about bringin' up
that nigger next year, and, when they do, by Jacks, I'm
done with baseball."*

Branch Rickey had signed Jackie Robinson to play for Brooklyn's minor-league team in Montreal, and, from what I had heard, Robinson had played well. I prayed I'd live long enough to see him play in the big leagues.

"I hope he's as brave as Timothy Moore," I said over my coffee cup, not thinking anyone could hear me, but that racist sure did.

"Who's that, you old fart? Who's Moore? You some niggerlover? Niggers got their own league, by Jacks. They don't need to be coloring up our game."

I paid for my coffee, and stood to leave.

"You ain't answered my question, mac. Who's this Moore feller?"

"C'mon, Richard, he's older than Methuselah. Let him leave," the barkeep said, but the racist blocked my path, beaming.

"Timothy Moore," I said, "was a freedman, played at Camp Ford."

"Camp Ford? That where the Browns went for spring trainin' durin' the war?"

Shaking my head, I ducked underneath him and exited that foul place, hurried back to my hotel, and began scribbling my thoughts on the tablet.

Timothy Moore. I remember the first time I saw him.

1,000 prisoners had been exchanged while I was in the stocks, and a few more than 500 transferred to Camp Groce while the Rebs held me in solitary. That brought Ford City's population down to about 3,300. Of that number, three were black, and another three Indians.

Head down, staring at the too big shoes on my

feet, I walked down Water Street, past the flowing spring, wondering if I would be better off if I just stepped over the deadline, let Sweet's Guards shoot me down. I hadn't seen Mike Peabody since his exile. No prisoner would shelter him, or help him now, not with that T branded on his face. The Secesh on the catwalks would probably even laugh at him.

"Watch out there!" came the alarm, and I whirled to spot a dark leather ball headed straight for my face. Reflexes took over; I squared myself, brought both hands up, and made the catch, the ball stinging my palms and fingers.

The man who had yelled the warning slid to a stop, and stared.

I stared back. I hadn't noticed a man of color in Ford City before. Nor could I remember ever seeing a Negro wearing the uniform of a Federal soldier. Sure, I had heard stories, had read newspaper accounts. Even my father had written about how proud he was of the 54th Massachusetts, and, back in camp in the fall of 1863, we had cheered and prayed for those soldiers who had been wasted so badly at Battery Wagner in South Carolina. Although I had never seen them, Negro troops took part in the Red River Campaign, and, since arriving at Camp Ford, we had learned, from more recent prisoners and Captain May's third-hand account in *The Old Flag* that black soldiers with the 11th U.S. Colored Troops and 4th U.S. Colored Light Artillery had been butchered, massacred, some of them while trying to surrender to Nathan Bedford Forrest's troops up in Tennessee.

Behind him, I saw another black men and two

dark-haired Indians watching anxiously. They were playing baseball, but not at Park Square. *Probably aren't allowed to play on Park Square*, I thought. The Negro closest to me just waited, only occasionally looking me in the eye. I guess he wanted to know what I planned on doing with the ball I had caught, likely expected me to toss it over the ditch across the deadline in some demented joke.

He was a tall man, thin but solid, wearing a dark blue blouse and light blue trousers, the bottoms frayed and ripped. No boots, no socks, and only a rimless black hat. The stripes down his trousers told me he had served in the cavalry. He chewed his bottom lip.

I threw the ball back, harder than I had meant to and a little high, but he leaped with ease and snagged it, pivoted, and relayed the ball to an Indian. Looking at me briefly, he nodded his thanks before breaking into a short run, but stopped after a few yards and shouted: "Hey, mister, that was a dandy catch!"

"You, too," I said. "Good throw, too."

His grin revealed white teeth, and he thanked me verbally and started to return to his game. For some reason, I wanted conversation, so I called out my name, rank, and regiment.

Turning back, he eyed me with curiosity. "First Sergeant Timothy Moore," he said, "First Kansas Colored Cavalry, First Squadron."

"You . . . you mind if I watch you play?"

Suspicion replaced curiosity, and several moments passed before he answered. "Suit yourself." He jogged back to the game.

With four players, it wasn't a real game, more

like batting practice, but I found it interesting. The Indian pitched to a striker, and two others played in the outfield, rotating hitters. They had no catcher, but used a one-seater outhouse as a backstop. This wasn't the fastest-paced contest I had ever watched, mainly because that Indian had an exaggerated wind-up and an awesome pitch, striking out more batters than allowing hits.

"You mind if I catch?" I asked Sergeant Timothy Moore after he connected on one of the Indian's pitches and sent it rocketing toward the palisade, stopping just short of the deadline.

"You don't want to catch him, mister," Moore answered. "Look at that privy."

Several pieces of wood had been splintered by the Indian's pitches, and once, when the other Indian had made contact with his bat, he had dropped the lumber and stood hopping at the makeshift plate, shaking his stinging hands and cursing his Indian friend as one mean-spirited Cherokee. The pitcher had just laughed. I didn't know Indians laughed.

"I'd like to give it a try," I said.

The second black man wasn't as friendly as Timothy Moore. "White folks got their own field over yonder," he snapped. "Why don't you go play with them?"

"Let him catch me," the Indian pitcher said. "I'll break every one of his damned fingers."

I smirked at the challenge. "You'll try," I said.

Well, Private Lewis Chockram did not break any of my bones, but he certainly bruised my hands, already aching from the knuckles I had jammed when I hit Mike Peabody in the jaw. The game, such as it was, did take my mind off the recent events, and I imagine I earned the begrudging respect of Chockram, Moore, Joshua Livinggoode, and Wesley Young Duck. After a couple of hours, we quit. Livinggoode, Young Duck, and Chockram went back to their she-bangs, Livinggoode taking the bat and Chockram the ball, and I followed Timothy Moore to the spring. Moore dropped to his belly and slaked his thirst while I soaked my throbbing hands in the cool water.

"Who did you play for before the war?" I asked, not expecting Moore's reaction.

When his chest quit heaving after the explosion of laughter, Moore shook his head and wiped his eyes. "Ain't you the funny one. Like any colored folks in Kansas ever heard of baseball. I learned from watchin' you boys at the Square. That's how we all learned."

"Even Chockram?"

"Definitely Lewis Chockram. You think Cherokees in Indian Territory play baseball?"

I felt like an utter idiot.

"So what made you want to play with us?" Moore asked.

Shrugging, I tried to think of an answer. "My father, I guess. He was an Abolitionist. It's because of him that I enlisted in the cavalry last fall."

"Well, I hope he's doin' better'n you, mister, you bein' a prisoner and all."

"He's dead. Killed at Gettysburg."

Moore frowned. "I'm sorry, Mister . . ."

"Don't *mister* me, or *sir* me. You're older than I am, and I am no officer. The name is Win."

"All right, Win. I am sorry about your father, sorry for any bad memories. How did you get captured?"

I told him, then asked for his details. That's common in a prison camp, the first question you ask. Where were you captured? And how?

"Up in Arkansas," he said. "We were escortin' a train foragin' for corn, food. Rebs seen us and attacked, screamin', howlin', shootin'." Moore's eyes closed as he shook his head. "Don't rightly know why they captured me. Most of us, them Rebs just shot down dead."

"Like at Fort Pillow," I said softly.

"I reckon. Done some horrible . . ." His eyes shot opened, and he washed his face. "Well, I'm here."

Moore rose, offered me his hand, which I took ever so gingerly, and he carefully helped me to my feet. "Win, you can catch for us any time you want, if your commander don't mind. Beats beatin' the hell out of our privy. That Chockram, he's done about knocked that dang' thing down."

I shook my still-throbbing hands. "Thanks, but I won't be there tomorrow. Maybe Friday. Don't tell Chockram, but I couldn't catch a feather right now."

Laughing, Timothy Moore jogged back toward the colored soldiers' shebang.

In late September, thirty-eight Iowans escaped through a tunnel from the Hawkeye Mess along the east wall, but twenty-two of those were recaptured, and as punishment, after two weeks in stocks and ten more in the Wolf Pen, they were forced to become our neighbors behind the privy.

One of those Hawkeyes was Ole Hendrickson, who we later learned was perhaps the best ballist in Ford City. Blessed with incredible speed, phenomenal hand-eye co-ordination, and muscular arms that could wield a bat better than Babe Ruth and Ty Cobb, Hendrickson amazed everyone, Union and Confederate. He would pay dearly, though, for his talent.

A few days after the escape, approximately 600 prisoners were exchanged, but none from the 3rd Rhode Island. Mike Peabody had disappeared, too, and no one knew what had happened to him, if he had been paroled among those 600, or what. Winter came late to East Texas, so we played baseball well into November. I'd catch for the Negroes and Indians once a week, and maybe play a game at Park Square. Some Union soldiers objected, and a few Secesh guards heckled me as a nigger-lover, but I didn't let their taunts bother me, and Captain McGee never said a word.

The big event, however, came in early October when Major Jon Rose's prayers were answered. All of those letters he had sent, to officials ranging from Union Rear Admiral David Farragut and Confederate General Kirby Smith to preachers and politicians North and South must have paid off, because boxes upon boxes arrived from New Orleans and Galveston.

Underdrawers, shoes, socks, pants, shirts, coats, and kepis, even blankets and, oddly enough, five dozen silk cravats. Those fashionable neckties weren't the strangest arrival, though, for, as Major Chauncey Perdue reported, when Sweet's Guards tossed one crate from the wagon, it broke open, and out spilled a dozen bats, several baseballs, even heavy canvas bags for the bases.

The equipment must have excited Major Perdue more than anything, because he exclaimed with joy at the sight, but Colonel Sweet told the guards to carry the baseball items to the hospital.

"Colonel Sweet," Major Perdue said, "I must protest. Recreation is good for morale, and those baseballs and bats are meant for us."

"Major Perdue," the colonel replied, "you must think me a fool to allow Yankee prisoners clubs. After your recent escape attempts, you should be grateful that I am allowing any of these items inside The Corral. But I am not about to give you weapons which you could use to crack open our skulls."

"Much as I hate to admit it," Sergeant Champlin said in our shebang after hearing Captain McGee's report, "the colonel has a point. Why, I'd love to stove in Sergeant Keener's head with one of those ash sticks."

Fall transformed into a mild winter, although some days turned frigid. Christmas and New Year's came with much celebration, something to break up the drudgery and stink, then faded from our memories. All those months, I thought of Jane Anne Bartholomew, wondering how she was doing, if she was thinking of me. I often found myself walking down Front Street, hoping the gate would open and I'd perhaps catch a glimpse of her. I thought of writing her, but figured my letter would never reach her. Inspecting all mail, Pig Oliver would make certain of that.

One pleasant day in February, while I patrolled Front Street, a Secesh called down from the cat-walk, aiming his shotgun at the compound as the gate opened. I looked outside, but the only person I saw, other than Confederates, was Fergal O'Hara, the baseball player from the 42nd Massa-chusetts, returning to Ford City after a few days in Major Rose's hospital.

I ran to greet him, thinking I might ask if Jane Anne had been helping the major, but he kept shaking and scratching his head.

"Damnedest thing I've ever seen, Mac-Naughton," he told me.

"What's that?"

"Them butternuts out there. They're playing baseball. New York rules."

Bitterly I shook my head. "With equipment meant for us."

"Yeah," O'Hara agreed, still perplexed. "But the thing is, those boys are pretty good at it."

That's what gave Conall McGee the idea.

Sitting in our shebang, eating panola for break-fast, we were discussing what O'Hara had seen and the other events of that fall and winter, when suddenly the captain tossed his bowl aside and hollered for Champlin and me to follow him.

We raced down Shinbone Alley, turned right on Battery Place, and left at Ten Pin Alley to Soap Street, where we found Professor Blevins, wear-ing one of those black cravats, not so new-looking after four months in Ford City, bartering with an Indiana lieutenant for some pipe tobacco.

"Professor," said a panting McGee. "We need to talk to you and Major Perdue."

Blevins told us to wait, finished his trade, and led us to Park Square, where we watched a baseball game in which the major was playing second base. That morning was cold, too chilly for baseball, and the wind made things uncomfortable to watch, but we waited. After the contest, the professor whispered in Major Perdue's ear, and the commander shrugged and walked to his shebang, the four of us right behind him.

After the major stoked his fire and warmed himself with a cup of Mr. Lincoln's coffee, he granted Captain McGee permission to speak. Champlin and I were as curious as Perdue and Blevins about McGee's plan, and our faces showed similar expressions after he briefly laid it out for Major Perdue's and Professor Blevins's consideration.

CHAPTER TWENTY

"Challenge the Rebs to a baseball game?" Perdue howled incredulously.

"Yes, sir." McGee's voice blared with enthusiasm. "Eighteen men, that would give us two nines, outside the walls. Armed with baseball bats."

"They'd have muskets," Professor Blevins added acidly. "And have you outnumbered."

"Aye, but the advantage of surprise we'd have, and, once we buffaloed a number of Secesh, we'd have their muskets."

Only respect and admiration for Captain McGee prevented me from rolling my eyes at such an unfathomable plan, but Major Perdue sipped his coffee, as if even considering this absurdity. "Go on," he said.

"Rebs left guarding the palisade walls wouldn't be paying attention to The Corral, watching the contest they'd be. A handful of hand-picked men . . . I'm guessing the muffin nine of our baseball club . . . would storm those walls."

"A two-pronged attack," Perdue commented with military esteem.

"Exactly, sir. We'll build ladders in our she-bangs, hide them in the roofs. Use those to storm the walls at the same time we mounted our offensive."

Emphatically Professor Blevins shook his head. "That's tantamount to suicide, man. Impossible."

"Difficult, sir," McGee said. "Not impossible. These aren't good soldiers guarding us. The Confederacy's dregs, they are. We have true soldiers in Ford City, and right is on our side."

"Right was on your side at Sabine Crossroads," the professor argued. "Right was on my side aboard the *Queen of the West*. Yet here we are. Right and God have been on our side since this damned war broke out four years ago, and how many young men have God and right let die!"

"Quiet, Zachary." Major Perdue scrutinized us 2nd Squadron representatives. "Eighteen men on the outside, you say?"

"Yes, sir, the first and second nines of the team."

"Perhaps we could get your muffin nine outside the gates, too, increase our numbers."

"No good, Major. Sweet isn't a bloody idiot. I'm not sure even eighteen prisoners he'd allow out of the gates, but I suspect he will. Southern pride. And if we had twenty-seven ballists, so would the Rebs. Eighteen is more manageable, sir, and less suspicion would it arouse."

"This is unsurpassed lunacy," Professor Blevins argued.

"Zachary, you wouldn't be saying that if Captain McGee adored your inane Massachusetts rules." Perdue cackled at his own joke, the only person who laughed, but his humor faded quickly. "It is terribly risky, potentially a disaster. You'd lose a lot of your athletes."

"Yes, sir, some of us will die. I'll hand-pick them meself. Volunteers only, and only men I can trust, men that can play baseball and do the job required."

The major shook his head with a short laugh. "Very well, Captain. I grant permission. You are in charge of picking your players, total control as manager, Mister McGee. With one proviso."

"What's that, Major?"

"You have your first two volunteers. I shall be your second baseman, first nine I hope, and Professor Blevins will play first base, if he dares lower himself to submit to New York supremacy."

"I submit to no such thing, Chauncey," Blevins said. "Respectfully. But I'll play your damned game. At least I'll die outside these stinking walls."

"We're getting ahead of ourselves, gentlemen," Perdue said. "First, we must throw down the gauntlet, and then Colonel Sweet has to consent to our challenge."

I firmly believe that Ruben Sweet would have laughed down such a dare had Captain Pig Oliver not been present when Major Chauncey Perdue, representing the Army prison body, Lieutenant Zachary Blevins, representing the Navy prison body, and Captain Conall McGee, manager of Mr. Lincoln's Hirelings, issued the challenge.

My one contribution had been the name of our team. Most wanted to call us something like the Camp Ford Federals or the Union Base Ball Club of Ford City, but I kept thinking about Jane Anne Bartholomew's words to me. *I guess you're not just one of Mister Lincoln's hirelings to me, Win.* Maybe the preposterousness of the name struck a cord with Conall McGee, as well, for he promptly adapted that moniker for us. Besides, McGee pointed out, President Lincoln loved baseball, so Mr. Lincoln's Hirelings it was, much to the detestation of Perdue and Blevins but to the delight of Lieutenant Colonel Ruben Sweet and Captain Pig Oliver. Perhaps that is another reason the Rebs acquiesced.

"Take 'em up on that, Sweet," Pig Oliver said after hearing the idea, this information coming to me second-hand from McGee. "We can lick them mudsills at their own game."

"That's *Colonel* Sweet, *Captain!*" the commander thundered indignantly.

"We'll nail their hides to the barn," Oliver added.

Sweet shook his head. "And where do you propose we play this contest, gentlemen? New Orleans? Perhaps Washington or Philadelphia?"

"Right here," Perdue said.

"Inside The Corral?" Sweet scoffed.

"Outside, Colonel. On your own field, your own terms."

"And how many prisoners do you think you would need outside the walls to play?"

Perdue pursed his lips as if considering this for the first time, then answered with a shrug.

"Twenty-seven, the first nine, second nine, and our muffin nine." The major knew Sweet would barter with him, which is why he set his figure so high.

"Not a chance, Major. Nine will suffice."

"No, colonel, that isn't fair. We need substitutes for injuries, just as your club will. Eighteen."

"Nine, or no game."

Perdue stood his ground. I'd hate to play poker with that man. "Then it is no game, sir." He snapped his heels, fired off a keen salute, and pivoted.

"Eighteen ain't nothin'!" Oliver almost begged. "We can beat these Yanks. That'd do wonders for our cause, get us writ up in newspapers, even in Richmond, Montgomery, Charleston. Hell, you'd be as big a hero as John Bell Hood. 'Sides, Yanks'll call us cowards if we don't do it, *Colonel*."

Running his fingers through his beard, Sweet considered Oliver's statement, a challenge really. Finally his head bobbed slightly. "When do you propose this game between . . . what do you call yourselves? Lincoln's . . . ?"

"Mister Lincoln's Hirelings," Captain McGee snapped in reply and salute.

The colonel sniggered. "And . . . ?" He glanced at Oliver.

"The Ford City Gallinippers."

"Nonsense, Mister Oliver," Sweet said. "You represent the Righteous Club of Lieutenant Colonel Ruben Sweet's Texas Battalion of Guards, Army of the Confederate States of America."

Oliver shrugged and spit. They'd be called the Ford City Gallinippers, anyway.

"When?"

"Spring," Perdue answered. "Let the weather warm up, give everyone ample time to be at the top of his game."

"It is agreed, then. But mark my words, Major Perdue, if anyone tries to escape during this . . . this truce, if you will . . . I will shoot you myself, and every one of your Mister Lincoln's Hirelings."

In March, baseball games at Park Square became more or less try-outs, under the watchful eye of Conall The Cat McGee. No one knew the real purpose of our game, just that a baseball club of prisoners would play against the Secesh guards in a month or two, and that had everybody excited. When McGee liked a player's ability, he would have a discussion with Perdue, Blevins, and Champlin, just to try to learn about these players, how much they could be trusted. If they passed that investigation, the players were approached, told the real purpose, and given the option of joining or not. Surprisingly, almost every one said yes.

McGee had penciled himself in as the first-nine left fielder, Professor Blevins at first base, and Major Perdue at second. I hoped I'd be catcher, but McGee rocked my gut when he announced Sharky the Seaman would fill that position.

"'Tis not that you cannot be trusted, Win," he told me back in our shebang. "I know you wouldn't ever repeat your mistakes. I trust you, lad. But . . ."

"I understand," I conceded. "Sharky's a better catcher than I am."

"'Tis not only that, son. Sharky and Blevins

have been inside these walls longer than most. They have the strongest desire to do the job we must do."

I wasn't so sure about Sharky, but I did not argue. Instead, I volunteered. "Well, sir, I hope you'll consider me as your muffin catcher."

When McGee gripped my shoulder, I almost broke into tears. *He wouldn't even let me do that!* Yet he smiled grimly and said: "No, Win. You'll be on the second nine."

Now, I know why. The muffin nine, storming the walls from inside the prison, would have the toughest assignment if anything went wrong. At least the eighteen players outside Camp Ford would have a chance at escape. Not much, but at least a chance.

Conrad Turner of the 47th Pennsylvania Infantry was chosen third baseman; Fergal O'Hara of the 42nd Massachusetts Infantry, shortstop; Ole Hendrickson of the 3rd Iowa Cavalry, center fielder; and Hans Jurgen of the 160th New York Infantry, pitcher.

Yet, I suddenly realized, Captain McGee had overlooked some of the best ballists inside Ford City.

"Negroes and Indians?" McGee shook his head after I offered my opinion in our shebang one rainy night. "I do not think so, MacNaughton. A bloody riot it would cause."

"Captain, I've never seen anyone pitch as hard as Lewis Chockram," I argued. "Joshua Livinggoode and Timothy Moore are great outfielders. Young Duck isn't as good, but he'd be a fine muffin outfielder."

"Can't be trusted, darkies and Injuns." Champlin spit. "And they aren't fighters."

"Tell that to the men of the Fifty-Fourth Massachusetts!" I snapped, no respect in my voice. "Or those Kansas horse soldiers serving with Timothy Moore gunned down in Arkansas. Moore and Livinggoode have more reason to fight and die than any of us. And wouldn't we want a Cherokee with us on the outside, if that plan works? An Indian would know the trails better than the rest of us."

"You insolent—"

McGee silenced Champlin by raising his hand. "I'll watch your friends, laddie. That's all, mind you, that I'll agree to do right now."

Three days later, Captain McGee announced that Lewis Chockram would be our second-nine pitcher, Joshua Livinggoode our starting right fielder, Timothy Moore our second-nine center fielder, and Wesley Young Duck a muffin-nine right fielder.

Conall McGee had been right. It almost did start a riot.

Hans Jurgen cursed, spat, and kicked mud all over the square, informing everyone in his harsh German accent that he would never play on any club with a colored man, and that Indians were not fit to lace up his shoes. Two other second-nine athletes and four muffins agreed.

"Then you're all off the team," Captain McGee said, "if that's the way you feel."

Everyone looked baffled, stunned, but Jurgen held his ground. So did Captain McGee. When Jurgen marched off the square, Captain McGee announced that Lewis Chockram was now our first-nine pitcher. In the end, only a second-nine shortstop from New Hampshire and all muffin players backed down. We replaced the rest, and kept a close watch on the quitters, in case one of those racists decided to become a turncoat razorback and reveal our true intention.

There was another surprise, too. Joshua Livinggoode said he'd be damned if he would play for our white team, and he cursed Timothy Moore for agreeing to a suicide mission, much less the stupid baseball game.

I was there, practicing with the Indians and Negroes, when Livinggoode, a sailor from the *Champion No. 3*, cursed Moore and the two Cherokees. When Timothy Moore slapped Livinggoode's face, I cringed.

"You're the damned fool," Moore said, squaring up against the sailor, who bested him by five inches and forty pounds. "I j'ined this Army to fight, mister, not for no forty acres and a mule, but to fight, for me, for my family, for all my brothers and sisters, and here's another chance. You want to cry about your past, you do that. You want to be a swamp-runnin' nigger all your life, you do that, too. But, damn you, Joshua, don't you ever cuss me, and don't you never belittle what Capt'n McGee is tryin' to do. For us, damn you. For all of us."

Joshua Livinggoode walked away, but the following morning, despite temperatures in the low 40s, he was back on Park Square for practice with Mr. Lincoln's Hirelings.

*   *   *

The biggest riot came inside the office of Lieutenant Colonel Ruben Sweet.

"It has come to my attention, Major Perdue," Sweet said, "that you have fielded niggers, both black niggers and prairie niggers, on your baseball club."

Hat in hand, Perdue verified the report, and Sweet spit into the fireplace with disgust.

"These terms are unacceptable, Major," Sweet said. "We are gentlemen, sir, and will not soil our reputations by playing with the likes of slaves and savages. They must be removed."

"I have no authority, Colonel. Captain Conall McGee makes all decisions regarding Mister Lincoln's Hirelings, and he has chosen those players."

"Tell him they must go, or there will be no game."

"Then, sir, there will be no game."

I wish I had been there, wish I could have seen the look on Sweet's face, but, again, this information comes to me from other sources.

"The hell with you, Major! The game is off."

"Very good, sir. I'm sure the readers of the Charleston *Mercury*, *Harper's Weekly*, and the New York *Herald* will enjoy learning that"—somehow, he remembered Sweet's preposterous name of his ball club—"the Righteous Club of Lieutenant Colonel Ruben Sweet's Texas Battalion of Guards, Army of the Confederate States of America, is scared that it would be defeated by a club with Indians and men of color."

Sweet almost struck him with a gauntlet. "You damned brigand. We'll play your game, and you will regret your insolence."

Major Perdue chuckled as he remembered the conversation in a discussion that night with McGee, Champlin, and Blevins. We didn't know then, however, just how dirty Ruben Sweet would play.

CHAPTER TWENTY-ONE

Baseball does wonders for a body's spirit. Naturally I've known that most of my life, but I guess a man forgets, only to be reminded of it, and I definitely was awakened at the train depot when the Cardinals returned to St. Louis. I've seen Presidents who didn't get that kind of reception, and this team hadn't won a thing. Fact was, the Cardinals would have to take the next two games to win the World Series, and odds-makers didn't think that likely. No one cared much, though, not on that pleasant day. Children, women, and men shook hands with manager Eddie Dyer and his boys, offering encouragement, bouquets, and beers.

Even I started to suppose that the Cardinals might pull this off, much as I had believed in another team's chances eighty-one years earlier.

During practice at Park Square, Mr. Lincoln's Hirelings felt loose. Try to figure that one out. We planned on attacking armed guards, man-killers like Pig Oliver and Ward Keener, with ash and hickory sticks in a daring escape attempt, yet there we were, joking, clowning around.

"Quite the crowd we've drawn," Captain McGee told Conrad Turner one brisk afternoon.

With a shrug, the Pennsylvanian picked up a Camp Ford-made pine bat. "Well, prisoners don't have much else to watch."

"'Tis not my meaning." McGee hooked his thumb toward the palisades, and Turner and I, catching for the second-nine, stared at the catwalk, filled with Rebel guards, all watching us practice.

"Doesn't seem fair, does it?" McGee said. "They spy on us, but we can't see the . . . what is it they are calling themselves?"

"Gallinippers," I answered.

"It wouldn't hurt, Captain," Turner suggested, "if we knew exactly what we were up against."

They sounded as if they thought we actually planned on playing the Rebs. I waited for McGee to get out of the way so I could catch and Turner could have his chance to strike.

"Trooper MacNaughton?" McGee said.

"Sir?"

"Don't you think you ought to have that Secesh sawbones check your fingers?"

Bewildered, I wondered what he was talking about.

"One might be broken, lad. All of them might be broken."

My fingers weren't broken. Sore, yes, but I could still bend them. The captain winked, and at last I understood. After calling out for Justin De-Car, our muffin catcher from the 1st Louisiana Cavalry, to replace me, I gripped my right hand in mock agony, and headed for the sally port, telling the guards that I needed to see Major Rose.

That's how we spied on the Ford City Gallinippers. Practically every day, whenever we could hear our opponents practicing beyond the log walls of our prison, a member of our team would come down with an ailment that required the attention of Major Jon Rose. We didn't get to see much of the Gallinippers, but it certainly helped.

Bantering and joking continued, and once Captain McGee even coaxed serious-natured Sergeant Champlin to take a turn with a bat. On his first cut, Champlin sent the bat slicing a vicious path over Lewis Chockram's head, and everyone burst out laughing. Everyone but Lewis Chockram, that is. Major Perdue picked up the bat near second base and returned it to the surly, but embarrassed, sergeant, who proceeded to duplicate his bat toss that sent Chockram diving for cover. After another explosion of laughter from us, and profanity from the Cherokee, McGee concurred that Champlin's batting practice had ended.

Practices continued until we felt we were at the top of our game. Ladders had been secretly built and hidden in the rafters of our shebangs, and the light-hearted mood waned, replaced by the foreboding soldiers feel before battle, matching the ominous look of the thunderheads, threatening us with rain but never producing.

Every Saturday after roll call, Major Perdue would request an interview with Colonel Sweet in which he asked to set a date for our game, and every Saturday the colonel would defer.

"What's he waiting on?" McGee snapped one night.

Nobody ventured a guess.

We found out the following week when Justin DeCar returned from his surreptitious doctor's visit with Major Rose. A Cajun who had refused, like a number of Louisianans, to join the Confederacy, Justin DeCar had played baseball with a club in New Orleans before the outbreak of hostilities. No, Abner Doubleday did not invent baseball, and, yes, the game was played in the South before the War of the Rebellion. Not much, certainly, as baseball's explosion did not take off until after the war, but games were played in Southern cities like New Orleans, Galveston, Houston, and, as I have written earlier, Jacksboro.

"They got a new player at first base," DeCar reported. "Swarthy gent, mean at the plate. Played against him, but I can't recollect his name, down in New Orleans. Got a new center fielder, too. Don't think I've seen him, but he's quicker than a rattlesnake. No chance to see him strike."

"So. . . ." Major Perdue let out a heavy sigh. "That's why Sweet has been slow to set a date for our contest. He's bringing in reinforcements."

DeCar went on to describe the two new players, what they looked like, how they played, what uniforms they wore. He hadn't heard any names mentioned, but he remained set in his belief that he had played against the first baseman before the war.

Ringers. That's what we started calling them toward the end of the 19th Century.

"That sneaky bastard," Professor Blevins said.

Sneaky. That wasn't the word for that son-of-a-bitch.

I managed my first hit against Lewis Chockram in two weeks on an overcast Friday afternoon. Once I connected, I knew my strike had been sweet, that this would be a great hit. That was the deal with our Cherokee pitcher. He threw the ball with such blazing speed and finesse, it proved nearly impossible to hit, but if you ever connected, and connected solid, you had an extra-base hit. Tossing my bat aside, I raced down the first-base line, looking skyward, trying to find that ball.

"Don't look for the ball!" Timothy Moore screamed. "Run!"

Ole Hendrickson and Joshua Livinggoode kept sprinting back, with no chance of catching that one on the fly, while Conall McGee limped around left field, laughing, ordering them to hurry. Bruce Few, the Wisconsin artillery private who played left field for the second nine, crossed home plate ahead of me and turned around. Bruce Few had reached first base when McGee dropped a fly ball. Now, he waved his arms and told me to slow down, that Hendrickson and Livinggoode were still chasing the ball.

Just before my feet touched the plate, a gunshot cut through the air.

Moments later came curses, screams, and shouts, and then every one of us took off running toward Front Street. Fingers pointed at the palisades, where Sergeant Ward Keener stood holding a smoking musket. Exhausted from all that running, I pushed my way through the crowd, looking at the guards before my gaze fell to the body of Ole Hendrickson, the best baseball player ever to set foot in Ford City, lying in a pool of his own blood, sightless eyes staring at the clouds overhead.

"Murderer!" Livinggoode screamed. "Murderer! You shot him dead. Shot him in cold blood."

Keener tossed his musket to an aging private, ordering him to reload it, pulled a revolver from his holster, and fired a round into the air.

"He crossed the deadline," Keener said. "You bluecoats know the rules."

"He never crossed no such thing!" Livinggoode said.

I located the ball, which had rolled into the ditch marking the deadline.

"If he crossed the deadline," Major Perdue began, "why is he lying here, on this street?"

Keener considered this for a moment, took the loaded musket from the private, and simpered. "Fifty-Six caliber I got," he said. "Wonder it didn't blow him all the way to your home plate."

Perdue spit across the ditch. "Like hell, Sergeant. I know a thing or two about physics."

Another gunshot silenced our rising voices, and Lieutenant Colonel Ruben Sweet joined Keener. The catwalk began filling with Confederate guards armed with shotguns, all aimed in our direction.

"What's goin' on here?" Sweet demanded.

"Your assassin murdered one of our men," Perdue said.

Sweet shot Keener a glance. "Sergeant?"

"The prisoner crossed the deadline, Col'nel. I hollered at him to stop, but he didn't pay no mind. Shot him with Ol' Landace here." He patted the barrel of his musket. "Ball knocked him to that patch the Yanks call a street."

"Your center fielder should have known better," Sweet said. "Couple of you prisoners fetch his body to the sally port and haul him to the cemetery."

A furious Fergal O'Hara almost stepped across the ditch himself, cursing the Rebel black-hearts, but Captain McGee jerked him back, and we crowded together into a huddle, O'Hara and Livinggoode crying for vengeance, McGee and Perdue begging everyone to cool down, that the Rebs just wanted an excuse to shoot down more of us.

"You've got to call this off!" a voice cried out, and I found Sharky the Seaman in the middle of us, tears filling his eyes. "It's hopeless, Major. They'll kill us all."

"Nonsense, Sharky," Perdue said. "Get a grip on yourself, sailor."

"Major," Sharky continued, lowering his voice. "Don't go through with this. Everyone will be killed."

"If you desire to be replaced on the first nine," McGee said bitterly, "just give the word. A brave man lies dead, and you're bawling like a coward."

"What chance will we have outside of those gates, Captain?" Sharky asked. "They'll shoot us all down like dogs."

"Then why did you volunteer?" McGee snapped.

"Listen to me," Sharky said. "They'll kill you all. Boys, they've got The Butcher out there. They've got—"

A snap of Justin DeCar's fingers silenced Sharky the Seaman. "That's the name. The Butcher. Played for the Royal Street Base Ball Club, didn't last but a year, but The Butcher was known in The Swamp as a man-killer and . . ."

DeCar frowned at the now silent seaman. I had

never taken my eyes off Sharky, and now he began sweating, backing his way out of our circle, but it closed in on him.

"How did you know his moniker?" Major Perdue asked.

Sharky made no reply.

"You said you threw dirt clods at the guards," I heard myself saying, "said that's how you wound up in the Wolf Pen with me." I choked out a hollow laugh. "You never threw anything at those guards, did you, Sharky? The Rebs sent you there to spy on me, befriend me, maybe learn about our troop movements. Right?"

Sharky's eyes locked with mine, but his face revealed no expression, and I had to look away, not because of Sharky, but because of another image, and suddenly tears plunged down my cheeks. "You were the tunnel traitor, Sharky," I almost wailed as I located Conall McGee. "Oh, God, Captain. We branded Mike . . . for nothing!"

A dark silence fell over us, broken up only by Sergeant Keener's command. "You Yanks gonna wait all day? Leave your pal to the flies? Get movin', boys. We ain't got all day to bury that dog. What are y'all jawin' about?"

I fought back the bile, the shame, made myself stop crying, tried to forget what we—no, what *I* had done to Mike Peabody. Waiting for an explanation, I glared at Sharky the Seaman.

"I've been rotting in this pigsty longer than just about anyone," Sharky started. "I'm trying to save your lives. You can't make it. . . ." He shuddered a couple of times, then made his back ramrod straight, and clutched the St. Christopher medallion with his trembling right hand.

"I'm sorry, Win," he said. "Sorry for everything."

"*Sorry?*" Captain McGee shot out with contempt.

Two men stepped forward, but Major Perdue blocked their moves. "Captain McGee," he said tensely, "have you your branding iron?"

"Aye, Major." Methodically McGee pulled the broken Barlow knife from his pocket.

The chain holding the St. Christopher snapped as Sharky jerked it, tossing the medallion at my feet. "That won't be necessary, gentlemen." Spinning with surprising speed, he shoved his way through the men behind him.

"No!" I screamed, charging after him, but Timothy Moore tackled me. I looked up, spitting out dirt, and, through tears, saw Sharky the Seaman, marching across the deadline, standing tall, proud, a Union sailor, a soldier once again. He was singing "Battle Cry of Freedom" at the top of his lungs when Sergeant Keener shot him in the head.

CHAPTER TWENTY-TWO

That night, clutching Sharky's St. Christopher medallion in my hands till my knuckles whitened, I leaned against the wall of our rank shebang, trying to stop shaking, trying to forget. Every time I closed my eyes, though, I saw Mike Peabody, in this very shelter, screaming for my help. We had called Mike a Judas, had branded him the traitor, when in reality I had betrayed my friend by not believing him. Hell, I had accused him. I had been the judge and jury and, to a degree, executioner.

Bruce Few, Wesley Young Duck, Fergal O'Hara, and Professor Blevins had taken Hendrickson and Sharky to the cemetery for burial. I wished they were burying me.

"He had money, MacNaughton," Champlin said from across the hut. "Hidden inside his blouse. Confederate script. What else could we believe? He didn't say . . ."

"We didn't give him a chance, Sergeant," I said weakly. "Captain McGee gagged him."

McGee sat in the corner in his grapevine chair, silently brooding, sipping a flask. Quinton Brett had wisely gone somewhere else. With a sigh, I stared at the ceiling, saw the ladder we had made and hidden. We wouldn't have much use for it now. Undoubtedly Sharky had told the Rebs what we planned, then had died for his sins, leaving the rest of us heavy with guilt.

" 'Twas my fault," Captain McGee said at last. "Me own knife and hand did the deed."

Unannounced, Major Perdue stepped inside the shebang, but no one jumped to attention. He considered us momentarily. "If Peabody wasn't a traitor then," Perdue said, "he is one now. Don't punish yourselves."

"What do you mean, Major?" Champlin asked.

"Blevins saw that one-armed louse himself. Outside the walls. Free as a bird. He's playing for the Gallinippers!"

This bit of information comforted Champlin and McGee, and they began cursing Mike Peabody again as a turncoat razorback, although they would later wonder just how a one-armed boy could play baseball. I didn't move, other than to bury my head between my knees and start sobbing again. We had driven him out, scarred him forever. I couldn't blame him for joining the Confederate cause.

Shortly after roll call and breakfast the following morning, Chauncey Perdue gathered Mr. Lincoln's Hirelings at the corner of Park Row and

Fifth Avenue. With Professor Blevins on his left and Captain McGee on his right, the major began softly explaining to the baseball players that there would be no escape attempt, no baseball game.

"Sharky betrayed us," Perdue said, his voice trailing off. "I commend you all for volunteering, but to continue, gentlemen, would be disastrous. We've given enough for our cause. The war cannot last forever. I . . ." Slowly he exhaled, and asked Captain McGee, as the team manager, if he had any comments.

Before McGee could speak, however, Timothy Moore stepped to the front.

"With all due respect . . . I . . ." He stared at his bare feet, kicking sod with his toes, lips trembling, eyes blinking rapidly, trying to choose his words. A few moments later, he ripped off that shell of a hat, stood at attention, and finished: "Well, it's this way. Escape? Major, we can dig tunnels any time. But, well . . . we ought to go on with that contest. We *gots* to go on. We gots to beat them Confederates. Call off the escape, sure. But please let us play. Give us a chance. Don't quit on us, sir. Let us play baseball."

Surprised, I realized I now stood beside Timothy Moore. "Let us play. Give us one more chance to fight the Rebs." I don't know why I said that. Later that night, I told Captain McGee I had been thinking of my father. After all, I had enlisted in the Army because of his death. The baseball game would help me cope, I said, and maybe there was some truth to that. Or perhaps, subconsciously, I just wanted a chance to apologize to Mike Peabody, to beg his forgiveness. Honestly I'm not sure, but, when I looked up, I found Bruce Few, Joshua Livinggoode, and Lewis Chockram beside us. Fergal O'Hara and Justin DeCar stepped out next, even though DeCar, as a muffin, wouldn't leave Ford City's walls if we played the Rebs. I don't know how many Hirelings stepped up with Timothy Moore—certainly not all—but Major Perdue stood a little straighter and again asked Captain McGee if he had anything to say.

"First nine," McGee barked, "take the field. Second nine . . ." He beamed at me. "Quit acting like a bunch of coffee coolers!"

The captain slowed to a jog as we headed to the field, waiting for Moore and me to catch up. "I need you to catch for the first nine," he told me. "Moore, you'll take over Hendrickson's place in center field." Grimacing and favoring his leg, he ordered Justin DeCar to find Champlin in a hurry. "We're going to conscript the sergeant," he said with a wink. "I have a chore for him."

Saturday came, and, as usual, Major Chauncey Perdue met with Lieutenant Colonel Ruben Sweet, who sat behind his desk, muddy boots in the corner, stocking feet propped on his desk next to a whiskey bottle, eating goober peas, tossing the shells into a spittoon.

"Good mornin', Major," Sweet said. "What can I do for you this day?"

"It is about the baseball contest, Colonel."

"You wish to call it off, I warrant."

"On the contrary, Colonel. I am here to demand that we set a date. We will not be delayed any more, sir."

Sweet almost choked on a peanut, coughed, swung his feet off the desk, and stared with disbelief. "Surely. . . ." He couldn't continue.

"What do you want of us, Colonel? To wait around till your guards kill the rest of our players? No, sir. I am here to demand a date. We'll play you tomorrow."

"That's the Sabbath, Major."

"Then Monday. Or Tuesday. But, by thunder, we will play a game, unless you, sir, call it off."

"Never."

"Then when?" Perdue shook his head. "Surely, you have your Butcher and center fielder brought in from afar. Do you wish to replace every single one of your Gallinippers? Is that it?"

With a smirk, Sweet swallowed a finger of whiskey, returned to his comfortable position, and opened another soggy peanut with his teeth. "You have not seen Sergeant Keener pitch, Major. Even The Butcher finds him difficult to strike against."

"When?" Perdue bellowed. "When shall I have the opportunity to strike against your man-killing sergeant?"

"Saturday! How does Saturday suit you, Major?"

"Saturday it is, sir!" He snapped a salute and spun to leave, but Sweet stopped him.

"A few more things, Major. At one o'clock in the afternoon of Saturday, your first and second nines will be escorted to our field. Stragglers will be shot, as will anyone trying to escape. And, Major, since your . . . muffins, I think you call them . . . since they will have no need of those ladders you have hidden in your shelters, kindly have them brought to your Park Square this afternoon. Build yourself a bonfire."

* * *

On Friday night, the first nine of Mr. Lincoln's Hirelings, Sergeant Champlin, and Bruce Few crammed into the 2nd Squadron shebang. I studied those dirty, hardened faces, wondering if we really had a chance against Ward Keener, Pig Oliver, Andy Griggs, The Butcher, and the rest of the Gallinippers.

Lewis Chockram could pitch, but could he keep up his blistering pace under competitive pressure? Would I be able to catch him for nine innings? How well could first baseman Professor Blevins and shortstop Fergal O'Hara, both who favored the Massachusetts game, play in a real game using New York rules? Suddenly second baseman Chauncey Perdue looked ancient, while nerves had turned Conrad Turner's face ashen. Timothy Moore and Joshua Livinggoode were sure to be relentlessly insulted, and would the pressure playing against Sweet's Guards be too much for them? Poor Captain McGee's left ankle still troubled him.

"No lengthy speeches, lads," McGee said. "Eat yourself a good breakfast in the morning. Don't exert yourselves. I won't take long tonight."

"Good," Fergal O'Hara said. "Your shebang smells of shit, sir."

We laughed nervously; a brief grin faded from Captain McGee's face.

"I have two small changes," McGee said flatly. "Sergeant Champlin, you are to take over as first-nine catcher. . . ."

That caused a rustle of voices. I said nothing, just stared, mouth open, confused. I had just been demoted in favor of a man who hated baseball, who couldn't hold onto the bat, and had never caught a ball in his life.

Someone complained to Perdue, but the major said he had given total authority to Captain McGee for baseball matters, although Perdue's tone and expression revealed his own doubts.

"Quiet!" McGee shouted. "The sergeant and I have discussed this matter in private. Some of you lads have seen Sergeant Keener pitch. All of us remember what he did to Hendrickson!" That extinguished most voices, and McGee continued. "I'm sure you all remember how well Sergeant Champlin strikes, you in especial, Mister Chockram."

Chuckles broke out, and Livinggoode jovially slapped the Cherokee pitcher's back. "You'll get one chance, Nicholas," McGee spoke directly to Champlin. "You told me once you'd like to stove in Keener's head. Well, the time has come. Throw your bat harder than ever. Tear the bastard's head off."

Once the cheering died, McGee's fingers began drumming the walls restlessly. "One other change, lads. I'll be reducing meself to the ranks." He stared at the dirt for the longest while, and a bittersweet stillness filled the shebang. "No sense in lying to meself. That leg's no good." Shaking his head, he sighed. As his eyes lighted on me, he smiled the saddest smile I have ever seen. "No longer The Cat am I. Mister Few, can I count on you to play left field tomorrow afternoon?"

"Yes, Capt'n."

"Jolly good. All right, lads, be gone with ye. A championship contest we have tomorrow."

I settled onto my lice-infested bedroll, only half listening while Sergeant Champlin explained his purpose to me. He would get one chance to strike, and once he laid out Keener with the flying bat, the Secesh would haul him off to the Wolf Pen—if Sweet didn't kill him—no matter how hard he pleaded that it had been an accident. After that, I would replace him as catcher on the first nine.

It didn't matter to me, though. I just observed Captain McGee, slouched in his chair, staring out the window, likely remembering all of his glories as a baseball player while trying to accept that it had all ended. I told myself I knew how he felt, but, in reality, I didn't. The depth of that kind of pain I wouldn't comprehend until the fall of 1879, after the Providence Grays' championship season, when manager George Wright met me in the hotel lobby and told me that my contract would not be renewed, that it was time to hang up my glove.

PART III

"I have observed that baseball is not unlike a war, and when you come right down to it, we batters are the heavy artillery."

Ty Cobb

CHAPTER TWENTY-THREE

Sunday, October 13, 1946—one of those perfect days for baseball. Temperatures in the low 70s replaced the near-unbearable heat from the first two games at Sportsman's Park, and Game 6 turned out to be a gem for the Cardinals' Harry The Cat Brecheen, pitching a seven-hitter and shutting the door on the Red Sox. With Boston trailing 4–1 in the ninth, Ted Williams gave the Red Sox some hope and the Cardinals a bit of a scare when he singled up the middle, but The Cat robbed hot-hitting Rudy York of a hit by getting his glove on the ball York drove up the middle. Second baseman Red Schoendienst fielded the ball cleanly to start a double play and force a seventh game.

The brass had me visit the Red Sox locker room afterward—Mr. J. G. Taylor Spink's way of proving The Sporting News was impartial, I guess—and I found Williams, York, and the rest of the players to be far from down. They'd go out and beat the Cardinals, they said confidently, get the job done Tuesday.

Duffy Lewis gave me the biggest surprise. Now a

Boston coach in his late fifties, Lewis had been a star outfielder for the Red Sox, and had also played some with the Senators and Yankees.

"Didn't you play with Emil Strickland?" he asked.

Well, I hadn't heard that name in years. Took me a moment to answer. "Played with him on the Grays for one season. Played against him, too."

"He hung out at the Huntington Avenue Baseball Grounds when I first came up back in Nineteen Ten. Had a heart attack and died there during a game. Cranky old reprobate. He played for the Red Sox, right?"

"Red Caps," I corrected.

"That when you played against him?"

"Actually I first played against him in Texas during the war."

The sally port opened Saturday afternoon, and Mr. Lincoln's Hirelings marched down the center of Park Square, lined by thousands of Union prisoners of war, cheering us with Yankee hurrahs.

We walked past the hospital and well past the field the Gallinippers had carved out near the prison stockade to a near field on the flats behind the buildings. The sight before us staggered everyone. It was a good thing we had called off our escape plans.

Armed Confederate soldiers in the bright red and blue uniforms of Louisiana Zouaves lined both sides of the field, and an artillery piece rested far behind home plate, aimed at The Corral. An open tent was set up near third base, sheltering two dozen women sipping lemonade while sitting in camp chairs. Children in homespun clothes played in the fields behind them. The air smelled of goober peas, and I spied Negroes stirring huge pots over hot coals. Bags of boiled peanuts sold for $5, Confederate. Shots of whiskey came cheaper. The lemonade was free.

"Too early to be boilin' peanuts," Timothy Moore said. "Must be boilin' dried peanuts, and they don't taste right."

"Nothing about goobers taste right," I remarked.

My mouth dropped open. It looked as if everyone from Tyler had come to see this baseball game, and once we passed the concessions—I guess you'd have to call them—reporters swarmed us like mosquitoes as our guards escorted us to the first-base side of the infield. A few newspapermen needed some background and rules on the game. Correspondents came from papers in New Orleans, Austin, Dallas, Shreveport, and Galveston; one man claimed to be with *Frank Leslie's Illustrated Magazine*. After a handful of questions, one of the reporters yelled out—"Look!"—and the swarm buzzed off to bombard the Ford City Gallinippers.

Once again, all we could do was stare. There we stood in our bare feet, worn boots or rotting brogans, filthy trousers, soiled shirts and blouses, hats (if we had them) battered beyond recognition. In contrast, the proud seamstresses of Tyler had outfitted Lieutenant Colonel Ruben Sweet's baseball players with new uniforms: butternut britches, gray shield-front shirts with yellow piping and sparkling buttons, and flat-crowned, flat-brimmed straw hats with wide black silk bands.

"Quite the dandies," Major Perdue commented. No one else said a word.

Totally psychological, I knew. Make us feel inferior in our dirty garb. Try to beat us down before we even took the field.

I didn't see Mike Peabody, though. Maybe, I prayed, Professor Blevins had been mistaken. Perchance Mike hadn't joined the Gallinippers.

"Hey, I know that fellow." Perdue pointed at a tall, young gent clowning around with Andy Griggs and Corporal Bobby Logan.

"That's their center fielder," Fergal O'Hara said. "The new guy, the one DeCar first saw."

"Strickland. That's the name. Emil Strickland." Perdue shook his head. "Played with the Champions in 'Fifty-Nine, then jumped from club to club. Fled New York, if I recall correctly, after the draft riots of 'Sixty-Three."

"He's good," O'Hara said.

"*Good?* He's the best."

Our escorts lined us up for introductions, Ruben Sweet being keen on pomp and formalities, and a blonde-headed lady in a gray and red dress began handing roses to the Ford City Gallinippers. Another woman walked down the first-base line and began giving the Hirelings flowers.

She stopped when she reached me, and my heart raced at the sight of Jane Anne Bartholomew.

"Don't try anything," she whispered. "Sweet knows about your escape plan. They have cavalry hidin' in the woods."

I took the flower and squeezed her hand. "We know. We're here to play baseball, nothing else."

She sighed with relief. "Beat them. My father has wagered heavily on the guards. Beat . . ."

"Jane Anne. Move along, honey. Don't converse with Northern ribaldry."

Never shall I forget that look on her face at the sound of those words. She moved away from me, quickly handing flowers to the remaining Hirelings while I sought out the man who had scared her so, the man who had to be her father. I wanted to see the cad's face, but he had turned, heading back toward the throng of press and Sweet's Guards. All I made out were the black silk hat and worn tan frock coat. My gaze tracked Jane Anne, however, as she retired to a seat in the front of the tent near third base. Then my eyes caught Pig Oliver glaring at me in jealous rage.

He spit out tobacco juice and shot a glance at Jane Anne before heading for the bench along the third-base side with the rest of his teammates.

Conall McGee and Pig Oliver, the team captains, decided on Major Jon Rose as umpire. Rules required a scorekeeper, and a journalist for the *Daily Picayune* named L. K. Struck agreed to perform that duty. "Struck," Conrad Turner said, trying to add some levity to the situation. "That's a baseball name, by grab." McGee won a coin toss, so we would take the field first, giving us the advantage of having the last at-bat. He explained the ground rules.

"One other rule," McGee told us. "Approved this year. There's a pitcher's box instead of a pitcher's line. Not a thing about it had I heard, but a New York sporting journal Sweet showed me, so I guess it's true. Is that going to be a problem, Chockram?"

The Cherokee stared at the twelve-by-three box chalked out on the field and shook his head. "I was pitching the old way before you white men informed me that I had to keep both feet on the ground when releasing the ball. Reckon that I missed seeing that 'Sixty-Three rule book. Box or line, don't make no never mind to me, Capt'n."

I sat beside Captain McGee as he made out the starting lineup, coaching me on his reasoning. Perdue and Professor Blevins would strike first and second, followed by O'Hara, Turner, and Few. "That'll give Sergeant Champlin time to watch Keener pitch, and give Keener time to find some rhythm, maybe relax. They'll be expecting something sooner. When the sergeant steps up to strike in the sixth position, they might let down their guard."

Livinggoode, Moore, and Chockram would follow in the seventh, eighth, and ninth positions.

"What do you think?" he asked me.

"Timothy and Joshua are fast runners, good strikers," I commented.

"Agreed, but I can't put Negroes and an Indian before white men, Win. It's policy and . . ."

He stared ahead, and I looked up. My stomach roiled. Two other players jogged to join the Gallinippers. I didn't recognize the tallest man, who turned out to be another one of Sweet's reinforcements, a first-nine right fielder named Captain J. C. C. Hopkins who had played a few baseball contests in Washington, D.C., before returning to Houston at the start of the Rebellion. I couldn't forget the other player, though, a heavyset second-nine boy with red hair and a peach-fuzz mustache, his right sleeve pinned up at the shoulder, those cold Peabody eyes full of hatred when he spotted me.

CHAPTER TWENTY-FOUR

Scowling at Lewis Chockram, Sergeant Keener picked up a hickory bat and stepped to the plate. As soon as he called for a high ball, Chockram began his windmill motion and fired the game's first pitch. Keener grunted as the bat connected, propelling the ball to center field, where Timothy Moore took one step and stuck out his bare hand to snag the ball.

Next came a loud snap and muffled groan as the ball dropped from Moore's hand into the grass.

Laughter exploded from spectators and Gallinippers, and Keener held up at first base as Moore picked the ball and fired it, left-handed, to Fergal O'Hara at second base. Turning to our bench and wiping his lips, Keener said with a sneer: "Red nigger can't pitch. Black nigger can't catch."

In center field, Moore gripped his fingers with his left hand, but shook his head adamantly when right fielder Joshua Livinggoode asked if he were injured.

"No problem!" McGee clapped his hands. "Go get them, Chockram!"

But The Butcher drilled the Cherokee's second pitch into right field for a double, and suddenly the Gallinippers had runners on second and third base.

When he came to the plate, Pig Oliver called for a low pitch and swung futilely at Chockram's first blazing, caroming fastball. That gave us reason to cheer, but Chockram's second pitch sailed over Sergeant Champlin's head, who made no attempt to catch it. That could have been disastrous except Keener was too busy on third base pruning for the ladies to notice he had a chance to score.

It didn't matter. He came home on the next pitch, when Oliver singled to left, and The Butcher moved to third base, bringing Emil Strickland to the plate.

The Gallinippers' second nine laughed at us, Mike Peabody the loudest. Women underneath the tent clapped politely, although Jane Anne just wrung her hands. We sat or stood, faces sullen, voices stilled.

Strickland motioned for low pitches, and Chockram gave him three wicked ones that the star player from New York didn't come close to touching. On the third pitch, Strickland swung so hard he spun and fell in the dirt.

"Three strikes!" Major Rose called. "First out."

I leaped from my seat, pumping my fist, cheering Chockram, who had finally showed the Rebels, and us, what he was capable of doing. That silenced the Gallinippers, except for the mumbling Strickland as he carried his bat to the bench.

Batting next, Andy Griggs asked for a high pitch, and popped up Chockram's second delivery. Fergal O'Hara positioned himself underneath the short fly, swallowed it with his big hands, and let the ball fall at his feet. The Butcher took off running for home, and, swearing vilely, Pig Oliver ran to second, but O'Hara's drop was premeditated, and Chauncey Perdue had read his mind. Perdue was already standing on second base when O'Hara dropped the ball, picked it up, and flipped it to Perdue, who caught the ball and threw quickly to first base, where Professor Blevins concluded the double play.

If you're a baseball fan, you'll likely question how that play materialized, and allowed Mr. Lincoln's Hirelings to escape the first half of the inning trailing only 1–0. It's simple: the infield fly rule, created to outlaw such chicanery, did not exist in 1865.

"Bully, lads! Bully!" McGee greeted our players as they hustled off the field to boos and curses from the Texians surrounding us. "Now let's show those butternuts how well we strike."

We showed them nothing. Before the guards could sell many bags of boiled peanuts or shots of whiskey, Ward Keener struck out Major Perdue, Professor Blevins, and Fergal O'Hara. O'Hara said it best as he handed me his bat and prepared to return to the field.

"Can't hit what you can't see."

Sergeant Harry Pate, playing left field, led off the second inning with a single in the right-center-field gap, and I thought we might have another long inning. Second baseman Alvin Coker, however, struck out, and O'Hara dived to his right and somehow managed to grab, and hold on to, a ball hit by Corporal Bobby Logan for the second out. Chockram struck out Captain J. C. C. Hopkins for the third out.

This would be the inning, I thought, sitting on the edge of the bench. This would be Sergeant Champlin's chance. I didn't look at him, didn't want to jinx him, just concentrated on Keener's wicked wind-up as he fired pitch after pitch past Conrad Turner and Bruce Few. Turner managed to get a piece of one toss, popping up weakly to a hooting Pig Oliver, who caught the ball for the first out. Bruce Few struck out, banging the bat against the dirt as he returned to our bench in frustration.

"Where do you want the damned ball?" Keener shouted after Champlin stepped to the plate.

The sergeant shrugged. "High."

I held my breath. Keener rotated his arm rapidly, delivered a pitch that bounced in the dirt before crossing the plate. Champlin swung, and the bat flew from his hands, hard, arcing viciously, but Keener ducked and the bat landed near second base.

"Foul! A foul move by Yankees!" Colonel Sweet's shout hid our loud sigh. Champlin had missed. He stood at the plate, not knowing what to do, before finally trotting onto the field to pick up the bat.

"Watch him," McGee told me. "He'll break Keener's neck as he runs past the pitcher's box."

No matter how much I despised Keener, I didn't want to watch that, and I breathed easier once Champlin returned to the plate without attempting to assault the murderer.

"Take that rascal to the Wolf Pen!" Sweet demanded.

"It was an accident, Colonel," said Champlin. "The bat slipped, is all."

The bat slipped on Keener's next pitch, too, only this time it somehow hit the baseball, and we just stared, struck dumb, as the ball landed in front of us, bouncing once before Perdue caught it and threw it back to Keener. Champlin picked up the bat and got ready to strike again.

This time, he hurtled the bat low. It moved like a tomahawk, almost breaking Keener's legs, but somehow the fiend leaped over the wood, landed with a thud, and rolled over as the bat skipped and hopped, digging up clods of dirt and grass, before coming to a stop in shallow center field.

"Third strike!" Major Rose called. "The striker is out."

Texians and reporters heckled Champlin as a Yankee felon, and Keener, dusting himself off as he rose and returned to the pitcher's box, called the sergeant a whole lot worse, ignoring the presence of ladies.

"The bat slipped!" Champlin protested, but this time Sweet ordered his guards to escort the sergeant to the stocks. "He'll spend a week there, then three months in the Wolf Pen!" the commander bellowed.

Dejected, maybe embarrassed, Champlin briefly looked at us. "Sorry, boys," he said before the Rebs roughly grabbed him and shoved him back toward the prison compound.

"How are we supposed to continue?" Captain McGee yelled.

"Bring in your second-nine catcher," Emil Strickland answered. "See if he can grip a bat-stick better than that oaf."

The Rebs laughed. On our bench, we looked sullen.

"Long odds they were," McGee said softly. "We'll just have to beat that bastard some other way. All right, Win. Take the field, lad. You have to catch for us now."

Taunts greeted me as I took my place far behind home plate to begin the third inning.

"You try that with Sergeant Keener, and we'll shoot you, boy!"

"Yankee reinforcement don't look so good, do he?"

"Judas! Look over here, you son-of-a-bitch. Look at my damned face, you gutless coward!"

I wet my lips, trying to block out Mike Peabody's voice, and watched Keener step to the plate.

"High," he said.

Chockram drilled one pitch past him, but Keener again connected for a single that stopped the heckles directed at me.

"Ser-geant Kee-ner! Ser-geant Kee-ner!" the Gallinippers roared.

Moments later, The Butcher doubled, putting runners on second and third base.

I had moved up closer to the plate after Keener

reached first, and now I waited for Pig Oliver to strike.

"Low," he said, resting the bat on his shoulder, concentrating on Chockram. I thought he was ignoring me until he whispered: "You keep away from Miss Jane Anne, MacNewton. Keep away, boy, or else."

He swung on Chockram's first pitch. The ball whirled to center field, chased futilely by Moore and Livinggoode, and I rose slowly, disgustedly, standing back as Keener and The Butcher scored easily. Oliver held up at second, clapping his hands before doffing his straw hat toward the ladies.

I moved back to let Strickland come to the plate. He, too, asked for a low pitch. Strickland had struck out in his first appearance against Chockram, but this time he singled, sending Oliver to third.

Next, Andy Griggs popped a foul behind me. I raced for it, diving, putting out my hand as the ball spun toward the ground. Somehow I grasped it before landing with a thud, closing my eyes as I rolled over and came to my feet, surprised to find I still held the ball, even more shocked to hear Major Rose rule: "The striker is out."

Pig Oliver spit at me, but I ignored him, and couldn't help but grin when I spied Jane Anne smiling at me. The grin widened when Griggs trotted past me and good-naturedly said: "I thought you was a friend, Yank."

Sergeant Pate struck out, but Corporal Coker drilled Chockram's second pitch to center field.

"Run!" Colonel Sweet yelled. "Nigger can't catch the ball. That—"

Timothy Moore hushed Sweet and the others when he ran down the ball, fielding it cleanly in the air with both hands for the third out.

He rolled the ball toward the pitcher's box as he jogged off the field, smiling at the praise we heaped upon him. When he picked up a bat, however, he grimaced and bit his lip. His fingers had swollen hideously, and I remembered the terrible sound when he had dropped the ball in the first inning.

"Your hand's broken . . . ," I started.

"Shut up!" he snapped. "Ain't nobody takin' me out of this game. You hear?"

Joshua Livinggoode popped out to second baseman Alvin Coker, and Moore slowly took his position at the plate. My, how determined he looked, how bravely he tried, but Keener struck him out on five pitches, and, dejected, Moore sat on the separate bench for our Negroes and Indian. It pained me, how he slumped there, staring at his feet, clutching his right hand, trying to hide his anguish. There were two outs as Lewis Chockram came to bat.

"Let's see if the Injun hits better than he pitches," Keener said.

Those were the last coherent words I ever heard from Sergeant Ward Keener.

Chockram drilled the Reb's first offering up the middle. I looked for the ball, but didn't see it, slowly comprehending that I had heard two *thuds*, the first from Chockram's bat striking the ball, and the second . . .

Face white, a doubled-over Ward Keener took a few steps to the right before he collapsed, clutch-

ing his groin with both hands, the baseball resting in the center of the pitcher's box. Chockram
stood on first base with a single while Keener
rolled to his knees and vomited.

"Lord have mercy!" a woman shouted. Another
lady fainted. Embarrassed, the other women
turned away or otherwise averted their eyes, although I caught Jane Anne Bartholomew grinning mischievously before she bowed her head.

Major Rose waddled toward the injured player
being comforted by Corporals Logan and Coker.

"Major," Logan said. "The sergeant thinks
they's gone. He wants you to check...." Keener
retched again.

"I ain't a-doin' no such thing," Major Rose announced. For one of the few times during my stay
at Camp Ford, I heard Jon Rose clearly. "Ain't
about to stick my hand in a man's britches, not
with ladies a-lookin'." He looked up. "Some of
you boys take him to the hospital. See you after
the contest, Sergeant. You'll live, most likely."

After the delay in which Sergeant Keener was
carried off the field and Major Rose assisted the
fainted woman, Colonel Sweet wanted to eject
Chockram, but Major Rose refused and ordered
the Gallinippers to bring in their second-nine
pitcher, a prematurely balding lieutenant named
Prosser.

"Well, well, well," Captain McGee whispered
to me. "Not the way we planned it, but ... well,
well, well."

Major Perdue tripled to left field, scoring
Chockram, and scored when Andy Griggs fum-
bled a slow roller by Professor Blevins. O'Hara

popped a foul out to third base to end the inning. We still trailed, 3–2, but we had put Keener out of the game.

Baseball's often a game of momentum, and suddenly we had it. Although Corporal Logan led off the fourth inning with a single, Captain Hopkins popped out to right field, and Chockram surprised everyone by striking out Lieutenant Prosser and The Butcher.

We didn't do much when we came to bat, mainly because I hit into an inning-ending double play, but Chockram had found his rhythm. Amazingly he struck out Pig Oliver to start the fifth inning, induced Strickland to hit a weak ground out to first base, and struck out Griggs.

"No harm done!" Ruben Sweet offered encouragement. "Their next strikers are blacker than a funeral of darkies in a thunderstorm!"

Joshua Livinggoode blasted Prosser's first pitch into the left-center gap. Ladies along the third-base line gasped as the black sailor trotted home. Minutes later, they gasped again when Timothy Moore, despite his broken hand, connected for another home run.

"If you can't pitch no better than that, Prosser," Pig Oliver snapped, "I'll shoot you dead right here and now."

I'm not sure that helped Prosser, for our next three hitters sent blasts to center field, but I begrudgingly gained respect for Emil Strickland. He ran down those would-be hits by Chockram, Perdue, and Blevins, catching each on the fly.

"Mighty hard that Strickland is working himself," McGee said. "I'd catch those balls on the bound for the outs, save me energy."

"Posturing for the ladies," Conrad Turner suggested.

The inning was over, but I felt good as I took my place behind home plate.

For the first time that afternoon, Mr. Lincoln's Hirelings led, 4–3.

CHAPTER TWENTY-FIVE

They sat me next to Phil Marchildon for the start of Game 7, figuring we had a lot to talk about. Marchildon, a right-handed pitcher, had left the Philadelphia Athletics after the 1942 season to serve as a tail gunner in the Royal Canadian Air Force. In the summer of '44, Germans captured him after shooting down his bomber. He almost starved to death until British forces liberated the POW camp in May of '45.

Well, we didn't say one word about the war, or our experiences. We talked about the worst fields we had ever played on—Phil named Sportsman's Park; I substituted one of the old Texas League parks in Camp Ford's place. Finally we settled back to watch the deciding game, the greatest I had seen in years. Still, my mind often wandered during that glorious afternoon to another game, another place.

The sixth inning passed quickly. My hands ached, and I had only caught Chockram for four innings.

"How are you holding up, Win?" McGee asked.

"All right," I said, although both little fingers were jammed so badly I couldn't bend them. Behind me, a panting Lewis Chockram drenched his oil-black hair with water. Pain masked the Cherokee's face from pitching fastball after fastball against some of the best hitters he had ever seen, but he said he'd make it through this game, or else.

Not that he had any choice. Rules prohibited the substitution of players unless they were injured or sick, or, I suppose, in the case of Sergeant Nicholas Champlin, hauled off to the stocks.

Gamely, Chockram took the field in the top of the seventh, striking out Prosser. Yet Chockram's hard pitches began losing their zip, and The Butcher blasted a shot to left-center field. Breathlessly I watched Timothy Moore chase down that drive, which landed a few rods in front of him and bounced high to the right. Moore sprang like a catamount, and, although the ball jumped slightly behind him, he somehow snagged it with his left hand.

On our bench, everyone jumped up and down, cheering Moore's name, yet The Butcher kept running, and I recalled that first baseball game I had seen back in Newport, when the local team did not understand Massachusetts rules. As The Butcher rounded second base, Moore looked on dumbly.

"Throw the ball in!" I screamed. "Throw it in!"

Moore threw quickly to Major Perdue, who shook off his confusion and relayed the ball to me. Pain shot from the ends of my fingers and up to my elbows when I caught it, guarding home plate, daring The Butcher to try. Smirking, he trotted back to third base.

"He's out!" Captain McGee demanded. "That ball was caught on the bound."

"Damnyankee don't even know his own game," Pig Oliver said with a chuckle.

"I know the rules." Fuming at Major Rose, McGee made his way to home plate. "And a ball caught cleanly on the first bound is an out."

"You know the old rules, you lame mick!" The Butcher screamed from third base.

McGee ignored the insult, focusing on Major Rose. I called for a time out before tossing the ball to Chockram. Once Ruben Sweet joined the debate at home plate, he fished a newspaper from his gray coat.

"Ambuscade," I whispered to no one in particular. We had been set up.

Sweet held out the New York *Clipper* sporting journal, with a headline circled in ink: THE BOUND GAME IS RULED OUT

One glance at the article revealed a rule change made at the National Association of Base Ball Players convention in March. Beginning with the 1865 season, all balls must be caught on the fly to be recorded as outs.

"This wasn't in the journal you showed . . ." McGee bitterly shoved the newspaper back in Sweet's hands.

I simply stared at Major Rose.

"Rules are rules," the umpire said. "Runner's safe."

"You knew this all along," I said softly. "I expected more of you, Major. I thought you were above hoodwinks, thought you were honest, could be trusted."

With a snort, the fat man put his hands on his waist. "Understand this, Yank," he said. "I'm a Texian, a Southerner. You're an enemy soldier, an armed invader, and this is my home."

Disgusted but defeated, Captain McGee returned to the bench, shouting out the new rule, and I took my place closer to home plate, disappointed with Major Rose, although I understood his position, which I suppose mirrored the feelings of most Rebs.

Pig Oliver tripled to right field, bringing The Butcher home to tie the score, and Strickland followed with a shallow fly to left. Oliver raced home, thinking that Bruce Few would never catch the ball on the fly, but the Wisconsin gunner dived and made an outstanding catch before sliding across the grass.

Oliver's grin vanished at the cries from his teammates, and he raced back to third base, barely beating Few's throw to Conrad Turner.

"I'll get home soon enough, MacNewton," Oliver said. "And when I do, boy, I'll rip your head off."

Griggs blooped an infield single to O'Hara, but Oliver couldn't score, and Chockram, now pitching on pure guts, struck out Sergeant Pate to end the threat.

I led off the bottom half of the seventh with a line drive to center field that once again Emil Strickland ran down and caught. Livinggoode flied out to right, and Timothy Moore grounded out to shortstop. At the end of seven innings, the score was tied, 4–4.

Chockram struggled a bit in the eighth inning, but we managed to get out without allowing any runs, then Prosser found his pitching groove, retiring Chockram, Perdue, and Blevins in order. The ninth inning began with the score still tied.

The Butcher flied out to center field, and how Moore held on to that ball with his broken fingers, I'll never know. One out. Pig Oliver lined two balls hard to right field that just landed foul, then popped a weak foul behind me. Despite tripping over Major Rose's big feet and crashing into the artillery piece, I caught the ball for the second out. I even managed to duck underneath the bat Oliver slung at me.

"It's a gentleman's game," Major Rose reprimanded Oliver as he stormed away.

Strickland singled with two outs, and Griggs leveled a line drive to center field. I covered home plate, watching Strickland race past second, round third, and come charging in for the go-ahead run. *Concentrate*, I told myself. *Watch the ball. Catch it first. He can't hurt you.* Moore gunned the ball to Perdue left-handed; the major pivoted and threw at the same time. As the ball came to me, I knew that Strickland planned on barreling over me.

Catching the ball, gripping it tightly with both hands, I swung, swung hard, bracing myself for the collision. Wind sailed from my lungs, and, now lying on my back, I spit out dirt and grass, my head buzzing.

"The runner is out," Major Rose announced. "The side is retired."

As my vision cleared, I found Chockram standing over me, a grin chiseled into his beleaguered face, and, once the ringing left my ears, I heard my name shouted by my teammates. I let the ball roll from my hand, and allowed Chockram to pull me to my feet.

"Let's win this game right now," Chockram said hoarsely.

Even eighty-one years ago, kids dreamed of ninth-inning heroics. Fergal O'Hara led off with a single, and after Conrad Turner struck out, Bruce Few doubled O'Hara to third. Butterflies danced in my stomach when I picked up an ash bat and stepped to the plate. A hit, even a fly ball to the outfield, would drive in the winning run.

"Low," I said.

"What's that?" a sweating, pale Prosser called out from the pitcher's box. "Speak up, Billy Yank."

"Low!"

I fouled off the first pitch. "You ain't nothin', boy," Pig Oliver whispered.

Despite numbing hands, I gripped the bat-stick as tightly as possible, dug in my heels, and waited. The ball spun toward me, and I swung through, barely able to contain my excitement as the ball snapped off the end of the bat. Knowing I had done it, I bolted for first base, but the loud groan from our bench quashed my joy. Head in his hands, Captain McGee doubled over. Lewis Chockram spun around and fell to the dirt, shouting Cherokee words of agony. Joshua Livinggoode, waiting to bat next, slowly shook his head.

"What . . . ?" I whirled with disbelief. "How?"

Behind me came Pig Oliver's sniggers. At third base, Corporal Bobby Logan held the baseball in his hands, although he hardly believed he had caught it. He shrugged as shortstop Andy Griggs kidded him, tossed the ball to Prosser, and tried to shake the pain out of his fingers.

"Son-of-a-bitch!" I hurled the bat angrily to the ground, and stormed off the base path.

"Watch it," Major Rose chided me. "There's ladies present."

"Tough luck," Captain McGee told me. Tears filled his eyes.

Still, we should have won the game in the bottom of the ninth, and I am not referring to being robbed of a hit by that lucky third baseman. Joshua Livinggoode followed my at-bat with an arcing fly to left field. Near the foul line, Sergeant Pate bobbled the ball before it rolled from his fingertips. Major Rose ruled it a catch, however, even though Pate never had control, and our side was retired.

We didn't argue. What was the point?

CHAPTER TWENTY-SIX

SEC. 26. The game shall consist of nine innings to each side, when, should the number of runs be equal, the play shall be continued until a majority of runs, upon an equal number of innings, shall be declared, which shall conclude the game.

Major Rose and Ruben Sweet, with help from Emil Strickland, explained that rule to the spectators as we prepared to enter extra innings.

Sergeant Pate led off the tenth inning with a blast to right field, and the Texians began cutting loose with Rebel yells. The sergeant rounded second and kept running, and I darted down the third-base line to back up Conrad Turner as Joshua Livinggoode fired the ball. Pate and Turner collided, falling into a heap, and I snagged the ball after the second bounce.

Only Conrad Turner stood up. Atop third base, Sergeant Pate lay spread-eagled, speaking gibberish.

More of Sweet's guards carted the good sergeant off the field after a quick examination by
Major Rose, and Pig Oliver called in a replace-
ment. The name made me shiver.

"Mike Peabody."

Grunting with satisfaction, my former friend
leaped off the bench and hurried to third base.
"Tear his head off, boy," Oliver told him, and I
walked back to the plate.

"You know what's coming!" Captain McGee
said.

I replied with a feeble nod.

Corporal Coker grounded to Major Perdue,
and Peabody, yelling at the top of his lungs,
dashed for home. I stood at the plate, and put out
my arms as Perdue's throw came smoothly, on
target. Instead of waiting, I ran to meet Mike
Peabody, ran as hard as I could, screaming until
the wreck staggered me. We both went down, but
I jumped up first, still clutching the ball, spinning
quickly to Major Rose to show him, daring him to
make a bad call.

"Runner's out," Rose announced glumly.

Blood poured from Mike Peabody's nose as he
lay there, and suddenly I felt repentant. After
tossing the ball back to Chockram, I held out my
hand, but Peabody spit at me, pulled himself up,
and limped back to the Secesh bench.

Bobby Logan grounded out, Captain Hawkins
flied out, and Mr. Lincoln's Hirelings came to bat
in the bottom half of the tenth.

Lead-off singles by Moore and even Chockram,
drenched with sweat, with nothing left of his
right arm but bone and sinew, gave us hope, but

Prosser got Major Perdue to ground out and forced Professor Blevins into a double play to end the inning.

Don't ask me how he did it, but Chockram struck out Prosser and The Butcher to start the eleventh inning. Yet Oliver singled, his fourth hit of the contest, and we shuddered when Professor Blevins dropped a pop-up by Strickland that would have ended the side. Angrily Blevins ripped off his broken glasses and tossed them to our bench.

"My fault!" he yelled. "My damned fault."

With runners on first and second, Andy Griggs loaded the bases with another single.

"It's all right!" Captain McGee called out to Chockram. "It's all right!"

I knew what he meant when Mike Peabody stepped to the plate. No one could believe it. Even the women began whispering animatedly at the sight of a one-armed boy coming to strike.

"Captain Oliver!" Sweet demanded. "Are you daft?"

Oliver did not reply.

Mike Peabody extended the bat with his left hand, took a measured practice swing, and announced: "High."

My mouth opened, but I couldn't think of anything to say. I felt sorry for my invalided boyhood friend as he swung pathetically at Chockram's first two pitches. The next throw sailed outside for a ball, and Chockram followed with a wicked, waving blast. When Mike Peabody swung, I could scarcely believe the *thwack*. To everyone's surprise, the ball looped weakly over Major Perdue's head and into center field.

"That one-armed turncoat!" a preacher shouted. "Great Scot, did y'all see that?"

What I saw sickened me. Oliver and Strickland scored standing up, and Peabody jumped up and down on first base, pointing a big finger at me, cursing the traitorous inmates of Camp Ford.

Joshua Livinggoode chased down Corporal Coker's fly ball to retire the side, but the damage was done. The Gallinippers led by two runs as we came to our last strikes.

Lieutenant Prosser announced that his shoulder was dislocated, verified by Major Rose, so a short, stocky private known as Pork Chop stepped into the pitcher's box. I've always figured Prosser and the doctor lied, faking an injury so the Rebs could bring a fresh arm to the pitcher's box.

When Fergal O'Hara greeted the chubby guard with a line drive, I leaped from my seat. O'Hara turned up his speed, rounding second base, third, coming home as Strickland ignored shortstop Andy Griggs and threw all the way home. It was a perfect throw, one of the best I've seen, especially when you consider he gunned a ball that weighed five and three-quarter ounces with a circumference of almost ten inches.

Pig Oliver batted the ball down, but he never touched O'Hara, and I forgot all about the presence of ladies when Major Rose called him out.

Typically one did not protest the umpire's call, but we not only protested, we cursed. Captain McGee shook his finger under the surgeon's nose, but to no avail. O'Hara was out, robbed of a home run, and we were down to our last two outs.

Conrad Turner lined a shot down the first-base

line, but The Butcher made the stab, and there were two outs. Spectators rose, cheering Confederate players as Bruce Few came to the plate, our last hope. He doubled easily, and Captain McGee nudged me.

"You're the striker, lad."

I walked to the plate, aware of nothing but my pounding heart until a voice snapped me out of the trance:

"Come on, Winthrop!"

My eyes darted down to third base, where Jane Anne Bartholomew stood, ignoring the indignant looks from other ladies. Beaming, she clapped and called out my name.

"I'm gonna kill you, MacNewton," Pig Oliver told me. "No matter what happens next, I'm gonna kill you. That girl's decent, too good for the likes of you. I'm gonna kill you."

Ignoring him, I swung on the first pitch, slammed the bat down, and cursed. You know when you've made that hit; likewise, a ballist can tell when he has popped up the danged thing.

I made myself look up while jogging down the base path, discouraged, fully realizing that Captain J. C. C. Hopkins would catch my muff.

"Run it out!" Captain McGee yelled. "You never know!"

At that moment, I saw the rider, galloping down the pike, whipping his horse in a frenzy, running straight down our outfield, yelling something I couldn't understand. All I could do was stare as Captain Hopkins came to a sudden stop, rods from the descending ball, forgetting all about the game.

"Run! Damn you, MacNaughton, run!"

Like a dream. That's how I remember it. The

rider kept coming, and I started running, in the corner of my eye seeing Bruce Few cross home plate to cut our deficit to 6–5. My teammates yelled for me to run while the Gallinippers cursed and shouted. Not until I rounded second base did I hear the Rebs clearly.

"It's a damnyankee trick! Throw the ball!"

What's a trick? I wondered.

The galloper tore a path across the infield, sliding his lathered gelding to a stop near Ruben Sweet.

"War's over! Lee's surrendered!"

I almost stopped running myself, Captain McGee's bellows—"Run! It's a Rebel trick!"— merely adding to my puzzlement.

Catching one brief glimpse of Jane Anne Bartholomew, I recovered and sprinted past third base, coming home, trying to tie the score, although not really understanding a thing. Pig Oliver stood there, his face equally confused, holding my bat-stick loosely, discouraged.

I pushed myself harder.

I never saw Oliver swing the bat. One second I was racing for home plate, and a moment later I lay on the ground, my head exploding, the rest of my body numb. At first, I couldn't see a thing, and barely made out the curses, shouts, sobs, hurrahs. Nor did I feel Pig Oliver slap my bleeding head with the ball that had finally been thrown in. Momentarily my faculties cleared, and I stared at Major Rose's slightly out-of-focus jowls, heard him, or maybe I just saw him mouth the words, and only thought I heard him before the world turned to midnight.

"Striker's out. Gallinippers win, six to five."

EPILOGUE

When Enos Slaughter came racing home from first base on Harry Walker's hit to score the go-ahead run in the eighth inning, turning Sportsman's Park to bedlam, the memories came flooding back. I cried so hard that a few Cardinals fans patted my back and offered me a beer, comforting, they thought, a Red Sox fan as Harry Brecheen, pitching in relief, took down the Red Sox in the top of the ninth, giving the Cardinals an improbable 4–3 victory and the World Series championship. Fishing a handkerchief from my pants pocket, I wiped my face, blew my nose, thanked them, and hurried to my hotel, found my Big Chief tablet and began writing. I wrote well into the morning, stopping only when I filled its pages. After breakfast, I bought another tablet to resume this narrative on the train ride home.

When I finally came to three days later, lying on a parlor sofa I remembered vaguely and smelling fresh-cut roses, I weakly called out Jane Anne's name. She didn't answer me. Conall McGee did.

"Gone under I thought you were, lad," he said, holding a cup of hot tea.

"What happened?"

"We lost the game."

"No . . ." I waited for dizziness to pass. "I . . . I mean . . ."

He grinned and sipped the tea. "War's over. Reb captain named Birchett confirmed the rumor. Lee surrendered to Grant at some courthouse in Virginia. Other Secesh generals have given it up, too." He held out the cup of tea, but I shook my head, regretting the move for the pain it caused. Gently I touched what felt like a half ton of bandages wrapped around my head.

"Sweet's Guards left once they heard, just opened the gate to Camp Ford, went home," McGee continued. "And headed to Shreveport are our lads. I'm supposed to haul you there when you can travel, get ourselves mustered out."

"Jane Anne?"

His face souring, McGee moved the vase of roses and sat on the table beside me.

"She's gone too, Win."

I tried to sit up—jump up, actually—but couldn't. "Why? Where?"

"Easy, lad, go easy. Told me we should stay here till you got on your feet, she did. That Reb sawbones, Rose, he's come over a time or two. Said you'd live."

"But Jane . . ."

McGee sighed. "She left, Win . . . with her father."

Nausea and dizziness returned swiftly, and for the first time in my life I truly felt heartbreak. "But . . . why?" I didn't wait for an answer.

"Her . . . father?" Determination suddenly possessed me. "I'll find her, by God . . . I'll . . ."

McGee's hand tightened on my shoulder. "Win, I'm not one to know the whys and wherefores about women, but she's troubled and . . . you'd never find her. Besides, she doesn't want you to." Sighing, he relaxed his grip. "A hold fathers have on their children. Some for the good, like yours, though you probably didn't know that till he died. But some, well, some aren't right. You're what, seventeen, no, eighteen? You'll find some corn-fed girl, Win, who'll love you back, who won't be haunted by—"

"I'll find her."

"She left on her own accord, Win. Her pa didn't drag her along."

"You don't know . . . I'll find her. . . ." The light began fading again, and I drifted off to sleep. Deep down, I guess I knew the truth.

So, we returned to Newport, where I learned of Captain Conall McGee's chicanery. Seems he had been writing my mother since our incarceration in Camp Ford, telling her I was all right. He had also written the Peabodys, lamenting how their son Mike had died fighting at Sabine Crossroads. Once we were mustered out, McGee took a job with the Easton shipping line until the Panic of '73 bankrupted my grandfather, then returned to his trade as a tattoo artist, much to Mother's consternation. McGee also managed the Newton Base Ball Club for several years, taught children the game, and dined with Mother at least three times a week. I think she loved him, and I know he worshipped her, but she remained true to

Henry Wallace MacNaughton. After Mother's death in 1885, McGee wandered, writing occasionally. The last I heard from him came in 1899 from the Klondike. Knowing him, he probably coached baseball in the Yukon more than he dug for gold.

In death, Father became one of Rhode Island's biggest heroes. The cannon that he had manned at Gettysburg, now called The MacNaughton Gun, went to Washington, D.C., until 1874, when it was returned to the State House on Benefit Street in Providence. A senator invited Mother and me, then catching for the Hartford Dark Blues, to the dedication.

I simply lost track of most players for both the Gallinippers and Hirelings. Sergeant Nicholas Champlin showed up after one of my games with the Grays, and we chatted briefly, but I never saw him after that. I heard that Chauncey Perdue managed a team in New York. Nor did I ever hear of Professor Blevins, Timothy Moore, Joshua Livinggoode, or Lewis Chockram. As I have mentioned, I played with Emil Strickland—we even became friends—on the Providence Grays in 1878, and against him many other times. The Butcher, I read in a Shreveport newspaper, was knifed to death in New Orleans a few weeks after the war, and Ward Keener, who survived his near castration, rode with Cullen Baker's black-hearts until a freedman killed him at Caddo Lake in 1867.

After losing my spot with the Grays in 1879, I returned to Texas, searching for Jane Anne Bartholomew. Fourteen years had passed, and I don't know what I expected to find. The plantation where she had lived with her immoral father, where she had killed three Confederate soldiers, lay in crumbling ruins, and none of the share-croppers on the spread now owned by some wealthy Texian had heard of the Bartholomews.

The forest had overtaken Camp Ford, whose remains had been destroyed by the 10th Illinois Cavalry in July of 1865. *It's all gone,* I thought. *Everything, everyone is gone.* But in a Tyler boarding house, I located an even older and fatter Jon Rose. The loss of all of his teeth made him more difficult to understand, and, although he lay on his deathbed, he recognized me immediately.

"How's your head, Yank?"

"It was fractured," I answered with a smile.

"Figured."

"Major, what happened to Jane Anne, Jane Anne Bartholomew?"

He frowned, and spoke clearly, although he took long pauses, gasping for breath after each sentence. "You was a-smitten . . . knowed it. They went to Gladewater for a spell . . . but come back. Only . . . bad story."

"Please, sir, tell me."

"Pig Oliver shot her daddy dead . . . right here in town. Don't know why. . . . Shot him, and rode out . . . her just a-standin' there. . . . She left . . . didn't even . . . see her . . . daddy planted. Don't . . ." Out of breath, Major Rose closed his eyes and drifted off to sleep. The last words I heard came faintly. "Let her go, Yank. . . . Under . . . stand?"

Perhaps I did, finally. Conall McGee had been right. I'd never find Jane Anne; she didn't want me to. But I had loved her. I'd like to think she loved me.

Pig Oliver, too, faded from my life, although I heard stories of a gunman in Coffeyville, Kansas, who enjoyed playing baseball when not rustling cattle or robbing stagecoaches, until a widowed seamstress nicknamed Kitty Cat Hall tamed him, married him, and carted him off to some Nebraska homestead. Perhaps because I know why he murdered J. Lyman Bartholomew, I'd like to think that gunman was Pig Oliver. Sure, Oliver came close to knocking out my brains, but he had rid the world of Jane Anne's father after undoubtedly learning exactly what that wretched man demanded of his daughter. Ulysses Oliver had loved her as much as I had.

Now, here I sit in the smoking car of a southbound train, ninety-nine years old, the pages of this last tablet almost filled, still thinking about baseball, all that it has won me, all that it has cost me. To a degree, it brought me fame, along with injuries and so much pain that writing these words with swollen, misshapen knuckles and fingers has been a challenge. It brought me my wife, a corn-fed Texas woman I met in 1889 in Dallas.

In a way, baseball also brought Mike Peabody back to me.

In October 1884, I was asked to umpire a game between the Kansas City Unions and St. Paul White Caps in Kansas City, Missouri. The Unions were horrible that season, but on that crisp autumn afternoon they beat the White Caps, 7–2, behind a powerful-striking, one-armed outfielder called Mike Thunder.

Locals said he had carved the T on his face himself; that's how tough he was. From church socials to the stockyards, Kansas Citians spoke Mike

Thunder's name in worshipful tones. He was so good with the bat-stick, they said, that he had cut off his right arm to give everyone else a chance. Of course, they couldn't quite explain the Unions' 16–63 record in '84. After the game, I found Mike Peabody in a bucket of blood not far from Athletic Field.

He kicked out a chair when he saw me, asking his followers if he could share a minute with an aging, worn-down umpire who couldn't play the game any more.

"You hit well today, Mike," I began.

"You ain't here to talk sports, Win. You want absolution."

I forced down the lump in my throat. "I . . . we found out that Sharky betrayed us, that you weren't the . . ."

"Knock it off, Win. Look at me."

"The money hidden in your coat. . . . It . . ." I couldn't finish. Here I was making excuses when I should be apologizing, begging his forgiveness.

His laugh sounded hollow. "Reckon I've let you rot long enough."

"I'm . . ."

"You ain't listening, Win. You never did. You said you could tell when I was lying, and you was right, almost. That money I had hid come when I told them guards about some micks that I had learnt was digging a tunnel. And I would have done the same to you, too, 'cept I got drunk on Rebel bark juice, passed out in my shebang." He laughed again before swallowing the last of his whiskey.

We stared at each other, and finally he lifted his glass. Taking the signal, I ordered another round.

"Make it a bottle," he said.

"A bottle," I agreed. "Of your best Scotch." As if a saloon of this class served anything other than forty-rod.

"Like when we was kids." Grinning, Mike Peabody shook his head.

Our eyes locked again, yet I couldn't tell if he were lying now, although I could not fathom why he would want to.

"Been gnawing at you, ain't it? Well, forget it. I look at it this way. I beat you in that game at Camp Ford. Hell, I laughed when Oliver practically caved in your skull. Besides, I owe you."

He laughed, this time with humor, at the look on my face.

"Owe me?" I asked.

"I wasn't worth a damn, Win. Do you know what I would have become if not for you? I'd be some walking whiskey vat back in Newport, a cripple, a nobody. But I hated you so much for what you done, for this T on my face, my missing arm, it powered me. Made me pick up a bat with my left hand, made me get better and better. Hell, I'm still playing ball, ain't no freak at no dime museum. By jingo, I can still strike the hell out of the ball, and catch, too. You seen it today. Folks buy me all the whiskey I can hold. Petticoats seek me. . . ." With a wink, he refilled his tumbler from the fresh bottle, and took another sip. "I give up hating you years ago, Win. I ain't gonna shake your hand, but I let you buy me a drink, so there's your absolution."

I left him there, paid for the bottle, and walked away. Maybe Mike Peabody was right. I had found my absolution. Anyway, ten years later I felt oddly comforted when I heard that Mike Thunder had died, still playing baseball for some dismal club team, but playing well enough that a San Francisco newspaper obituary lauded his talent, his overcoming of adversity, his generosity and humor.

When I put my hand on the batwing door in that Kansas City saloon, he called out: "MacNaughton!"

As I turned, he lifted his glass in toast. "You played a hell of a baseball contest, MacNaughton."

"So did you, Mike." I touched the brim of my hat before walking outside into the fading light.

> Respectfully submitted,
> Winthrop H. MacNaughton
> October 16, 1946

AUTHOR'S NOTE

The highlight of my Small Fry baseball career came at Sardis, South Carolina, in 1972, when Coach Perry Stokes turned to the dugout and admonished us bench-warmers to hush, that there were only nine players on our team who knew what was going on during the game that night, and they were on the field. Perry paused, then added: "I'm wrong. There are ten players. Johnny's paying attention to the game." That boost of confidence overshadowed my .000 batting average and the splinters I earned riding the bench.

The highlight of my high school baseball career came during my junior year, when Coach Butch Anderson let me, team manager and statistician, take batting practice, and I proceeded to send line drives into the outfield, causing Butch, who had played Double-A ball, to comment: "That's a hit in any league." Suddenly comparing myself to George Brett, I began having reservations about not trying to make the team until Al Jordan announced he would throw a curveball, and my pathetic swing left Al, Butch, and practically everyone else laughing.

My most memorable baseball career highlight, however, came at the major-league level in 1991 while working as assistant sports editor at the Dallas *Times Herald*. Mark Hartsell, a diehard Detroit Tigers fan, and I, a longtime Kansas City Royals fan, decided to make a road trip to Missouri and catch a Tigers-Royals game. Victor Galvan, who worked on the metro desk with Mark, tagged along. Neither the Royals nor Tigers had much of a team that year, and we were worn out from all-night traveling, pigging out on barbecue, and watching bad baseball when, late in the game, the announcer informed the crowd that in Arlington, Texas, Nolan Ryan was only a few outs from recording his seventh career no-hitter, a feat he reached, shown on the DiamondVision screen in K.C. Mark, Vic, and I exchanged glances and groans. We had driven 500 miles to miss the game of a lifetime.

I never was much of a baseball player, needless to say, but I always enjoyed the game.

Baseball was played at Camp Ford, Texas, as well as other prison camps during the Civil War, among Union prisoners of war, but, as far as history recalls, POWs and Confederate guards at Camp Ford, a.k.a. Ford City, never played a game, and there were no teams known as Mr. Lincoln's Hirelings or the Ford City Gallinippers.

Recommended reading for early baseball includes *Baseball in Blue & Gray: The National Pastime During the Civil War* by George B. Kirsch

(Princeton University Press, 2003); *Playing for Keeps: A History of Early Baseball* by Warren Goldstein (Cornell University Press, 1989); and *Beadle's Dime BaseBall Player: A Compendium of the Game* by Henry Chadwick (a 1996 Sullivan Press reprint of the 1860 original). My primary sources for the Red River Campaign were *Red River Campaign: Politics & Cotton in the Civil War* by Ludwell H. Johnson (The Kent State University Press, 1993) and *Disaster in Damp Sand: The Red River Expedition* by Curt Anders (Guild Press of Indiana, 1997). I turned to *Camp Ford, C.S.A.: The Story of Union Prisoners in Texas* by F. Lee Lawrence and Robert W. Glover (Texas Civil War Centennial Advisory Committee, 1964) and *Twenty Months in the Department of the Gulf* by A. J. H. Duganne (J. P. Robens, 1865) for information on Camp Ford. Other sources include *Portals to Hell: Military Prisons of the Civil War* by Lonnie R. Speer (Stackpole Books, 1997); *When the Boys Came Back: Baseball and 1946* by Frederick Turner (Henry Holt, 1996); *Ninety-Four Years in Jack County 1854–1948* by Ida Lasater Huckabay (Texian Press, Centennial Edition, 1974); and the online version of the *Baseball Almanac*.

Many thanks to the Vista Grande Public Library staff in Santa Fé County for tracking down some of the scarce titles mentioned above; Sandra Allen of the Newport Public Library, Kirwin M. Roach of the St. Louis Public Library, the National Baseball Hall of Fame Museum, and friends Mike Goldman, Kurt Iverson, T. R. Sullivan, and Jim R. Woolard for research help; and my wife, Lisa, and son, Jack, for strolling with me along the site of

MAX BRAND®

TROUBLE'S MESSENGER

Peter Messenger is made for trouble. He is specially trained in the art of death, even though he's never killed anyone. But his skills with his hands, a gun, or a knife are undeniable. And there is only one person he plans to use them on: Summer Day, the wily medicine man who has tortured and killed a defenseless white. But to get to the one he seeks, Peter will have to take on the whole Blackfoot nation…and hope his extraordinary talents are enough to stay alive against the wrath of an entire tribe.

ISBN 10: 0-8439-5858-8
ISBN 13: 978-0-8439-5858-4 $5.99 US/$7.99 CAN

THE BLAZE OF NOON

Tᴉᴍ Cʜᴀᴍᴘʟɪɴ

The blistering road through Arizona Territory is called the Devil's Highway for a good reason. And now Dan Mora knows why. He's met all kinds of challenges on the trail, and he'll be in big trouble if he doesn't soon find water. Hugh Deraux knows the same stifling thirst. Breaking out of prison was easy compared to this trek through the unforgiving desert. But both men are driven by more than thirst. They hunger for the riches rumored to be found along the dangerous trail. And nothing will stop them from claiming the treasure—not each other, not Apaches, not even...*The Blaze of Noon*.

ISBN 10: 0-8439-5892-8
ISBN 13: 978-0-8439-5892-8 $5.99 US/$7.99 CAN

RAVEN SPRINGS

JOHN D. NESBITT

Just outside the small town of Raven Springs there's a curious little inn. Is it just a coincidence that a number of missing people spent their last night there? That's what Jimmy Clevis aims to find out. He's tracking down a man who seems to have vanished into thin air—and his trail stops dead at Raven Springs. Jimmy has no choice but to check into the inn and find out for himself what mysteries are waiting behind its doors. But will he be able to do what others before him couldn't? Will he survive his stay?

ISBN 10: 978-0-8439-5804-9
ISBN 13: 978-0-8439-5804-1 $5.99 US/$7.99 CAN